The Last Hurrah

A Dreadball Novel

by Robert E Waters

The Last Hurrah
Cover courtesy Mantic Games
This edition published in 2020

Zmok Books is an imprint of

Winged Hussar Publishing, LLC
1525 Hulse Rd, Unit 1
Point Pleasant, NJ 08742

Paperback ISBN 978-1-950423-01-9
Ebook ISBN 978-1-950423-51-4
LCN

Bibliographical References and Index
1. Science Fiction. 2. Action Adventure. 3. Games

For more information
visit us at www.wingedhussarpublishing.com

Twitter: WingHusPubLLC
Facebook: Winged Hussar Publishing LLC

This book is published under license from Mantic Games.

Dedication

To Jamie Chad Brandon, Archeologist, Anthropologist, and a Lifelong Friend. You will be remembered. You will be missed.

Welcome to the Warpath universe!

Humanity rules the galaxy through an organization known as the Galactic Co-Prosperity Sphere (GCPS). Thousands of suns and hundreds of thousands of planets revolve around this economic and technological juggernaut. Life is good.

But within this comfortable co-prosperity lies a relentless drive for self-governance. Alien races, for centuries having suffered under the corporate yoke, rebel against the GCPS and take what is theirs. War is constant. Nothing is truly safe... or prosperous.

Thus comes DreadBall, the deadliest sport in the entire universe. Teams from all over the GCPS commit their best and brightest players in a do-or-die struggle for fame, glory and wealth. Heroes and legends rise and fall in the DreadBall arena, while their corporate sponsors line their pockets with unimaginable wealth. DreadBall is a test of wills that only the bravest, only the strongest, survive.

The strikers are the ball-carriers, the scorers, the most nimble, most agile of the DreadBall elite. They lack the power of the guards, but their abilities in the arena are the subject of the most awe-inspiring legends in the GCPS. If you need a score, strikers are your best option.

The guards are the muscle, the sledgehammers of the DreadBall arena. They are not equipped to carry the ball, but they wouldn't deign to anyway. Their hands are for slamming, choking, hitting, and if the DreadBall Governing Body (DGB, or 'Digby' for short) continues to allow it, for killing. Entire teams have been wiped out by a guard on a rampage.

The jacks serve the DreadBall arena in a wide variety of ways. They are, in essence, a combination of the other two specialists. Reasonably agile and fast, they can score, though their ball-carrying skills are not as refined as those of the strikers. They often serve as field captains and assistant coaches, and they have a talent for blocking opponents from scoring lanes.

Welcome to the Warpath universe!

Humanity rules the galaxy through an organization known as the Galactic Co-Prosperity Sphere (GCPS). Thousands of suns and hundreds of thousands of planets revolve around this economic and technological juggernaut. Life is good.

But within this comfortable co-prosperity lies a relentless drive for self-governance. Alien races, for centuries having suffered under the corporate yolk, rebel against the GCPS and take what is theirs. War is constant. No one is truly safe... or prosperous.

Thus comes DreadBall, the deadliest sports event in the universe. Teams from all over the GCPS commit their best and brightest players in a do-or-die struggle for fame, glory, and wealth. Heroes and legends rise and fall in the DreadBall arena, while their corporate sponsors line their pockets with unimaginable wealth. DreadBall is a test-of-wills that only the bravest, only the strongest, survive.

The 'strikers' are the ball-carriers, the scorers, the most nimble, most agile of the DreadBall elite. They lack the power of the guards, but their abilities in the arena are the subject of the most awe-inspiring legends in the GCPS. If you need a score, strikers are your best option.

The 'guards' are the muscle, the true hammers of the DreadBall arena. They are not equipped to carry the ball, but they wouldn't want to anyway. Their hands are for slamming, choking, injuring, and if the DreadBall Governing Body (DGB, or 'Digby' for short) continues to allow it, for killing. Entire teams have been wiped out by a guard on rampage.

The 'jacks' serve the DreadBall arena in a wide variety of ways. They are, in essence, a combination of the other two specialist roles. Reasonably agile and fast, they can score, though their ball-carrying skills are not as refined as those of the striker. They often serve as field captains and assistant coaches, and they have a talent for blocking opponents from scoring lanes.

And finally, the DreadBall glove. Every striker and jack wears a special glove in order to catch, carry, and throw the ball which can oftentimes move at speeds of up to 200 miles per hour. Every race and team has a specially-designed glove to fit their physiology and play style. Without this glove, a lot of hands would be ripped away. DreadBall is a bloody sport, indeed, but let's not get carried away!

So, now you know some basics of the game. The teams are assembled, the ball is ready for release. Grab a snack, a drink, find a comfortable seat in the stands, and get ready to cheer.

DreadBall begins...now!

Prologue

981AE, Trontek Arena, Semi-Final Match

Leeland Roth snatched the weapons-grade titanium ball out of the air with ease. Blue-white sparks popped off the ball's hardened casing as he scooped it into his glove and held it firm against his body for added support. He put his head down and rushed toward the strike zone. The crowd roared, and the arena shook with kinetic energy. In his peripheral, Leeland saw his coach frantically waving him forward toward the strike zone. His fellow Trontek 29ers mowed the path before him, a guard and a power jack in front, pushing aside with ease Jade Dragon defenders foolish enough to try to block. All of the Jade Dragons were foolish in Leeland's eyes, just mere amateurs who got lucky and found themselves in the semi-final with the best corporate team in the First Sphere, the best team anywhere. And he would prove it in a few seconds.

Leeland smiled as he ducked a swing from a Dragon guard and a futile leap-tackle from one of their rookie jacks. He thought about kicking the helmet of the jack and delighting in the satisfying crack of the young boy's jaw within. He didn't. Leeland was a striker, and strikers did not concern themselves with such tactics. He would leave the heavy violence up to his guards and jacks. He paused a moment to allow the tangle of bodies before him to subside. When it did, he launched himself into the air and came down perfectly in the

Dragon's back strike zone.

Now, he thought, as he angled himself to the left to get a better view of the goal.

The Dragons had tried to set up a standard three-player castle of their back goal, the three-point/four-point goal. The 29ers had eliminated that threat early, but there were still too many bodies in the way, and Leeland preferred an unfettered strike lane.

He moved closer, gnashing his teeth angrily at giving up an attempt at the higher four-point score. But even closer to the goal, his three-pointer would put them a point ahead, and in a match as desperate and definitive as this one had been, one point could make all the difference.

The strike lane cleared as his blocking guard threw a Dragon striker across the Neodurium pitch and into the wall ablaze with bright flashing league sponsorship. Leeland turned his head from the blood spray from the man's cracked helmet and skull. He firmed his stance, bent at the knees, raised the ball high, fought against the pain in his shoulder, and threw.

Someone behind him caught his arm and snatched the ball right out of his glove.

Leeland turned and glared at the face of the thief. "Victor! You lousy Zwerm! That's a foul. Foul!"

Leeland's cries were matched by his coach, his players, and nearly everyone in attendance, and the stadium again rocked with the collective rage of the 29er fans. The cybernetic ref and its Eye in the Sky assistant, however, did not bother to call it as such, because stealing the ball from an opponent was not a foul; but in Leeland's experience, it never hurt for a player or a team or an entire stadium of fans to scream foul even when none had occurred. Confusion and trickery was an important part of the game.

Enraged, Leeland took off after his brother. But Victor was fast, much faster, and by the time Leeland caught up, his brother had scored.

The ball disappeared and was immediately shot back into play at the centerline. A Trontek jack scooped it up and moved to score. Leeland did not care.

"Are you serious?" He pushed Victor hard. "Why would you do that?"

Victor recovered, pushed back. "This isn't pre-school baby DreadBall, Leeland, where everyone plays soft with no hitting. This is *real* DreadBall. If you can't take the pressure, retire."

"You're taking advantage of information I told you in strict confidence."

Victor shook his head. "No, I'm maximizing my play on intelligence. Perfectly legal."

Leeland gnashed his teeth, his anger growing. "You're going down, you little zit. You and your Dragons are gonna be wiped out. I'll break you."

Victor smiled and nodded. "Bring it... you son of a Zee!"

His brother disappeared in the rush of bodies as the ball bounced away from the Trontek jack, who now lay flat on his face with a Dragon guard's boot jammed into his back. The grav-pulsor in the ball's belly made it bounce erratically, and everyone on the pitch scrambled for it.

Leeland jumped in head first, pushing, kicking, biting, punching, all to gain access to a ball that seemed impossible to acquire. His violent actions were, strictly speaking, against striker rules, but in the chaos of the moment, he hoped that the ref would not notice with so many arms and bodies flailing. This ball was extremely difficult to snag; everyone had to commit. Perhaps it had been tampered with; perhaps someone had hacked the ball's grav-pulsor programming.

That was not an uncommon act to fix the game. But he went for it nevertheless, at great risk to himself, and it did not matter what he had to do to get it.

In the roiling pile, he found it, snatched it up, and called for help. "Pull me out!"

Mungo 'Madeye' Birk, the 29er's star guard, heard the order, grabbed Leeland by the scruff, and pulled him free. Now the chase was on, as everyone began to notice that the ball had been acquired. The screaming in the arena reached a level that Leeland had never heard before. His head, his injured right arm, his entire body, shook in excitement as he raced again toward the Jade Dragon's deep strike zone.

He had a free lane of movement. A skittish jack, which had just come out of the Subs Bench, tried to block his path. Leeland twisted one-eighty and left the boy in dust and shock. He now had no one in front of him and a clear line of sight to the goal.

His brother stepped into his vision. Victor had cleverly pulled himself out of the fray and positioned himself to thwart any attempted throw on goal. Leeland saw him. His anger grew as Victor's mouth curled into a derisive smile.

You're not going to take advantage this time.

Leeland halted in the strike zone. Victor closed. Leeland shifted slightly to the left to get a better angle for a score attempt. He raised his arm to throw.

At the last second, he turned and threw the ball straight into Victor's face.

Victor, not anticipating the attack, froze in shock, tried to duck, but took the ball square in the helmet at one hundred and fifty miles an hour.

The speed and force of the throw knocked Victor off his feet and into the wall. He crumpled like a flower.

Yes! Leeland was joyous, and a little smug, but his attack had lost him the ball and the chance to score.

"*Leeland Roth!*" The Eye in the Sky assistant referee bellowed his name. Red warning lights flashed across the pitch and klaxons sounded. "*You have committed a foul. You are out of the game! Leave immediately!*"

But Leeland ignored the order and went to his brother who was cuddled up against the wall. He offered his hand. "Good game, Victor. You played well, but I told you I'd get you." Victor didn't answer. Leeland's brow furrowed. "Victor? Hey, Vic?"

Leeland knelt and pulled the cracked helmet off his brother's head. The force of the strike had sent shards of the helmet into Victor's scalp. Blood poured down his face.

"VICTOR!"

"Out of the way!"

Play was stopped, and a tin-voiced medibot pushed its way through the gathering players. The medibot knelt beside Victor, scanned the savage cut along his head, checked his vitals, his pulse. It raised its hand, tapped data into its forearm display, and spoke dispassionately into a microphone at its wrist. "Code black. Code black. Victor Roth, Jade Dragon striker, is dead."

Chapter One

[illegible], The [illegible] Vitale, [illegible]

Saomi Rapoor found her father alone in his private box at the Vitale Dinner Theater, a half-eaten plate of Mugnini Portofino and a glass of Black Muscat sitting on a small round table at his side. He was coughing again, as he obviously did these days. It sounded worse every day.

She entered quietly, her neatly cropped black hair bobbing at her shoulders, her purple pantsuit looking smart, clean, and freshly pressed. It was the kind of professional look that her father preferred for the family business, and she waited like an obedient child until he had collected himself, wiped his mouth, and took a long drink of Muscat. Even from where she was standing, she could smell the food, almost taste the wine. She was hungry herself, and a sip of grape wouldn't hurt. But that wasn't why she had come.

"Come here, Saomi," Damon Rapoor said, waving her forward with his handkerchief. "Would you like some wine?"

There was a second of hesitation, and Saomi took it without comment. She held the glass daintily as her father's withered hand struggled to keep the bottle from shaking. She provided support with her own delicate fingers and smiled as the dark, sweet liquid swirled into her glass. "Thank you," she said, and took a seat on the other side of the table.

Damon Rapoor leaned in his chair, cleared his throat, and waved again at the stage beyond the bulletproof glass of the

Chapter One

986AE, Third Sphere Industrial World Vitala, Zaigor System

Saanvi Kapoor found her father alone in his private box at the Vitala Dinner Theater, a half-eaten plate of Mughlai Paratha and a glass of Black Muscat sitting on a small round table at his side. He was coughing again, as he always did these days. It sounded worse every day.

She entered quietly, her neatly cropped black hair bobbing at her shoulders, her purple power suit looking smart, clean, and freshly pressed. It was the kind of professional look that her father preferred for the family business, and she waited like an obedient child until he had collected himself, wiped his mouth, and took a long drink of Muscat. Even from where she was standing, she could smell the food, almost taste the wine. She was hungry herself, and a sip of grape wouldn't hurt. But that wasn't why she had come.

"Come here, Saanvi," Damon Kapoor said, waving her forward with his handkerchief. "Would you like some wine?"

There was a second glass nearby, and Saanvi took it without comment. She held the glass tightly as her father's withered hand struggled to keep the bottle from shaking. She provided support with her own delicate fingers and smiled as the dark, sweet-smelling liquid swirled into her glass. "Thank you," she said, and took a seat on the other side of the table.

Damon Kapoor straightened in his chair, cleared his throat, and waved again at the stage beyond the bulletproof glass of his box.

"Do you understand this play? I have seen it twice, and I still don't understand it."

It was a modern Vitalan comedy-of-errors depicting three twenty-somethings, living together in a small apartment and trying to make it work. Each actor depicted one of three ancient gods of Old Earth mythology: Vishnu, Shiva, and Brahma, which represented the so-called Trimurti. One was the creator, one the preserver, and the other the destroyer. But like her father, Saanvi could never remember who was who, and in terms of comedy, it was very light on that score.

"Why do you bother watching it, then," she asked, "if you don't understand it?"

Her father shook his head. "I don't know... somehow, it relaxes me. Reminds me of simpler times."

Saanvi rolled her eyes. *Simpler times?* "I apologize then, for coming and disrupting your quiet reverie. I shall leave."

He coughed again and shook his head. "No. We need to talk, and this is the best place for it. No eyes, no ears. We can speak openly here... and honestly."

She swallowed another sip of wine. "Very well. What do you want to talk about?"

He turned to her, and Saanvi could see how his illness had made his face drawn, gaunt. The loose skin below his eyes was nearly black, his pale lips thin and haggard. There was still a spark in his eyes, however, and that gave her comfort. He tried to smile, but he was never very good at it.

"I hate to be so blunt with you, Saanvi, but you know as well as anyone: I'm dying. And when that happens, I want to ensure that Kapoor Industries moves forward, unfettered, into the future."

"You have created an empire," Saanvi said, "whose systems and corporate culture are so strong as to be nearly unbreakable."

He nodded. "And you have done very well in your brother's stead and in my absence. As far as I can tell, we move forward at pace. But it's your brother I wish to speak about."

Saanvi rolled her eyes again. "What has Aryan done this time?"

Damon coughed into his kerchief. "It's not what he has done, Saanvi. It's what he hasn't done. He hasn't lived up to expectations.

"I've heard the media refer to him as 'wasted seed.' I won't go so far as to say that about my only son, but he has wasted his life, and his talents, for sure. He drinks. He womanizes. He whiles away his life partying and who knows what else. We have tried again and again to bring him back to respectability, to make him live up to his familial and corporate obligations, but he has failed every time. He spends his trust fund like it's water. I'm to blame for that, I suppose. I should have cut him off years ago.

"As long as I was healthy, vital, his behavior could be ignored and, at worst, tolerated. But I'm dying, and the only son of Damon Kapoor can no longer be an impediment to the corporation."

"I can run the company, Father," Saanvi said, reaching over and patting his hand. "Don't worry about Aryan."

"I know you can, but that isn't good enough. With respect, Saanvi, you don't have the experience and the relationships to handle the politics of our board. Our strongest asset—over the decades that Kapoor Industries has functioned here on Vitala—is the strength of our family name. When I go, that strength will be in jeopardy, and I promise you, when they smell blood, the wolves will pounce. They will eat you alive."

"And you think getting Aryan involved in the company will make any difference?"

"No, of course not, but if we can get him back onto a respectable path, get him out of whatever gutter he's lying in now, then at least in the eyes of the public, the Kapoor family will be seen as strong;

and the board is very cognizant of public opinion. The pulse of the Vitala economy runs through our family, Saanvi, and it does not work without the family being stable. And that requires a stable Aryan.

"He trusts you more than me. If I approach him again, he'll simply close down and run. But you can get through to him. I know you can."

Saanvi felt a wave of nausea. Was it the wine or her father's words? A little of both, probably. This was not the conversation that she imagined when she had walked in. She had thought, perhaps foolishly, that Father would announce her as his successor, and while he did not close the door on that possibility, he wasn't holding it wide open either. Saanvi knew that in his heart, Father did not trust her with the company. Not because he was overtly sexist; had he been so, he'd have never trusted her with executive authority these many years. No. But family tradition had it that the oldest Kapoor son took over the company when his father died, and this tradition had held from the beginning. Now, that archaic tradition was in threat of disappearing; and Damon Kapoor, as wise and as capable as he was, did not have the intestinal fortitude to break with that tradition. Perhaps Father was intending for her and Aryan to run the company together. The board would probably agree to such an arrangement.

But not me…

Saanvi stood and went to the window. Intermission had been called. The lesser folk, those below, scrambled for drinks, a toilet, a bite to eat, pleasant conversation. Slowly, the window of their box grew a foggy opaque blue, and then advertisements rolled past like images in a dream. She hardly cared about joining the armed forces of any corporation, the latest hair products, concerts and operas being planned in the Vitala Cineplex. The Kapoor Industries advertisements caught her attention. Her family's business dabbled in everything: pharmaceuticals, steel beams, weapon systems, agricultural equipment, asteroid mining. Vitala was the industrial complex in the Zaigor System.

The man who sat atop that empire was dying before her eyes.

Another advert caught Saanvi's attention. She read it as it formed out of the blue fog in the glass. She read it again and again, until the truth of it began to make sense.

She turned to her father and pointed to the advert as it dissipated and the overhead lights flickered to indicate that intermission was ending.

"Let's do that," she said.

Damon Kapoor squinted. "Do what?"

"Let's give Aryan a DreadBall team."

"A team? How is he going to—"

"He's loved the sport since he was a boy. You used to take him to games yourself, remember? He even tried out for the Brimstone Bashers, though of course he got cut. Let's give him a team."

Damon Kapoor stood slowly, with pain. He waved off help and stumbled to the window. He looked down upon the people who were enjoying an afternoon of theater in a house Kapoor money had built. He kept himself from falling by leaning against the lip of the rail.

"Very well," he finally said, coughing, "if you think it'll work."

"Of course it will," Saanvi said, "and I'll see to it. I have the right connections."

She helped her father back to his chair and act two of the play began. Saanvi paused to see if her father would say anything more. When he didn't, she bid him goodbye with a soft kiss on his forehead, and then left.

It was a good plan, even *if* Aryan failed. It was a better plan if he failed, for Father did not realize that, in his absence, his daughter had already discussed the future of Kapoor Industries with 'The Board,' and they were as anxious as she was to see Aryan Kapoor fail. There were powerful interests in the wide galaxy other than the Co-Prosperity Sphere, and if Saanvi could find an avenue through which resources could be funneled to effectuate those interests, then all the better.

Aryan's little sports team would be that funnel… and Aryan would take the fall if things went bad. Saanvi smiled to herself.

I am indeed my father's daughter.

kill. There were powerful interests in the wider galaxy other than the Co-Prosperity Sphere, and if Sharvi could find an avenue through which resources could be funneled to effectuate those interests, then all the better.

Aryan's little sports team would be that funnel, and Aryan would take the fall if things went bad. Sharvi smiled to herself.

I am indeed my father's daughter.

Chapter Two

Abandoned Warehouse District, Planet Scorn, Fourth Sphere

The Marauder jack's face seemed to peel from the bone as the hidden bomb exploded at its side and sent the tiny goblin smashing into the pile of crates filled with bits and pieces of sharp scrap metal. Its uniform, a patchwork of red wool and gunmetal gray armor stitched together with wire, erupted in a volcano of deadly shrapnel.

Rohl Leandet anticipated the explosion and was ready for it. He skirted the edge of the blast zone and watched as the concussive explosion ripped the ball from the little creature's glove. It was propelled through the hot, stagnant air of the warehouse and right into Leandet's waiting glove. Then he moved accordingly.

Burlak's Bruisers were now down to six bodies, and three of those were Orc guards. Leandet's own Scorn Insufferables weren't faring much better, but they still had two strikers, and one of them was Leandet. He took the ball, dodged the green meaty paw and roar of a Bruiser guard, and headed up the dilapidated flight of rusty stairs toward the enemy strike zone.

There was no room in the warehouse for fans, and so a relatively complex series of cameras and screens had been set up in the girders of the ruined building to catch all the action. Like the building itself, the leads off the cameras were old, and they popped, sparked, and threatened to catch fire by the minute. Not that that was a big problem, for in the Xtreme version of DreadBall, the more violence and chaos, the better. But Leandet had seen one of those lines spark before and send an electrical charge right through a line of Insufferable jacks, cooking them to the bone. Burlak's coach and sponsor was not above trying something like that again, so Leandet kept a jaundiced eye toward the cameras and gave them a wide berth.

A Burlak jack nipped at his heels. Leandet kicked back and smashed the bugger's nose. *Serves him right*, he thought, as he gathered his footing and reached the top of the gantry. Just ten minutes ago, the same little monster had cut Leandet's forehead with its razor-sharp claws, sending an ocean of blood into his eyes. Even though he managed to wipe away most of it, his vision was still fuzzy, and it hurt when he blinked.

The gantry was, for all intents and purposes, nothing more than a narrow bridge. And at the other end of that long bridge stood the Bruiser's most defended strike zone. The Insufferables had tried to score on it once already, but the jack who had tried was now draped in sweet splatters of crimson across the metal barrels that had survived the first hidden bomb. One, perhaps two, bombs lay in those barrels somewhere, Leandet knew, and perhaps he'd be lucky enough to find one, and his long nightmare would finally be over.

"Throw me the ball!" the other striker on the team, Hal 'Spartacus' Grubb, called. He was positioned beneath the gantry on the pitch floor, shadowing Leandet's movements, and his idea (Leandet knew) was to try to assault the strike zone from the other end of the makeshift arena. But there were too many bodies over there, both alive and dead. It would require more than guile and speed to get through it all, and they didn't have enough bodies left for such a push. No. The best way was to do it alone, atop the gantry, where they least suspected a striker like him to try. *I'm not afraid*, Leandet thought as he streaked down the gantry, his steel-toed boots clapping madly along the bridge's iron joints. *I'm not afraid.*

Waiting for him, alongside the steel barrels, was Mucky Vook, a Bruiser star guard whose skin was a pus-riddled green gray. The sight of him made Leandet's stomach turn, but he kept sprinting forward, dodging goblin jacks who were jumping up from below to grab his feet.

Vook roared, bared his foul black teeth, slapped his fists together, and charged. Leandet kept his eyes on the brute, and as the gantry began to vibrate under the rush of the Orc guard, Leandet high-stepped it forward as if he were about to take flight. Luckily, Vook wasn't the brightest bulb in the package, and so he saw Leandet rise on his tip-toes and naturally tried to match the maneuver, hoping to perhaps slam the Insufferable striker right off the gantry. At the last minute, Leandet dropped to his knees and slid, letting the steel pads protecting his knees and shinbones carry him through Vook's wide stance and on to the other side. Vook, now totally confused and more than a little enraged, tried to stop, turn, and respond. But the impetus of his weight carried him right over the gantry and onto the concrete floor of the warehouse.

Leandet ignored the loud fan cheering being piped in on speakers, though he felt inclined to smile for those watching. Through his long, thick black beard, it was hard to see the gesture, but he did it anyway. Anything for the fans, right?

He regained his feet, and now, with no further impediment, he reached the end of the gantry and jumped his first barrel.

Jump, jump, jump. It was like being in a steeple chase, and the runner had to be careful where to place his feet. One false placement and the barrels would ignite. But wasn't that why he had chosen this route to score? Didn't he want to ignite the barrels? Didn't he want to go out with a bang? Yes, yes, a thousand times over... yes. And yet, something in him made the correct jumps, made him place his feet in the correct locations after each jump. Something within told him to play, to be professional, to win.

He jumped the last barrel. It wobbled a little when he landed, but not enough to ignite any hidden bombs. Leandet paused to ensure nothing would happen and that no other Bruisers were in the way, and then he stepped into the strike zone, drew back to throw, and let the ball fly.

Score!

***

Aryan Kapoor was sweating, and he didn't know why or from what source. He wasn't drinking, nor was he approaching his proverbial 'doom': his father or someone to which he owed extreme money. He knew the man he was approaching; not personally, of course, but someone he had admired for a long, long time. *It should be easy to approach him*, he thought, as he paused in the hallway just outside the locker room. He ran his soft fingers through his spikey-black hair. He lifted his arms to smell his pits to ensure he didn't, at least, stink. He breathed deeply to calm himself. Then he stepped through the door.

He found Rohl Leandet alone in the locker room. It was more of a chop shop, really, with tortured metal carcasses of trucks and Lancer battle tanks hanging on massive chains from the ceiling. Engine parts and old, rusty cannon barrels, ruined anti-grav pods, and outdated armorweave meshes were stacked twenty high along the walls. Old chairs and cabinets were strewn about the vacuous room as if an explosion had occurred. And perhaps it had. In other connected rooms, artillery shells had penetrated the building complex, and rubble was piled sky high. But not here. Here, in the center, lay a line of small abused metal lockers, a dripping shower with no curtain, a line of wet carbonwood benches, and a lone Xtreme DreadBall player.

Aryan clapped his hands as he approached the solitary man. The sound echoed across the room like thunder. Leandet either did not hear or did not care. He did not flex a muscle.

"Very good, Mr. Leandet," Aryan said, his voice echoing as well. "Congratulations on your well-earned victory. That was a sweet move you pulled on The Vook. It will take quite some time for the medibots to patch him up."

The striker turned and stared up at Aryan through a forest of unkempt, sweaty black curls. He wiped his face with a dirty towel and said, "Who are you?"

Aryan paused, suddenly nervous again and unsure of his decision to seek out this man. He swallowed, collected his thoughts, and said, "I am the answer to your prayers."

Leandet grunted, got up, pulled a flask from one of the lockers, and took a generous swig.

Aryan could smell the whiskey three meters away. He wriggled his nose, longed to take a sip, but continued instead. "I am Aryan Kapoor, son of Damon Kapoor of—"

"I know your family," Leandet said. "Who doesn't out here?"

"Yes, well, I am he. And I am here to make you an offer. An offer, I hope, you won't refuse... Leeland Roth."

The man stopped in his tracks and ruffled his brow as if he didn't know the name, but Aryan knew he had him. If the man thought his thick beard and artificially darkened skin were going to hide the truth from him, he was sorely mistaken. "Yes, I know who you are, Mr. Roth. I've been a fan of yours since I could walk. Perhaps you can hide the truth from others, but not me. I was there at your 979AE championship victory over the Draconis All-Stars. I saw you pull off that miracle against the Nemion Oceanics a year later, only to lose in the semi-finals against the Shan-Meeg Starhawks. I saw you valiantly break The Great Pile-On against the Keoputki Kolossals just five years ago. And... I saw your last game against the Jade Dragons. That one, I must say, was a difficult game to watch. For many reasons."

Roth moved as if here were going to throw a punch, and Aryan stepped back a pace, not sure if he had pushed the man too far. He swallowed back his fear and kept talking. "You even signed a poster that I still have hanging on my wall. Yes, indeed. I know all about you."

"What do you want? I'm not interested in selling my life story, or giving some interview about my brother, or confessing anything. I have no interest in whatever it is you are after." Leeland's body seemed to shrink at the realization that he had been discovered. Aryan could see him shake, as if his blood sugar was low. The striker seemed confused, not sure what to do. He stepped back a pace himself, and waited; his dark, angry eyes glaring.

"I am not interested in any of those things either, Mr. Roth. Honestly, I could care less about your personal life, your personal anything. I'm here for one reason only: I want to hire you for my DreadBall team."

Leeland huffed, threw up his hands, turned around, and returned to his flask. He drank even more generously this time. "Leeland Roth doesn't play DreadBall anymore, boy. All he's good for these days are back alley brawls, gutter fights, and this..." He held up his flask and winked.

Aryan chuckled, "Yeah, I've up-ended my fair share of bottles. Trust me, I sympathize. But I've no interest in seeing you play, Mr. Roth. Despite your excellent moves today, you seem pretty banged up. No. I want to hire you to be my coach and general manager."

"I don't coach, and I definitely don't make personnel decisions."

"Oh, come now, Mr. Roth. My father may think me a fool, but I *know* you. You were the Trontek 29er's captain for years, and that position demanded that you make a lot of decisions for the team, including personnel decisions. You were, for all intents and purposes, the team's *de facto* coach as well, since the goon they had at the time was as useless as a dead dog. Your 29er teams were unstoppable, due in large part to you. You were more involved than you wish to admit."

"Not anymore," Leeland said. He took the last sip from his flask and then tossed it away. "Go away and leave me alone. I'm not interested."

Aryan moved to protest, to argue, then paused. *No, think before you speak, idiot,* he thought, trying to hear the advice his sister Saanvi had given him before he had set out to find Roth. '*Don't screw this up like you have everything else, Aryan. This is your last chance. Father will not tolerate another failure.*'

He took a deep breath, then said, "I understand. You have moved on. You want to forget it all. You want everyone to forget you. I understand. You find more comfort in that fancy flask than in anything else. Perhaps you even find some comfort in the arms of a different lady every night." He chuckled. "Trust me, I know. We're a lot alike."

"You're nothing like me," Leeland said, his teeth snapping as if he were a dog. "Have you ever caught a metal sphere at two hundred miles an hour? Ever have your face bashed in by an angry Forgger? Stomped near half to death by a Siren? Ever... kill a man?"

Aryan shook his head. "No, but I know you have. That, and a lot more. Look... here's the deal. The First Sphere Intergalactic DreadBall League is going through an expansion. They want to add two Second Sphere teams and one Third Sphere team by next season. A tournament will be held in both spheres to determine the winners, who will then be given an invitation to join the FSIDL. My father and sister have decided that it is in the best interest of Kapoor Industries to enter the competition. There will be thirty-two teams that make up the tournament for the Third Sphere tryout. My team will be one of them, and I want you to be a part of it."

Leeland nodded. "I see. So, your daddy waves a lot of money in your face, and you thought, 'Why not?' What else do you have to do with Daddy's money, right?"

Stay calm, stay calm… "If you wish to berate me with personal insults, Mr. Roth, that's fine. Perhaps I deserve it. But full disclosure. This is my last chance too, as I think it might be yours. I screw this up, and I'm out, cut off, no longer a part of Kapoor Industries, and perhaps the family as well. I considered refusing and just living in the gutter like you seem happy to do, but this is the first time that my father has given me a job that I actually want to do, and I thought—perhaps foolishly—I could lure you back into action. The silly dream of a silly boy, I guess. But the offer is out there, Mr. Roth. It's yours if you want it."

Leeland considered, and it seemed for a moment that perhaps he would bite. Then he said, "Thank you, no, Mr. Kapoor. No amount of money will bring me back into the game."

Aryan pulled a pen and a pad of paper from his coat pocket, scribbled down a number, tore off the sheet, and handed it over. "How about this?"

Leeland looked at the number, huffed, and let the slip of paper fall to the cold floor. "Don't waste my time, boy."

"Okay," Aryan said and scribbled another amount. "How's this?"

Leeland ripped the second offer from Aryan's hand and looked at it. A small sliver of a smile brightened the old striker's face. Then he changed his expression quickly, back to the stolid, uncaring visage that he must have perfected over his years in exile. "Come on... now you're joking."

Aryan shook his head and winked. "I never joke about spending my father's money."

Leeland paused and it seemed as if he were about to reject the second offer. Then he crumpled up the paper and tucked it into his pants pocket. "So, what's the name of your team?"

Aryan shrugged. "I don't know... Aryan's Awesomes?"

Leeland puckered as if he were about to puke. "Well, we'll work on it."

Leeland paused and it seemed as if he were about to rejecting second offer. Then he crumpled up the paper and tucked it into his back pocket. "So, what's the name of your team?"

Arjon managed, "I don't know. [illegible] awesome!"

Leeland puckered as if he were about to puke. "Well, we'll work on it."

Chapter Three

The red dot of the laser rifle rested on Leeland's forehead. He ducked as the sniper fired and hit the target a centimeter off the bullseye.

"Get off my target range, you idiot!"

Leeland stood upright in front of the target and held his arms out as if he were the Vitruvian Man. He answered the woman's order with one of his own. "Carla, my love, you've lost your edge. Six years ago, you'd have taken my head off."

The rifle cracked again, and this time, he felt the buzz of the bullet across his ear. He whistled. *Close!*

He jumped down to the long, empty grass field between him and the woman doing the shooting. He walked toward her, not quite certain exactly where she was hidden among a hillock of sage brush sixty meters from his position. He breathed deep and kept walking. *I hope she remembers who I am.*

She emerged from her hiding spot. Carla 'Bullseye' Bock, the tallest, strongest, most impressive woman Leeland knew. Even in her retirement, now pushing sixty, she was still formidable at such a distance, in her green-and-gray fatigues, soft felt cap, hefting a five-foot Sinor Sniper with tripod. She carried the rifle with barrel down in one hand like it was a pencil.

"Who are you?" Bullseye called. "And how did you get on my property?"

"Your security owed me a favor."

They paused in front of each another, Leeland at least a head shorter. He looked up at her, thankful that her broad body blocked the hot sun. Her face was a little rounder than he remembered, her arms a little less 'cut,' as she might say. Bullseye's jet-black hair was streaked with gray, but her velvet eyes still beamed with that sharp intensity she had always brought to the pitch.

She recognized him, dropped the sniper rifle, and took Leeland in a bear hug that cracked his ribs. "Okay... okay, Carla... that's enough." He struggled to breathe. "I've missed you too."

"By the stars, where have you been?" she asked. "We thought you were dead."

She let him go, and Leeland drew a deep, painful, breath. "I tried to be, many times. No such luck, I'm afraid."

"You're *lucky* I didn't part your eyes, you sorry Zwerm. That was ten times foolish jumping in front of my target."

Leeland nodded. "But I knew you wouldn't shoot. This isn't a battlefield, and you're no longer a corporate marine."

"Once a marine, Leelee, always a marine."

He winced at his old nickname. He never liked that name, hated it in fact, but he let it go. "And once a Siren, always a Siren?"

She ignored his question, wrapped his arm with hers, and said, "Come, come. Let's get you a proper drink."

To Bullseye, a proper drink was green tea with a touch of lemon. Leeland considered asking her if she had anything stronger, but the foul expression on her face stayed his request. He accepted the steaming teacup humbly and took a seat on a stool in her fancy kitchen.

The whole property, in fact, was fancy, from the stone cut walkway they had taken up to the house, to the neatly-trimmed beds of red, yellow, and white flowers lining their path. In the house itself were clean and lush accommodations that rivaled the best hotels in the First and Second Spheres. And was that a golden chandelier hanging in the foyer? An antique 'smart' grand piano in the living room? Leeland was most impressed.

"The Sirens paid you better than the 29ers ever paid me, it seems. Nice digs."

Bullseye took a stool across from him. She blew on her tea and took a sip. "You didn't stay long enough for the pension."

That was a dig, but he let that go as well. "I had to leave, Carla, you know that."

"I know nothing of the sort, Leelee. You walked away, disappeared. Over a stupid mistake. Over an accident."

"Can we not get into this right now?"

He could see that she was growing angry, frustrated. Bullseye put her teacup down, spilling a drop. "Fine! But where have you been? What have you been doing?"

He told her everything. As much as he was willing to tell her, anyway, which wasn't everything, of course, but enough to allay her anger. He told her about the exciting—and oftentimes dangerous—world of Xtreme DreadBall play, something that she was familiar with conceptually, but hadn't tried herself, much to her own credit. Bullseye was no fool.

"It's a whole different dynamic in the seedy warehouses and back alleys of the universe," he said, laying out the details for her. "Death is a reality in the DreadBall arena as you well know. It's even more so in Xtreme. The fans actually get angry with you if you don't die."

Carla spared a chuckle. "You did okay by yourself, looks like. At least you're still alive."

Leeland shrugged. *I was unlucky.* "I was lucky."

He left out all the stuff about the women and the excessive drinking. Bullseye frowned against prurient details like that.

She took another sip. "But surely you didn't come out of hiding, and all the way here to the First Sphere, just to tell me all this. I'm glad you came, Leelee, but why are you here?"

Leeland smiled. "Because I need you, Bullseye. I've been hired by Kapoor Industries to coach and to manage their new DreadBall team."

He told her everything he knew about that as well, everything Aryan Kapoor was willing to confide in him and to put into his contract. He told her about the upcoming tournament and the plans for the FSIDL expansion. Bullseye knew about the expansion, having seen the details on news feeds.

"I'm quite comfortable in retirement, Leelee," she said. "I have my target range, all my firearms, my tea. More money than I can ever spend in a lifetime. Why would I ever get back in the game?"

"For ten years you were the Void Sirens' best guard. Three of those years you served as their captain. The Kapoors want me to make personnel decisions, and I can do so on the offensive side of the ball. But you were—still are—the best when it comes to defense. You understand that delicate transition from offense to defense, when the ball switches sides on a knife edge. You proved that time and again in your career. That's a part of the game I don't understand."

Bullseye rolled her eyes. "Strikers never do."

"I need your help in picking guards and jacks. I want you to be my second."

Bullseye took another sip of tea, held the cup close to her mouth and let the steam and aroma cover her face. She breathed deeply. She sipped again, then said, "Okay, so what's your offensive philosophy?"

Leeland considered. "Well, we need fourteen players, but not all can be stars. Our money's capped per tournament rules, so we have the budget to field perhaps four, maybe five, truly exceptional players. The rest will be slam-fodder, minimum-salary guys, at least at the beginning. I was thinking two key strikers, two jacks, one guard."

Bullseye shook her head. "That's bunk, Leelee. Jacks are your true slam-fodder. A dime a dozen. Two strikers, one jack, two guards."

Leeland smiled. He had said two jacks just to rile her up, to get her engaged immediately in the decision-making; he knew as well as she did, although Jacks were considered the 'jacks' of all trades on the DreadBall pitch, they were true utilitarian players. At least on human teams, anyway. Other races, like the cybernetic, slightly green and monkish Tsudochan, hired only jacks, while the sallow-grey and infinitely brittle Judwan hired only strikers. But human teams were a mixture of all three of the main positions, and it was vital that human teams (if they wished to be successful) have good diversity across the positions.

"That's fine," Leeland said, nodding. "So, you're in?"

"I don't know, Leeland," she said. He knew she was getting serious by not using his nickname. "Going all the way out to the Third Sphere, and it all may be over within a few months. That's a big commitment for an old lady like me."

"Old!" Leeland waved off such nonsense. "If you hadn't broken your leg in your final season, you might still be in a suit. You were one of the best guards I'd ever seen. Surely, somewhere amidst all that gray hair on your head, you still remember how the game's played. And you still love it."

He winked and flashed a smile at her, and that was probably why he was still upright. One didn't so easily insult Carla Bock in her own home, especially about her hair. But if their friendship meant anything, surely it meant that he could give her a good ribbing once in a while.

"You little punk," she said, shaking her head. "I wish we had played at the same time. I would have loved slamming you silly."

And indeed she would have, but she had retired a year before Leeland had begun his career. Luckily for him; health-wise, at least. "I'm sure you would have, and with ease, but now we can be on the same side and do something constructive with our lives again. The gods know, I need to. So what do you say?"

Bullseye took some time to consider. She got up, paced the kitchen, sipped more tea. Then she said, "There is the matter of my salary. I may be rich, Leelee, but I'll be damned if I traipse all the way out to the hinterland on my own dime."

Leeland fished around in his pocket. He pulled out a small scratch of paper, unfolded it, and handed it to her. "I've been instructed to offer you this..."

Bullseye took the offer and stared at it. Her mouth dropped open. She tried to shut it before Leeland noticed, but he said, "I know. It's incredible. These guys are serious, Carla. They mean business."

Bullseye handed the offer back to him, said, "Okay, I'm in. So, where do we start?"

"Well, as soon as you're ready," he said, taking the last sip of tea and setting the cup down, "we'll jump out of Kobau Station to Vitala, meet with Aryan Kapoor, sign your contract, and—"

"No," Bullseye said, closing her eyes and shaking her head as if she were a schoolteacher correcting a student. "That's not how we start. We start, my coach, my friend, by first visiting the Halcyon-Pleasance Sanitarium."

Leeland ruffled his brow. "A sanitarium? What for?"

Chapter Four

The Halcyon-Riverdale Sanitarium (or the HRS, as it was referred to by the masses) was the largest and most notable physical and mental health institute in the First Sphere. Cut out of the sheer cliff side of the Burobos Escarpments on the planet Wisteria, it was five levels of solid granite and steel. Some considered it the strongest fortress in the galaxy, and rumor had it that if the Council of Seven ever needed somewhere safe to hide, this would be the place.

He and Bullseye climbed the one hundred steps of the visitor entrance on the left side of the complex. Leland did not doubt it.

"Again, why are we here?"

Leland was growing annoyed with asking the question and not receiving a full answer. "You'll see," was all Bullseye would ever say, with a lilt in her voice and a tiny smirk on her lips.

"You do realize, Carla, that I'm your boss now? You have to tell me."

"You'll see."

They were admitted with no fanfare by a stooped, bald man who wore white scrubs, a paper mask, and blue prophylactic gloves. Leland then followed this man and Bullseye through the twisting corridors of the facility. He got lost once due to pausing to gawk at the patients that ran everywhere, from small children to the very old and infirm. Parts of the facility were calm, warm, and pleasant, more like hospitals and spas in other cities, on other planets. But as they

Chapter Four

The Halcyon-Pleasance Sanitarium (or the HPS, as it was referred to by the masses) was the largest and most notorious physical and mental health institute in the First Sphere. Cut out of the sheer cliff side of the Barabas Escarpments on the planet Wysteria, it was five levels of solid granite and steel. Some considered it the strongest fortress in the galaxy, and rumor had it that if the Council of Seven ever needed somewhere safe to hide, this would be the place.

As he and Bullseye climbed the one hundred steps of the visitor entrance on the left side of the complex, Leeland did not doubt it.

"Again, why are we here?"

Leeland was growing annoyed with asking the question and not receiving a full answer. "You'll see," was all Bullseye would ever say, with a lilt in her voice and a tiny smirk on her face.

"You do realize, Carla, that I'm your boss now? You *have* to tell me."

"You'll see."

They were admitted with no fanfare by a stooped bald man who wore white scrubs, a face mask, and blue prophylactic gloves. Leeland then followed the man and Bullseye through the twisting corridors of the facility. He got lost once, due to pausing to gawk at the patients that ran everywhere from small children to the very old and infirm. Parts of the facility were calm, warm, and pleasant, more like hospitals and spas in other cities, on other planets. But as they moved deeper into the rockside, the way grew darker, starker, until they reached barred doors with ominous words etched in perfect red letters above the doorway.

The Fullsham Center for the Criminally Insane.

Leeland's heart skipped a beat. "Umm, I think it's time for you to tell me what the—"

"Shh!" Bullseye said, raising a long finger to her lips. "I don't want to spook him. We're almost there."

The bald man handed them over to an armed guard in a pitch-black uniform. The hand-over was unceremonious, and the new man, without expression, said, "There are specific rules that you must follow when visiting a patient here. Do you know those rules?"

Bullseye nodded. "I do. I've been here before."

"And you?"

The question shook Leeland from his glassy stare at the words above the doorway. "Actually, no." He glared at Bullseye. "My companion has been very coy about everything."

"Very well. I'll explain them." The guard sighed, as if he were bored with their discussion. "Don't lean on the bars in order to give the patient a chance to grab and/or strike you. Don't make promises to the patient. Don't discuss with the patient anything that you have discussed with the medical staff. Do you understand these rules as I have read them to you?"

Leeland nodded.

"Very well. We had an attempted breakout a week ago. There was a riot. People were injured, inmates killed. Your boyfriend was in the thick of it."

"Boyfriend? What does he mean, Bullseye?"

She ignored him once again. "I understand, sir. You may let us in now."

The man unlocked the doors, opened them, and stepped aside. Bullseye led, Leeland followed.

"What did he mean by 'boyfriend'?"

Bullseye shook her head. "Nothing. A figure of speech. I've been here a few times to visit the same patient."

"What patient?"

They were escorted by an armed guard to a small cell one left turn and three right turns from the front door. The way was dark with a hint of moisture and mildew in the air. Cameras everywhere; nothing, not even an ant, could move without someone watching. With all the surveillance and the wet, humid air, Leeland found it hard to breathe. He shook his head. *No wonder these people are insane, he thought. I'd be insane too if I had to endure these conditions.*

A few of the patients/inmates tried to speak to them as they passed. Leeland just kept his head down and followed Bullseye's order not to make eye contact, which was specifically against the rules. Some of the inmates were women who propositioned him as he passed. It was difficult not making eye contact with them, but he did his best, kept on Carla's heels, and made it through the gauntlet.

The cell that they stopped in front of held a solitary man. As tall, if not taller, than Bullseye, though it was difficult for Leeland to know for sure. The man sat on the hard, rocky floor in the lotus position, without socks or shoes. He was naked, save for an orange loincloth. Around his neck lay a spiked iron shackle fixed to an eight foot chain that was bolted to the wall behind him. He was built like a brick tomb, all muscle and mass. He was bald, with red-and-green tattoos interlaced across his forehead, wrapping around his ears, and ending on his head in sharp tips of venomous fangs. His eyes were closed as if he were sleeping.

Bullseye tapped the iron bars of the cell's door with a fingernail. The sound echoed in the stale air. "Hello, Backhoe," she said. "It's good to see you again."

Leeland's jaw dropped and his heart skipped another beat. "Backhoe? Brutus 'Backhoe' Bertuchi? The Triple-B?"

The man's eyes opened, and he looked at Leeland with a watery expression as if the mention of his full name both excited and saddened him. He nodded. "That was what they called me, yes."

Leeland stepped back two paces, eyeing again the iron collar wrapped around the man's neck. "He's dangerous, Bullseye. Volatile. We shouldn't have come here."

Triple-B had once been a star guard on the Convict team known as the Long Rock Lifers. Like all Convict teams, their players wore collars around their necks that, when activated, could electrocute others around them at a specified radius. It was quite a devastating attack if pulled off at the right time. Triple-B's collar, unfortunately (for him, anyway), had been sabotaged and replaced with high explosives. But nobody knew when it would blow, and it was determined that if they tried removing it, it would ignite and wipe out the lot.

"If you think I'm going to put this beast on our team, you've another—"

"He's not criminally insane, Leelee," Bullseye interrupted. "He has anger issues, yes, but he checked himself in. He can leave at any time."

"He's a ticking time bomb," Leeland said, finding the courage to walk back to the cell bars and stare at the beast again. "He could blow at any minute and wipe out our entire team. Besides, didn't the guards say that he was involved in a riot recently?"

"Not my fault! I got swept up in it. I tried to stop it. Not my fault!" Triple-B shouted and climbed to his feet, confirming his height. He rushed the cell door, got caught by the chain, and held a couple meters away. He reached out with his massive hands and swiped the iron bars. The entire door rattled with his pounding. Leeland stepped back. Bullseye held her ground.

"Brutus... release!" She said, and it was like night and day. Suddenly, Triple-B calmed, put his arms down, and stepped back until the chain was dragging the floor. He blinked, several times, and smiled. "It's nice seeing you again, Carla. I've missed you."

Bullseye seemed to blush. "I've missed you too. How have you been holding up?"

Triple-B shrugged. "Okay, I guess. Our news vid viewing privileges are limited here. I don't know what's going on in the FSIDL. I'm not aware of what's going on in the game at all these days. Can you catch me up?"

Bullseye told him everything she knew about the state of the game, and about the Third Sphere tournament. Leeland filled in where her details were lacking.

"The game's played in the same manner you're familiar with," he said with a shrug. "Standard Digby rules still apply. Scoring is still the same and the goals and their locations on the pitch haven't changed. I'm sure you've seen it, but it seems now more than ever that young punks are trying to go for the easy high score in the back goal, but the front two are just as good with a strong arm. They think a heavy tip of the score in their favor won't tip it back the other way; but scoring four points on a team that's up by three still swings the score back to one the other way. Can't beat simple math."

By the end of their conversation, Triple-B was staring at them like a child enraptured by a bedtime story. Just a simple reminder of how the game was played seemed to fill the big guy with joy.

"You see," Bullseye said, taking Leeland aside, "he's all about the game. He longs to get back in."

"Yeah, but he's... well, he's old. No offense, Bullseye, but he's as old as you are. He's still built like an ox, yes, but the game has gotten faster, more brutal, since your time."

"There was no one better than Triple-B, Xtreme or otherwise," Bullseye said, "and you know it."

She wasn't lying. No one could take over a game like Brutus 'Backhoe' Bertuchi, save for perhaps Firewall or Kal Terza, or maybe even 'Lucky' Logan. The stories about Triple-B were even more legendary than Bullseye's. Leeland hadn't seen many of his games, but the old guard's reputation was undeniable. But... he was in a facility for the criminally insane, and whether or not he was admitted involuntarily or had checked himself in by choice, the truth could not be denied.

Triple-B was a walking bomb.

Leeland shook his head. "Too risky. We can't afford the risk."

"Do you want victory, Leelee, or safety? We've got one shot at this. One and done, isn't that what you said? We can't afford to play it safe. We need the best."

"And there are no other qualified guards that we can recruit? In all the galaxy? It's got to be Triple-B?"

Bullseye nodded. "Oh, of course there are others. But I know Brutus. He knows me. We can work together, and I know how to control him. Watch..."

Bullseye stepped back up to the bars. "Brutus..." she called, "attack!"

Triple-B bared his teeth, roared, and pulled his chain straight, doing exactly what he was told. The bolts that held the chain in place buckled, and dust flew from the wall. For a moment, Leeland thought the chain would break, but Bullseye said, "Release," and the guard calmed again.

"Guard!"

With that command, Triple-B paced his cell, mumbled about the game, the set-up, the rushes, the slams, the scoring, everything.

He paced and mumbled as if he were a coach himself, going over in his confused mind the details of some game that he had played in the past. Watching him was both painful and mesmerizing to Leeland, as years of experience and the memory of games played exploded out of the big man's mind.

"Okay, okay," he said. "Make him stop."

"Release," Bullseye said again, and Triple-B became as calm as a flower.

"Very well, Carla, I'll take him. But he's your responsibility, you hear? If things go wrong..."

"On my honor, I promise to keep him stable."

Leeland nodded and started going over in his mind all the legal ramifications of getting this brute of a man out of the facility and onto his team. He turned to Bullseye and asked simply, "How do you know all those commands, anyway?"

Bullseye shrugged and blushed again. "He talks in his sleep."

Chapter [illegible]

[illegible]

They were blinded by camera flashes and wolted by too many questions. Leeland didn't want to answer any of them, certain that he didn't have the answers right now that the media would accept. No, we don't have a team yet. No, we don't have a name. No, we're not ready for the first game. Aylyn insisted, however, that they face the press immediately upon return, more for a photo op than anything else, Leeland figured. Early publicity had its value, indeed, but it was far too early.

"[illegible], will you have a team ready [illegible]?"

"Ahh, soon. Soon."

"There is a rumor that you [illegible] gram. Is that true?"

"No comment."

"Why did you come out of hiding?"

"I wasn't hiding. I was simply on a hiatus, getting my head clean. Nothing more."

"Sig [illegible] owner and general manager [illegible] [illegible] would [illegible] [illegible] [illegible] they [illegible] Do you care to respond?"

"No."

"Do you [illegible] this [illegible] with [illegible]?"

Chapter Five

Kapoor Family Complex, Vitala

They were blinded by camera flashes and pelted by too many questions. Leeland didn't want to answer any of them, certain that he didn't have the answers right now that the media would accept. *No, we don't have a team yet. No, we don't have a name. No, we're not ready for the first match.* Aryan insisted, however, that they face the press immediately upon return, more for a photo-op than anything else, Leeland figured. Early publicity had its value, indeed, but it was far too early.

"*So, when will you have a team ready and fielded?*"

"Ahh, soon. Soon."

"*There is a rumor that you've acquired Brutus Bertuchi as your star guard. Is that true?*"

"No comment."

"*Why did you come out of hiding?*"

"I wasn't hiding. I was simply on... hiatus, getting my head clear. Nothing more."

"*Sir, Trontek 29ers owner and general manager, Horus Ruth, was asked if he would bring charges against you for breach of contract, since you violated your contract with them and did not play in your last game. He said they are looking into it. Do you care to respond?*"

"No."

"*Are you doing this in honor of your brother's memory?*"

That one stung. "I'm doing this because I was asked by Aryan Kapoor and Kapoor Industries to field a team for the tournament. That is all."

"*Yes, but…*"

It went on like that for another thirty minutes until even Aryan saw that Leeland was about to blow. An end to the questions was called.

"My apologies, Leeland," Aryan said, as he ushered them out of the press conference, "but this is big news. My family has never done something like this. *I've* never done something like this. It's a big deal. People need to know about it. And with you and Carla and Brutus heading the show, the other teams are beginning to scramble to find personnel with as much star power as you three."

"That's ridiculous," Leeland said. "We've only one player. We don't have a team yet or much of a coaching staff. Three has-beens don't make a team, Aryan."

Leeland didn't know why he was being so grumpy. The press conference probably. The question about his brother rankled. The others as well. He'd never been very good in the spotlight. That exalted position was always left to his brother. Victor had been good at that sort of thing. All Leeland wanted to do was field a team, and he had no time to preen in front of cameras. He'd leave the pomp and flash and politics of a team to someone like Aryan. All he wanted right now was to get the ball rolling, no pun intended.

He was about to ask that very thing when Aryan took him and Bullseye into a large building that had clearly been used in the past as some kind of steel processing plant. There were piles of rusty girders and iron tubes lining the wall. Cold, empty smelting vats and bull ladles hung from chains on the ceiling, and there was a scent of magnesium in the air. But the guts of the building had been torn away, and in its place, a make-shift DreadBall pitch had been painted on the concrete floor.

"It's primitive, I grant you," Aryan said as he presented the pitch with a wave of his hand, "but there was no time to construct anything better. This will have to do until we actually field a team and begin to draw revenue. What do you think?"

Leeland didn't like it. He could tell at a glance that the pitch was uneven, that it would be slick in places and too rough in others. A player's footing would be compromised all the time.

Over his long career, Leeland had trained on such pitches, so he understood that sometimes one had to make do. In the brutal arena of Xtreme, conditions were even worse. But there was an expectation there; it was understood from the beginning that you were practicing, and playing for, in effect, organized crime. With real DreadBall, the expectation was different. And with the Kapoor family being one of the richest in the Third Sphere, Leeland was surprised that accommodations weren't better right out of the chute.

"It'll be fine," Leeland said, stepping out onto the pitch to get a feel for its grip. Not good. "No worries."

"Then I leave you to it, Mr. Roth," Aryan said, clapping his hands and turning to leave. "You and your staff have two weeks to build me a DreadBall team."

***

Throughout the next several days, scores of potential players arrived at the Kapoor family complex for tryouts. Leeland was surprised. Despite his disdain for the spotlight, it seemed as if their little impromptu press conference had spurred an avalanche of wannabes and post-glory day players eager to climb back into their suits and go at it. Most were incompetent and ill-equipped, playable only as slam-fodder or fill-ins. Some were not even that competent. While

Bullseye and Triple-B served as screeners for the less capable, and helped to separate the chaff from the grain, Leeland tried to convince two veterans to come in for a shot.

The first was Conner Newberg, the so-called 'Jack of all Trades.' Leeland had played with him in the last couple years of his career on the Tronteb 29ers and found him to be just that: one of the most competent and experienced jacks in the game. Problems with his knees, however, had lessened his prowess over the past couple years; at present, he had been waived by the 29ers and was looking for a new home.

"I have at least two, perhaps three, good years left in me," he told Leeland over vid-comm.

"Then come out and give it a go with us. What have you got to lose?"

Conner chuckled. "Everything, Leeland. My career, my reputation, my name, my life... everything."

But he did show up, and despite a little rust beneath the hood, he was perfect for what Leeland needed: a veteran jack who could function both as player and as assistant coach.

Surprisingly, that's exactly what Triple-B was becoming as well. With Bullseye's careful control over the brute's emotional stability, he was proving to have a keen eye on talent. And the one person he recommended came as quite a surprise to Leeland.

"No," Leeland said when the name was suggested, "absolutely not. He's a jerk."

Triple-B nodded. "You're right. Shyler Coch is arrogant. He's a drama queen. He cares only about himself. Just like all strikers, right?"

Leeland shook his head. "I was never those things."

Even Triple-B laughed at that. His guttural voice sounded like an avalanche, and Leeland cringed to keep from getting swept up in it.

"With respect, Boss," Triple-B said, finishing his laugh, "I saw you lose your cool more than once on the pitch."

Leeland nodded. "Of course, in the heat of battle, that's to be expected. But Coch is an arrogant Zwerm from sun up to sun down. He brings too much baggage."

Bullseye sighed and rubbed her face which was growing redder by the second. Leeland could tell she was about to blow. The last several days, the breakneck speed at which they were all required to field a team was beginning to wear her down. "Look," she said, "I understand your apprehension, and if this were a normal recruitment, I'd be with you. But it isn't. We have to put a team on the pitch in real competition in less than five days. Shyler Coch is available right now, but I can assure you, that won't last long. Other teams will come sniffing. Our mission here is not to field the perfect team, but to field one that can win the tournament. Shyler Coch can help us do that."

She was right, of course, but there was more to it than that. If this team managed to survive the tournament and was given that invitation to join the FSIDL, Leeland would need players that jelled together, not perfectly, but well enough to maintain their cohesion through lean times. Personal chemistry between players was vital for the long-term health of the team, and no way was Leeland going to put a paper tiger on the pitch just so that it could win the tournament but then lose the war. Leeland was not going to put a team in the FSIDL that was going to be anyone's punching bag, especially for the Trontek 29ers. A guy like Shyler Coch, though brilliant, could be a major disrupter of that needed harmony. And besides, the arrogant punk reminded him too much of his brother Victor.

"Fine," he said, just to move on to the next crisis. "Bring him in, but I swear, if he causes trouble, I'll kick him out quick."

Triple-B struck an open palm with a meaty fist. The smack echoed across the pitch. "Don't worry, Boss. If he's trouble, I'll do it myself."

Shyler Coch showed up two days later and was every bit as brilliant as he was advertised. Age and wear and tear had gutted his speed, but he had the canniest sixth-sense that Leeland had ever seen. The man literally had eyes in the back of his head. He just knew instinctively where the danger spots were on the pitch, and he avoided them all. His lack of speed could, in time, prove seriously detrimental, but he had good throwing skills as compensation. So, as long as someone was waiting for the ball, Coch could throw it out of danger with a quick and efficient release. Leeland was also relieved that the man was behaving himself. He had been kind and courteous, willing to take advice, listen to the assistant coaches, and so far, he had not even complained about all the grueling practice hours needed for such a short recruitment period.

All that changed, however, when the second starting striker was announced.

Frank Marbary, or 'Little Frankie' as Bullseye was calling him due to his short stature, had the speed that Shyler lacked. He was a nobody, a walk-in who was trying out on a dare from his friends. But when he got on the pitch, his speed, his quickness, became immediately obvious.

Handling a ball thrown at you at two hundred miles per hour on average was not an easy skill to master, and Little Frankie had difficulty working his glove to catch the ball in stride. Once he got the hang of it, he became quite a late game threat due to his speed. Shyler Coch was less impressed with the young man's improvement.

"He's got ball control issues, Leeland," Shyler said. "I can't reliably throw the ball to him late in the game, when everything's on the line, and expect him to perform."

"He's getting better each day," Leeland said at his desk as he put his signature on the last few contracts for the non-starters that they had selected. "He'll be ready for the Sledgehammers. Besides, you're the veteran on the pitch. You know how this game's played. Train him. Teach him. Guide him. Take him under your wing."

"That's not what I signed up for."

Leeland rose from his chair and faced Shyler. The champion striker was taller than him, so it felt a little awkward trying to strike a stance of authority. "What did you sign up for, Shyler? Tell me, I'm confused."

"Well, I didn't sign up to play nurse-maid to a newbie who's going to get himself killed on the first rush. He gets banged around out there, Leeland. You've seen it. He may have the speed, but he's too thin. He doesn't have enough muscle yet. And it won't be just practice drills soon. It'll be the real deal, and any Forge Father team is going to bring the hurt, and you know it.

"The best thing to do is to let me be the lone striker to start and field an additional jack or guard to cover the empty slot. Perhaps you can bring him in when numbers decrease, but to start?" He rolled his eyes. "The knives are going to be out for Little Frankie, Leeland, and they won't stop cutting until he's ready to roast."

"So, you're telling me how to coach now?"

"You've been out of the game for a long time."

Leeland nodded. "Yeah, playing Xtreme, which is far more brutal than anything you've ever played."

"Fair enough. Compromise and making do are standard issue in that game... but not here. Here, you have to field the best right away."

"It's all we've got!" Leeland felt his anger rise, and he wanted to alleviate the pressure in his chest with a quick jab to Shyler's throat. But he didn't. Instead, he stabbed verbally. "You're too slow these days, Shyler. As good as you are at sensing danger and moving accordingly, you're going to have trouble outrunning pursuers.

That's a fact, whether you wish to accept it or not. You're going to get swarmed, and who do you give the ball to then? Conner? Great player, but I'm not going to put the fate of this team in the hands of a jack. I need strikers, good ones, and you and Frankie are it. So, I don't want to talk about it anymore. The matter is closed. Shut up, buck up, and deal with it."

"Gentlemen!"

Aryan Kapoor's voice rang out at the doorway. How long he had been standing there listening to them argue, Leeland did not know. Hopefully not very long.

When Shyler saw the owner of the team, he backed off, put up his hands in surrender, and said, "Very well. That's all I have to say about the matter." He nodded. "Good day to you both."

When he was gone, Leeland fell back into his chair, closed his eyes, and rubbed them with thumb and index finger until they began to hurt. He then stopped, blinked several times, swiveled his chair around to face Aryan, and tried to smile. "What can I do for you today, Mr. Kapoor?"

"Having difficulties with players already?"

Leeland shook his head. "Just a simple misunderstanding. Nothing I can't handle."

Aryan nodded, went to the front of the desk, and took the seat there. "So, the first game is against the Saltborne Sledgehammers. Will you be ready?"

"We will. We have a couple 'prospectives' we want to look at, then the last few contracts to sign. Then it's set. No going back."

"Anyone I may know by name?"

"Shadrack Menapi." Leeland handed over the young guard's file.

Aryan thumbed through it. He raised his eyebrows. "Interesting consideration, but as I recall, he's been plagued with injuries."

"Impressive early career," Leeland said, accepting the file back. "Spine seriously injured against the Glambek Ghosts. Acquired an opioid addiction due to that and was pretty much drummed out of the game after only three years. He's been healthy and drug free now for a while, but no one seems willing to give him a shot. He's fallen into that chasm common in this game: his star power has come and gone, and no matter how good he still is or was, nobody talks about ol' Shadrack anymore. The game has moved on. But Carla wants to bring him in for a try. That'll happen tomorrow."

"Very well." Aryan fished around in his pocket and produced a small piece of paper. He unfolded it and handed it over to Leeland with a guilty expression on his face, and said, "I'm sorry, but I'm going to have to make your day a little less joyous."

Leeland took the paper and read it. It was a name.

"Who is this?"

"A man that will fill one of your last jack positions."

Leeland crumpled up the paper and tossed it onto his desk. "No, sir. Sorry, but you agreed to leave me and Carla alone to pick the players that we wanted."

"Yes," Aryan said, nodding, "and I promise that this will be the only time." He leaned in. "Look, I owe his father a debt. I either pay up in money I don't have, or I put his son on the team. You don't have to use him at all. Just let him warm a spot on the bench, and if we win the tournament, we can boot him off. This is only temporary, I promise."

Only temporary. Famous last words by any rich person rich enough to make promises they could (or would) never keep. Leeland had seen it before. This was the first interference that Aryan was making. It would not be the last. And how long could he put up with it? The idea of losing the tournament early became more appealing with each passing day.

"Fine!" Leeland leaned back in his chair, frustrated. "Anything else, sir?"

"Yes, there is. The Kapoor Industries board has decided on a name for the team. Now, initially, they were in favor of using 'Kapoor' as the first name and also the symbol of our corporation. Something like 'The Kapoor Kolossals', but my father was able to sway their decision. Honestly, he doesn't want our brand associated with the team in case it—in case I—fail miserably."

Leeland huffed sarcastically. "Splendid father."

Aryan nodded. "He's an acquired taste, no doubt about that. So, they've decided to go another way. They still like the alliteration of their first option, but instead, they want to let the name represent the entirety of our fair planet.

"Here it is..."

Chapter Six

The planet of Vitala got its name, Leeland came to find out, from the undead creature of ancient Old Earth mythology, which was sometimes associated with vampires, bats, serpents, or demons. A Vitala, according to legend, served Kali, The Goddess of Destruction, and could secrete a deadly venom through its sharp fingernails. And so, the Kapoor Industries board thought it right and proper to give its team a name suitable to this mythology and as a goodwill gesture to the citizenry of a planet from which it took so much.

The Vitala Vipers' team logo was the head of a snake, baring its fangs through a starburst of red and gold. The official uniform, which was revealed publicly at the same time as the name and logo, was a mixture of red and gold as well, the helmet a dark red with gold streaks running like lightning over its curves. The new shininess of the uniforms struck Leeland with surprise; he rarely ever saw DreadBall uniforms in their virginal state, so clean, pristine, and untouched. That would change soon, he knew. But for today, he was enjoying the spectacle. And thankfully the team, with the exception of Shyler, seemed to like the name and color scheme.

The final reveal was the special DreadBall glove that all strikers and jacks wore in order to catch the ball. Without time to get the engineers and tech people to design one specifically for the Vipers, they opted for the standard model for most corporate teams: a crescent-shaped launcher on the back of the wrist. When the ball drew near, a holographic scoop was projected outward, aided by an electromagnetic pulse that funneled the ball into and out of the launcher as required. The actual glove that this devise was attached to was a bright gold color with the teeth of a viper painted down the fingers. Since the guards' primary job was to protect the ball carrier and to knock heads, their gloves were just big and heavy gauntlets, with no scoop and ball launcher for handling the ball; when they made a fist, the entire head of a Vitala struck its enemy with titanic force.

Three days later, the Vitala Vipers took to the pitch in their first official scrimmage.

Through rigorous negotiations, the FSIDL agreed to allow the teams participating in the Third Sphere tournament a small pre-season of three games, so that they might have an opportunity to take to the pitch and work out personnel and gameplay issues before the official tournament began. Leeland liked and disliked the idea. It was perfectly fine to get in some more practice before the real matches began, but there were no rules governing play in these pre-season, skirmish-like events. It was full on contact DreadBall, and half his team could be wiped out before the tournament even began. That's why Leeland held in reserve a list of names of prospectives that almost made the cut; he hoped that he wouldn't need them.

The purpose of these skirmish games was to also determine the seeding of the tournament, and the FSIDL officials would weigh ranks based upon the final number of wins, points scored, and the number of injuries and kills each team accumulated by the end of game three. All the team names were fed into a database, and opponents were randomly selected. The good news was that they didn't have to win any of these games; though if not, their seeding would be very low, and presumably they'd be facing off against far superior teams. So, winning was important, and the first team that the Vitala Vipers would be facing was rotten luck, in Leeland's estimation anyway.

The Saltborne Sledgehammers was a Forge Father team whose members were miners from the saltpans on Miradan Wake, a tiny planet a few light years from Vitala. Neither Miradan nor Vitala had an official DreadBall stadium (that would be built if either team won the tournament), so they agreed to use a near orbit GCPS ship that had an old, but functional, pitch. Leeland was happy to agree, for the on-board pitch provided was not much better than the one that the Vipers had been training on for weeks. *Finally*, Leeland thought, *we've caught a break.*

So, both teams took to the pitch, and Leeland held his breath as he gave each of his six starters a thumbs up, a fist bump, and words of encouragement.

"This is our first game," he said, speaking loud enough so that everyone could hear and feel the energy in his voice. "This is not an elimination round, but every game counts. They're going to disrespect us out there because we're a corporate team full of rookie *human* players. Green as grass, they'll say. Wet behind the ears. I say bull to all that! You're the Vipers, and there is no team better equipped, better trained, then you. So you get out there and knock heads, and most importantly... strike goals! I want to run up the score on these tiny bastards. I want to see them drop from exhaustion. I want to see them beg for mercy. You can do it. I trust you. Bullseye trusts you. Kapoor Industries trusts you.

"Now get out there and show the Third Sphere how deadly a viper's venom can be!"

They roared their satisfaction of his pep talk. Leeland had to admit to himself that such a speech was a little corny, but it sometimes took a while for a coach to get the feel, the vibe, of his players. He'd get better, the team would get better, and everything would fall into place. Hopefully...

"Not bad," Bullseye said as she winked and followed the team into the arena. "You come up with that all by yourself?"

Leeland blew her a raspberry, followed, and poked her in the side.

He was feeling good about their chances.

Then the Saltborne Sledgehammers took to the pitch, and Leeland's heart stopped.

***

"Painmaster," Leeland said when he was able to breathe again. "They have Painmaster as a guard?"

Bullseye sighed. "Apparently so."

Yurik 'Painmaster' Yurikson was a Forge Father guard and decidedly one of the toughest defenders to ever take the pitch. His normal area of operation was the First Sphere, moving from team to team, growing bored with one team when his financial and play options with that team declined, and then he'd move on to the next team, and so on. He was a loner, and nobody knew much about him save for his skills in the game, and those skills were legion.

"Don't worry," Bullseye said, patting Leeland on the back, "Triple-B can handle him."

Leeland nodded wearily. "I hope so."

The teams took to the pitch, the ball was released on the center line, and the game began.

Conner Newberg snagged the whirling ball first; his new glove allowed him to constrain its volatility without fear of his arm being shredded. He held the ball close to his body and waited for his defensive shield to take shape, with Triple-B taking the lead in that capacity. Conner's plan was to move quickly to the first, and closest, opposing goal and try a quick score, as per the game plan. But a

Sledgehammer guard named Thorgus Oakbiter undercut Triple-B's legs and took him down. This left Conner exposed to Sledgehammer jacks who raked at his glove to try to dislodge the ball. Conner was a professional, however. He kept the ball tucked tightly against this body, fought his way through their jacks, and reached the strike zone in good order. He took a shot on the goal, but Sledgehammer striker Borus Dakport flew into the arching shot and snatched the ball out of the sky.

The Sledgehammers were now on the move, but their first strike on goal went wide and bounced into Shyler Coch's glove.

The game wavered back and forth like that for a time, with each team taking shots on goal but having little success. Then, on the Sledgehammer's fourth rush, Triple-B and Painmaster met in the middle.

Yurikson started the rush doing something that many guards often do – he feigned being tripped and fell onto the ball. Due to their lack of a ball-handling glove, guards could not catch and/or carry the ball, and so by default, it scattered. It was even odds as to where it might scatter, but since more Forge Fathers were around the area where it occurred, the odds were in their favor.

And indeed, the ball dropped handsomely into the possession of one of the Sledgehammer's strikers, whose launcher was affixed to the actual palm of the glove. The teams collected themselves and went after the ball-carrier. Triple-B did not.

Angered by Painmaster's trick, Triple-B decided to conduct his own 'trick' by putting his boot into Yurikson's face while he was still prone. Luckily, the referee's attention was diverted, so Triple-B's move was not detected. Less fortunate for Triple-B, however, was Yurikson's legendary speed, despite his mass. Triple-B's boot struck Yurikson's face, and Leeland heard the crack of the guard's faceguard and saw a light spray of blood through the broken bars, but when Triple-B pulled his boot up for another strike, Yurikson moved quickly and grabbed the leg and twisted.

The roar of pain from Triple-B echoed across the pitch, and he went down. At first it was hard to know if Triple-B's knee had been dislocated by the twist, both brutes now writhing on the floor, trying to push the other away. When Triple-B finally gained his feet, he seemed no worse for wear. Leeland was relieved. That good feeling, unfortunately, did not last.

Yurikson rolled away from Triple-B, recovered his footing, and went in for the kill. The Forge Father lowered his head and rushed the human guard like a bull, holding his meaty punching gloves forward as if they were horns. Luckily, Triple-B was familiar with the move, having seen it, apparently, on CorpsNet. He held his ground, but at the last moment, when the Painmaster tried to thrust his fists up into the soft spot beneath Triple-B's chest armor, the spot where the sternum lay waiting, Triple-B turned to the left and caught the upper cuts in the side armor of his uniform. No bones were shattered, thankfully, but the strike lifted Triple-B off the ground. Yurikson did not back down; he kept those fists where they struck and pushed Triple-B into the wall.

A little way down the pitch, but coming on strong, was a cluster of men and Forge Fathers trying to gain advantage and the ball. The ball had switched sides a few times since Triple-B and Painmaster had been going at it, but now it lay firmly on Little Frankie's glove, and Shadrack Menapi was doing his best to keep the rookie from being slammed.

"Finish him!" Leeland screamed at Triple-B through the roar of the crowd. "Protect the ball carrier!"

Triple-B and Yurikson were trading blows. Triple-B was pounding the Painmaster's neck and shoulders with strikes that would paralyze any normal man. Yurikson continually slammed Triple-B into the wall, such that the wall itself had cracked; if it collapsed, and if they fell through that gap, both players would be ejected from play.

"Finish him!"

The cluster was growing closer, and Triple-B made an attempt to break free. He kicked up with his left knee and took Yurikson in the gut. The strike dislodged the Forge Father just enough for Triple-B to grab him and toss him aside. Yurikson hit the pitch hard and tumbled away. Then he lay still.

"On the ball!"

But Triple-B had other plans. Seeing the Painmaster lying there, still and quiet, he went to finish the job. As the spread of players drifted by, Menapi screamed at Triple-B to 'plow the field' while Shyler waited in the Sledgehammer's back strike zone for Frankie's pass. "On the ball! On the ball!" Leeland kept shouting at his star guard, but Triple-B walked up to Yurikson and lifted his boot for another stomp.

"No... don't do it! Don't—"

Triple-B's boot struck the Painmaster's head once more. The Forge Father's helmet cracked, though it did not appear as if the contents were damaged in anyway. Triple-B raised his foot again for another head crusher.

Foul sirens blared, and Triple-B was marked with red light. A metallic female voice announced his fate. "*Brutus Bertuchi... you have been ejected!*"

In the midst of Triple-B's ejection, Menapi was slammed by Forge Father jacks and taken down. Frankie made a desperate attempt at throwing Shyler the ball, but without guard protection, his legs were swept, his pass was off target, and he threw an interception.

Three rushes later, the Saltborne Sledgehammers won the game by three points.

***

Leeland found Triple-B in the locker room. "Didn't you hear what I said? Was there too much blood in your ears to hear me?"

Triple-B, sitting on a bench, looked up at his coach, leaned right, and spit blood in a nearby spittoon. Sweat glistened off his iron collar. "You said finish him, and that's what I was trying to do."

Leeland shook his head. "That's not what I meant, and you know it. I said finish him and then protect the ball. You should have moved to protect Frankie. As it was, we lost the game because we gave up that score. Now, the next time I tell you to do something, you do it. Do you understand?"

Triple-B stood, and despite being covered only in a towel, his presence was intimidating. The amount of muscle on display was more than Leeland had ever seen, and he found it difficult to show resolve. The bruises on Triple-B's shoulders, stomach, and flanks were both impressive and terrifying. A few more rounds of punishment like that, and Triple-B would have been the one being finished.

"Do you understand me?"

Bullseye intervened. She placed her hand on Triple-B's forming fist, said, "Release, Brutus. Please. Go shower and clean up. I'll find you in a minute, and we'll talk."

Triple-B relaxed but stood a moment more to stare angrily at his coach. Then he turned toward the showers and walked away. The rest of the players in the room went back to normal activity.

"What's the matter with you, Leelee?" Bullseye whispered. "You can't embarrass him like that in front of everyone. He's a proud and strong man. He won't put up with it."

"He screwed up, and we lost the game."

Bullseye nodded. "Yes, he did. He should have listened to you. He made a mistake. It cost us the game, but it won the crowd. He took the Painmaster out of the game, and I doubt he'll be back for this tournament. That matters, Leelee. Now every coach is looking at Triple-B and trying to figure out how to beat him. Every team is scared to death of us right now, and that'll go a long way in the future."

She was right again, Leeland knew. But with only three scrimmages for seeding, victories mattered more than anything else. Yes, injuries and kills would help, but victories, victories, would be the basis on whom they played against in the first round of the tournament. They needed a high seeding, and right now, their prospects looked dim.

"You have to find a better way to talk to these men, or you'll lose them."

"I know!" He didn't mean to snap at her. He was more frustrated with himself than with her or even with Triple-B. He'd let his emotions get the better of him. Next time, he promised himself, it'd be better.

"Everyone shower up," Leeland said, ignoring Bullseye's strong stare, "dress, and get ready. We leave on a shuttle for Vitala in an hour."

this tournament. That matters, Leelee. Now every coach is looking at Triple-B and trying to figure out how to beat him. Every team is scared to death of us right now, and that'll go a long way in the future."

She was right again. Leeland knew that with only three games for seeding, victories mattered more than anything else. Yes, injuries and bills would help, but victories, victories would be the focus on whom they played against in the first round of the tournament. They needed a high seeding, and right now their prospects looked dim.

"You have to find a better way to talk to these men, or you'll lose them."

"I know." He didn't mean to snap at her. He was more frustrated with himself than with her or even with Triple-B, but he let his emotions get the better of him. Next time, he promised himself, he'd be better.

"Everyone, listen up," Leeland said, ignoring Bullseye's strong stare. "Dress and get ready. We leave in a [illegible]. We'll [illegible] hour."

Chapter Seven

The Vipers' next game was against a Rebels team called the Polmak Resisters. Leeland considered benching Triple-B, at least for a short time, as punishment for insubordination, but took Bullseye's advice and put him smack in the center of the starting line. Three rushes later, he had sent one Gaelian jack, one Sorak jack, and two Ralarat strikers into the Sin Bin. All came back onto the pitch in time, save for one of the Ralarat strikers, who refused to face Triple-B and quit on the spot. Near the end of the game, Triple-B was ejected again for fouling, but by then, it was too late for the Resisters. They lost by four points.

Their next and final opponent in the skirmish round was the Hardshell Pulverizers, a Teraton team that loved using their teleport special technology to great effect. As a matter of course, Leeland made a formal complaint about the use of the technology to the tournament's advisory and rules board but knew that nothing would come of it. It had been established a long time ago in the Digby by-laws that non-human participants in DreadBall could utilize their species' so-called 'inherent traits' during DreadBall competition. Teleportation was considered one of those traits and thus, it was allowed. But Leeland hated it; hated it so much, in fact, that he considered simply forfeiting the game, taking the loss, and accepting a lower seeding. But it was quite possible that they would have to face the Teratons again in the official tournament, and there would be no backing out then. The best move was to play them, get a good sense of their strengths and weaknesses, and hope for the best.

He sat Triple-B out for the match. The aging brute was so banged up after his first two outings that he needed a rest. Besides, he had developed a nasty contact abrasion underneath his iron collar, and there was fear of infection. The man's body was simply not used to such punishment anymore, but he'd be back soon enough, after the skirmish round and after the longish break between the last seeding game and the official tournament. The bulk of the guard duties, then, fell to Shadrack Menapi. As one of the guards picked up during recruitment, Menapi was doing yeoman's work against a relentless and hostile Teraton team.

But the true star of the Vipers in the game was Conner Newberg, The Jack of All Trades. Down a star guard, the Viper jacks, with Conner's guidance, stepped up to fill the gap.

Having played against the Ukomo Avalanchers many times as a Trontek 29er, Conner understood how to play against a team where every player could blink out of existence and then rematerialize right behind your lines; short jumps, but oh so annoying. It was a frustrating tactic that drove many coaches mad, even those as skilled and knowledgeable as Bullseye.

"Trust me on this one," Conner said, trying to convince her of his plan. "Let me coordinate the team's defense on the fly. I know exactly what they're going to do."

"Are you suggesting that you know more about defense than me?" Bullseye said it in a way that sounded more like a jest than a real challenge to Conner's request.

He winked. "They don't call me 'Jack of All Trades' for nothing."

Bullseye rolled her eyes. "You're the only one who calls you that these days, you goon." She gave him an affectionate nudge. "Okay, but keep an eye on me for tactical adjustments during the game. Understood?"

Conner gave her a nod, a little peck on the cheek, another wink, and slammed his helmet into place. "I'll watch you like a hawk."

Conner got to work. He ordered himself and any other jacks that came into play to remain on the Viper's side of the starting line, and some deep, so that, when a Pulverizer jack suddenly popped up in a Viper strike zone, there was at least one—and often two—Viper jacks in position to intercept it instantly.

The downside to this strategy was that Viper strikers had to rely on their guards alone for down-the-pitch protection. Shadrack and his fellow rookie guard did their best, but serious pressure was placed on Shyler and Little Frankie to deliver scores, and both wanted to be the chief scorer of the game. Their on-pitch rivalry, however, ticked Leeland off such that he benched Little Frankie for a short time to tamp it down. Shyler was happy about that, but in response, the Pulverizers began holding back some of their jacks to prevent the Vipers from scoring on the long ball; and in the final two rushes, the Pulverizer's counter-tactic worked, sending Shyler into the Sin Bin for the rest of the game.

Luckily, Shadrack managed to dislodge the ball from a Teraton jack. It bounced right into Conner's hands.

Never known for being a high scorer, Conner proceeded to violate his own order. He crossed the centerline and into Pulverizer territory. One juke and one fake out later, he was standing in the closest strike zone.

One of the Teratons that he had embarrassed on the juke blinked out of sight. Anticipating where the tortoise-like brute may rematerialize, Conner threw the ball as hard as he could. The Teraton guard reappeared right where Conner threw, and before it could raise its gloves for protection, the ball slammed into its head and ripped half of it away. The ball was travelling so fast, however, that the strike didn't force it off course. It simply blasted through the creature's skull and right into the goal. The crowd erupted in cheers and the Vipers went up by one.

Time expired.

Before the game was officially called, however, the referees took another look at Conner's throw to see if it was a foul. They determined in the end that it was not, since the poor Teraton was *not* in the line of the throw when Conner had made it. Leeland was obviously happy with the ruling. The Vipers had finally caught a break.

Even Triple-B imbibed in the champagne that was uncorked in the Viper locker room afterward, and for a few fleeting moments, Leeland felt good about their prospects in the coming tournament. A two-and-one start wasn't bad and should ensure them a reasonably high seeding. Who would they play first? It was hard to know in a thirty-two team one and done, but that conversation would begin tomorrow morning.

For now, he and Bullseye and Triple-B and Conner and all the others enjoyed their sweet victory.

Until a small knock came to the locker room door, and a gray-suited man, with hefty security, stepped in and handed Leeland a letter.

Leeland took the letter and read it to himself. His joy was gone. It was a cease and desist letter from the Trontek 29ers.

Chapter Eight

"Mr. Newberg's contract with the Ironton 29ers clearly states that he may not play with any team, nor be in competition with the Ironton 29ers for a full standard year of [illegible] relations."

The Vipers' lawyer read through the fine print in the contract that the delegation from the 29ers had delivered to them, while both legal teams stared daggers at each other over the long, wide table at the Kapoor Family Complex. A representative from Uggy had been called in, and sat at the head of the table to the right. Academy Trainer Newberg sat between Leeland and Buckley. Aqua was not present. Erec, perhaps more so than the [illegible], and Desh Vetter, [illegible] Leeland the most.

"But Mr. Newberg is not in competition with the 29ers," the Viper lawyer said. "He is on the Vipers, which has no direct [illegible] with your team."

The 29ers lawyer set the contract on the table, [illegible], then said, "Yes, but this tournament in which you are currently involved may result in your victory. At which point, the Vitala Vipers would be in direct competition, and Gunner Newberg's contract would prevent him from playing in the FSDL."

The Vipers' lawyer nodded. "And we agree, if the Vipers win the competition, then Mr. Newberg would have to sit out the required number of games until he has satisfied the time requirement as outlined in the clause and [illegible] letter."

Chapter Eight

"Mr Newberg's contract with the Trontek 29ers clearly states that he may not play with any team that may be in competition with the Trontek 29ers for a full standard year after release."

The Vipers' lawyer read through the fine print in the contract that the delegation from the 29ers had delivered to them, while both legal teams stared daggers at each other over the long, wide table at the Kapoor family complex. A representative from Digby had been called in, and she sat at the head of the table to the right. A steaming Conner Newberg sat between Leeland and Bullseye. Aryan was not present. That, perhaps more so than the bogus cease and desist letter, angered Leeland the most.

"But Mr. Newberg is not in competition with the 29ers, sir," the Viper lawyer said. "He is on the Vipers, which has no direct contact with your team."

The 29ers lawyer set the contract on the table, sighed, then said, "Yes, but this tournament in which you are currently involved may result in your victory. At which point, the Vitala Vipers would be in direct competition, and Conner Newberg's contract would prevent him from playing in the FSIDL."

The Vipers' lawyer nodded. "And we agree. If the Vipers win the competition, then Mr. Newberg would have to sit out the required number of games until he has satisfied the time requirement as defined in the cease and desist letter."

"No, that is not satisfactory. The contract clearly states, '*may* be in competition.' That is the operative word here. The Vipers may be in competition within a standard year with the Trontek 29ers, and therefore, Conner Newberg may not play."

"This is nonsense!" Conner shouted, throwing his copy of the contract across the table. "You gonna seek out and remove every ex-29er in the tournament? There are several that I know of by name, and—"

"We have, Conner," said Horus Ruth, interrupting. "We have reviewed them all. Everyone else, including your boss Leeland Roth, seems capable of reading and following a contract. All but you."

Leeland had to hold himself back from climbing over the table and punching the teeth out of Ruth's smarmy little mouth.

Horus Ruth was the current owner and general manager of the Trontek 29ers. He was the kind of owner that players liked come payday - he had the good sense to know that money speaks loudly in the game - but loathed in private. Short in stature but large in petulance, his father had been owner and general manager before him, and Leeland had had a good relationship with the senior. Not so with the son, who had assumed his father's responsibilities a few years ago. But Leeland remembered Horus the Second as a mustachio-twirling jerk even when he was a teenager. Looking at the boy over the table, Leeland was beginning to grow weary of dealing with the less-than-stellar children of great men.

The 29ers lawyer jumped in. "You are the only ex-player, Mr. Newberg, that is in violation of his contract, and we are exercising our right to enforce that contract."

Leeland was about to jump in, but Bullseye touched his hand. He calmed and held back. Bullseye turned to the Digby representative and asked, "What does Digby say about this?"

Her name was Tasha Marnes, and she sat in the chair like a thin slice of granite. Leeland wondered at first if she was a plant from the 29ers, someone acting the part, because who out here in the Third Sphere had the knowledge and wherewithal to know every DreadBall representative? It would be easy to fake the role. But no. She had all the proper credentials from the governing body of DreadBall; Leeland was more than familiar with those documents. She was legitimate, and the fate of his team rested in her hands.

Tasha Marnes cleared her throat and averted her eyes from the Vipers' side of the table. Leeland's heart sank.

"It is the decision of Digby," she said, "to agree with the interpretation of the contract that the Trontek 29ers have put forth. Mr. Newberg is in violation of the contract that he signed with the Trontek 29ers' organization, and therefore, is ordered to stand down as jack on the Vitala Vipers, until such a time as a full standard year has transpired from his departure from the 29ers; at which point, he may resume his role as a full member of the Vipers' team."

"By then it will be too late!" Conner said.

"Can we appeal?" Leeland asked before the team lawyer could ask the same question.

Marnes nodded. "Yes, you may appeal this ruling."

"Then we do so," the Vipers' lawyer said. "And can this ruling be held in abeyance until our appeal goes through?"

Marnes shook her head. "I'm afraid not. Since three games have already been played with Mr. Newberg as a starting player, in violation of his contract, Digby considers those games time served on his appeal. He must now sit out until the ruling on the appeal goes through."

"And when will that be?"

Marnes looked at the ceiling as if the answer was there. Her thin lips moved silently as if she were calculating days in her mind.

Then she nodded. "Thirty-five standard days."

A collective moan went up between Leeland, Bullseye, and Conner. But there was nothing else they could do. Marnes ended the meeting and left without further comment.

Leeland pushed himself away from the table and walked into a corner. His throat was dry. His head pounded. He needed fresh air, but more importantly, he needed to know what had just happened. Something wasn't right.

He'd been a member of the Trontek 29ers for years, and there had been many members of the team that had left early and had played on other teams, in *direct* competition with the 29ers. And that same boiler plate clause about non-compete in Conner's contract had been in every one of their contracts as well. And the team had never bothered to enforce it. Why now?

New management. Leeland considered. *Old man Ruth was out, the son was in.* It was possible. In his self-imposed exile for the past five years, he hadn't kept up with his old team's legal shenanigans. But it didn't make sense, especially out here, so far away from any direct contact with the FSIDL. The chances of the Vipers actually getting through such a rigorous tournament were slim at best. Why waste time and treasure bringing up a legal case when, like the Vipers' lawyer had said, the smarter play would have been to wait and see how the tournament played out, and then apply a strict interpretation of the contract. No, something - someone - was purposefully trying to sabotage their play even before the tournament began.

Who?

Leeland turned to leave. Horus Ruth was waiting for him. Leeland wasn't the tallest man in the galaxy. Horus Ruth was even shorter.

The boy smiled up at him as if they had been life-long friends. "It's nice seeing you again, Leeland. It's been too long."

"Nice seeing me again, eh? Could have fooled me. I'm not familiar with the idea of being kind to someone right after you've stabbed them in the back."

"A contract is a contract, Leeland, and if we don't enforce them, they are worthless. My Father never understood that."

"Your father was a great man, Horus. Far better than you'll ever be."

Ruth's pleasant smile was replaced with a frown. "Well, at least my father never had to carry the shame of seeing his son kill someone."

Leeland moved forward, his rage intact, and put his angry, reddening face close to Ruth's. "What did you say?"

Ruth pulled back a pace. "I think you're still young enough to hear clearly, my old friend. You're lucky the statute of limitations has run out on your contract; otherwise, we would have sued you as well, to recoup all the money we had to spend cleaning up your dirty deed."

Ruth chuckled, and that craven smile appeared again. "But I think you've suffered enough. Thinking about it every day. Reliving the roar of the crowd, the anticipation of your score. But wait! What's this? An opportunity to strike back at your own brother? For what violation, I wonder. What violation could have been so egregious that it required murder?" Ruth chucked again. "I'm sure the ghost of Victor Roth haunts you every—"

Leeland swung at Ruth's tiny head. Bullseye blocked the punch and slammed him against the wall. "No!" she said, shouting into his face. "Not here. Not now."

He struggled, but she was strong. His movements were chaotic, unfocused. In his rage, Leeland could not push her away. All he could do was stand there with her forearm in his throat, listening to Ruth's nasty little chuckle.

The Trontek lawyers pulled their client away. "Have a good tournament, Mr. Roth," Ruth said as his men ushered him out of the room. "I'll be watching."

When everyone was gone, Bullseye let him go. "Are you an idiot? If you had hit him..."

"Buzz off!" Leeland said, pushing Bullseye away.

"What's wrong with you?" she asked, her expression more of surprise by his tone than his anger. "Are you purposely trying to sabotage the team?"

"Oh, I think that's already being done. We're screwed."

"We've got plenty of jacks to fill the gap until Conner comes back."

Leeland shook his head. "None that are as good as he is."

"True, but we adapt, we persevere. We've got a game in three days, Leeland. We have to move on. We've got practice this afternoon, so get your head clear and let's get to work."

Leeland pushed her aside. "No, not today. I'm not doing a thing today."

Bullseye called for him as he left the room. Leeland ignored her. He paused in front of the elevator. When it opened, Aryan Kapoor's anxious face greeted him.

Aryan stepped out. "I'm sorry I'm late. What was decided?"

Leeland felt rage all over again, and he pushed the boy to the floor. He stood over him, fists clenched. "You're late, and they've just determined our fate. We'll be lucky to win a single game now."

Leeland stormed onto the elevator and watched the door close as his body shook in anger.

***

He ducked the first fist with ease. The second, not so much.

Leeland felt a trickle of blood down his chin and was worried that the blow had loosened a tooth. But that didn't stop him from joining the fray.

The man that had struck him in the bar that he had gone to took a chair on his back from another patron who just happened to be in the right place at the right time. Or vice-versa, depending on one's perspective. From Leeland's, it was a good thing, for the drunken rage in the man's eyes as he was about to deliver another strike on Leeland's face was a frightening sight indeed. That second punch would have broken his jaw, Leeland knew, for he had received such blows on the pitch; but with the protection of a helmet, they usually amounted to just a bruise or a headache. The chair strike against the man took him down. Leeland was grateful for the assist.

His gratitude did not last for long, however, as another two amateur pugilists entered his space and began dealing out more pain. Leeland ducked one of their fists and then delivered his own on both, a glancing blow against one man's nose, and a solid strike to the top of the other man's head. Leeland howled in pain as his knuckles cracked against thick skull. Then he realized that it wasn't a man, but a Brokkr. Made sense, when he thought about it, as many of the patrons in the bar were from rival teams.

Brokkr players were, like their Forge Father cousins, hard as iron with a low center of gravity that made them near impossible to take down in a straight up one-on-one. The little monster in front of him was as thick and wide as he was tall, and his face was a tangle of black and gray whiskers arranged like barbed wire.

The Brokkr took the strike as if he'd been tickled by a feather, then delivered a thick fist against Leeland's ribs that picked him up and threw him against one of the last upright tables.

The table splintered and collapsed as Leeland fell into it. The Brokkr pursued, but Leeland was ready for him, despite the ample amount of alcohol coursing through his veins that impaired his vision. It looked like two Brokkrs were coming at him. Too bad there weren't three; if so, he'd simply target the middle one. But he had to make a decision, and he kicked out at the groin on the Brokkr to the right.

He was wrong.

The real one on the left picked him up and began delivering countless blows against his head, shoulder, and neck. Leeland fought back as best he could, acting like a cat and scratching at the Brokkr's eyes and face. He drew blood and screams from the little fellow, though those screams were more shouted obscenities than cries of pain.

"I want to say," the Brokkr said through his insults, "that it's an honor to be beating the hell out of you. I'm a big fan."

"Thank—thank you," was all Leeland could muster through a puffy lip and bleeding gums. "I'll give you an autograph if—"

He wasn't able to finish his sentence, as the large shadow of Triple-B came into view. The big man plucked the Brokkr off Leeland like he was a grape and tossed him across the bar and into a bloody mass of men trying to exit as sirens from Vitala law enforcement began to blare. Then Triple-B picked Leeland up like a sack of dirty clothes and tossed him over his shoulder.

They fled out the back exit, down a small street, and into a dark alley, where Backhoe dropped his cargo hard onto the cold, dirty concrete. Leeland yelped as his bruised hip struck solid pavement. Then someone tossed a handkerchief into his face.

"You're lucky we found you," Bullseye said, out of breath. "Another minute and you would have woken up in a Vitala jail cell, or a hospital, or both."

Leeland steadied himself against a pile of discarded cushions and broken chairs. The alley smelled of grease, oil, and piss. He was surprised he could still smell things, given the condition of his nose. He began wiping blood away from his mouth. "Didn't I tell you to leave me alone?"

"Not with so many polite words, no," Bullseye said, daring to crouch down beside Leeland, "but for some inexplicable reason, I feel obligated to keep you out of trouble."

"Are you my mother?"

Bullseye huffed. "I guess I'm gonna have to be."

The thought of his mother brought Leeland to tears. He tried covering them up by wiping them off as they flowed through streaks of blood coming from his nose and the laceration at the base of his scalp. Bullseye saw them.

"Brutus... release," she whispered. "Give us a minute, please."

Triple-B came down from his adrenaline high, nodded, and then trundled out of the alley. To where, Leeland did not know, but he was glad that the crazy guard was on his team.

What a beast!

"Okay, Leelee," she said, sitting down and crossing her legs. "No more attitude. What's bothering you? And don't tell me it's about losing Conner. We have other jacks; we'll get by. Tell me the truth. Is it what Ruth said to you?"

Leeland wiped his eyes clear, blinked a few times, and waited for his vision to return. There was still a line of blood from the cut on his mouth running down his chin, but it was drying quickly. He moved his jaw. It was sore but functional. The teeth that he was worried about losing seemed fine as well.

"Do you remember my last season with the 29ers?" he asked her. "You were out of the game by then, but were you keeping track?"

"Of course I was. I always watched your games."

Leeland nodded. "Then you know that it wasn't supposed to be a good season for us. We had lost a number of stars in the off-season. I was really the only one left after the purge, and so, it was supposed to be a rebuilding year.

"It started off like that for sure. We lost our first three games, and then our newbies began to get it together. We were able to string along a number of three-score games, and suddenly, we were being talked about as a potential wild card in the playoffs. I was having one of my best years, in terms of scoring, and we were riding high going into the playoffs.

"But the press - you know how they are - had decided at the beginning of the season that we weren't supposed to be there, that the Trontek 29ers were out, and at the end, when we defied their expectations, they grew angry. They never gave us a break. Whenever we'd win, the press would say, 'They can't possibly win two games in a row, not after that brutal a game'. And then we would, and then they'd say, 'Well, they can't possibly win the next game,' and so on and so on. I was still a star in their eyes, but a star who had lost a step. I wasn't the man I had been just a year before. They were relentless in their criticism of me as well.

"But we weathered it all and made the playoffs. But as you know, so did my brother. The Jade Dragons came out of nowhere. Only in our league three seasons and suddenly taking the number two spot in the bracket. Victor was the rising Roth brother, and I, the falling star. The press was relentless on that comparison as well."

Bullseye shrugged. "It didn't seem to bother you, though. At least not on the pitch."

Leeland shook his head. "Not on the pitch, no. But off the pitch, I admit, it bothered me a lot. Not jealousy for Victor's skills; I knew that he'd eclipse me... given the chance. No. It was the artificial rivalry that the press created through their desire to see us play against each other. They acted like it was fated to happen, and of course, Victor was the darling in that scenario, and I was the grizzled old veteran who wasn't supposed to be there. They pretty much gave the win to Victor before the game even started, before we had progressed enough along the bracket to even have a chance to meet.

"Well, long story short, we both made it to the semi-finals, as predicted. But along the way, the 29ers faced the Koeputki Kolossals in the game right before our semi-final match against the Jade Dragons. Against the Zee, the rotator cuff on my throwing arm was damaged."

Bullseye couldn't contain a smirk. She chuckled. "You let those little apes injure you?"

"Hey, don't knock the Zee, Carla. In swarm, they can be quite deadly, and you know it.

"They swarmed me late in the game, as I was preparing to throw the ball at the goal. This was supposed to be the winning shot, but three of them reached up and blocked my arm, and in motion, I felt and heard a snap, and I dropped the ball. Luckily, we managed to recover the ball and win, but I was out of commission at that point, though I didn't tell anyone. How could I? We were heading to the semi-finals against the Jade Dragons. It was fated that I meet my brother on the pitch.

"All those six days prior to our match against the Dragons, I worked on my arm, my throwing motion, trying hard to get it back into shape. But it was painful, so painful, and suddenly I started to wonder if perhaps the press was right: was I past-it? Would I have to sit it out while Victor got all the glory? But no, I couldn't let that happen. I had to play. I had to.

"So, I did. I sucked it up, popped a few pills for the pain, and took to the pitch."

"Drug use is illegal, Leelee."

Leeland shook his head. "Not all drugs are illegal. You can take a dose of a sanctioned painkiller so long as it's monitored and recorded. My dose is on record, but not for the rotator cuff. I made up some bogus excuse that my ankles were sore and that I needed a little. Then... I popped a couple more right before hitting the pitch. That was illegal, but necessary. I couldn't have played with the pain I was in."

"So those drugs made you kill your brother?"

Leeland was surprised at the frankness of Bullseye's question. It startled him, in fact. But then, she was never one to show too much overt sympathy and tact. She had a directness that he hated at times but loved as well. Sometimes.

"No, not at all." Leeland cleared his throat and spit a gout of blood. "The night before the game, Victor and I met at a bar, much like the one you just pulled me out of, for a final drink and bull session. This was a big deal for the Roth family. Mama Roth's sons were both big-time DreadBall stars. So, we wanted to get together for a little brotherly comradery, throw back a drink or two, shoot the breeze, and wish each other luck.

"One drink led to two, led to three, and so on; and by the end of the night, I was feeling pretty good, open, relaxed. No pain in my shoulder, let me tell you. No pain anywhere. I felt so good in fact, that I confided in him about my rotator cuff. We were both so baked and laughing and having a good time, that I thought he hadn't really heard me about the injury. But in the game, he made it clear to me that he knew, and had heard every word.

"From the very beginning, he was agitating my throwing arm, my shoulder. When he couldn't steal the ball, he would just bump into me, swipe me with his free hand as he ran by. Over and over. And then when he stole the ball from me on that last shot, I lost it. I was so angry that he had violated my trust, that he was using my injury against me that I—"

"There is nothing in the rules that says that a player cannot take advantage of another's injury. It's part of the game, Leelee."

"I know, but he was my brother, dammit! My own flesh and blood, taking advantage of insider knowledge. I couldn't take it anymore. I snapped and, well, you know what happened after that. Everyone knows. And I couldn't be convicted of it either, for the kill had happened on the DreadBall pitch, and death is something that happens as a matter of course in the game." Leeland chuckled. "I even tried to check myself into a prison, much like Triple-B had done. They laughed me right out the front door.

"I killed my brother, Carla. I killed Victor. And I can't seem to shake the guilt."

Bullseye moved closer and took Leeland's hand. She squeezed it tightly, lifted it to her lips, and kissed it. "Then why did you come back? Coming back into the light just brings it all up again, and you must have known that that was going to happen. You can't run from it if you are constantly standing in front of people who are going to remind you of it every day. Why did you come back?"

"Because I thought, perhaps if I did something big, something bold, you know, something I could dedicate to the memory of Victor, that it would go away. All the pain, the guilt, would just disappear. But it isn't working. Seeing Horus Ruth today, fighting with him, just brought it all back up again.

"I don't know what I'm going to do, Carla. I don't know if I can go on."

There was silence, and then Bullseye said, in the calmest, most gentle voice that Leeland had ever heard the ex-guard use, "You're not alone, Leelee. You have me, and Triple-B, and Coch, and Frankie, and Menapi... all of us. And Victor too. He's here in spirit. I know he is. I didn't know your brother well, but I'm sure that he would have never wanted you to hide away from this. That is a betrayal of his memory, and with respect, a betrayal of us. We're here because of you, each one of us, at the end of our careers. Most of us, anyway. This is our last hurrah, if you will, like you, and we all have pain in our past. Don't get me started on Triple-B's past. You'd shoot yourself in the head if you heard it all."

Leeland half snorted, half laughed at that. "That's a story I'd like to hear someday."

She stood and offered her hand. "Come, let's face it together. And if we fail, so be it. We'll at least have the satisfaction of knowing that we tried. Isn't that enough?"

Was it? Leeland wasn't sure, but her voice was so sweet, so confident, like a mother's would be when faced with a grieving child. And that's what he was, in a sense, a grieving child. And Leeland hated himself for it. He'd prided himself for always being strong, tough, working in a brutal sport, and never showing fear, uncertainty. But now... It's true what the experts say: the mind is far more delicate than the body, and mental health, mental strength, was just as important in DreadBall as physical strength.

Leeland took her hand. He stood. He was a little woozy from the beating he had gotten, not to mention the alcohol, but Bullseye put her arm around his waist and helped him out of the alley.

Standing there, next to Triple-B, was the Brokkr that had just delivered that beating. The little fellow stood there, like a rock, with a pen and piece of paper in his hands.

He held them up to Leeland, a shy grin across his broad face. "May I?"

If he were feeling better, Leeland would have broken out in laughter, but it hurt to smile. He smiled inwardly instead, signed his name to the paper, and handed them back over. He winked at the Brokkr, smiled as best he could, and then said, "I'll see you in the tournament, you little maggot."

hurrah, if you will. Like you, and we all have pain in our past. Don't get me started on Triple-B's past. You'd shoot yourself in the head if you heard it all."

Leeland half smiled. Half laughed at that. "That's a story I'd like to hear someday."

She stood and offered her hand. "Come, let's face it together. And if we fail, so be it. We'll at least have the satisfaction of knowing that we tried. Isn't that enough?"

"Is it?" Leeland wasn't sure. But her voice was so sweet, so confident, like a mother's would be when faced with a [illegible] child. And that's what he was, in a sense, a grieving child. And feeling that [illegible] himself for it. He'd [illegible] himself for always being in control, working in a brutal sport, and never showing his vulnerability. But now... it's true what they always say: the mind is far more delicate than the body, and mental toughness, mental strength, was just as important in DeadBall as physical strength.

Leeland took her hand. He stood. He was a little woozy from the pounding he had gotten, not to mention the alcohol, but Bullseye put her arm around his waist and helped him out of the alley.

Standing there, next to Triple-B, was the [illegible] that had just delivered that beating. The little fellow stood there, [illegible] with a pen and piece of paper in his hands.

He held them up to Leeland, a sly grin across his broad face. "May I?"

If he were feeling better, Leeland would have busted out in laughter, but it hurt to smile. He smiled inwardly instead, signed his name to the paper, and handed them back over. The [illegible] smiled as best he could, and then said, "I'll see you in the tournament, you little mugga."

Chapter Nine

"The Blue Weasels... what do we know about them?"

Leeland, Bullseye, Triple-B, and Aryan were sitting in Leeland's office at the Kapoor Industries Complex, looking over the roster of their first opponent in the tournament. The two-meter vid screen was playing footage of the brightly-colored Veer-Myn team on loop.

Bullseye shrugged. "They're strange, we know that. They ritualistically shave themselves before every match and then wash in blue ink."

"Why?"

Bullseye shrugged again. "Who can say? Perhaps they think it makes them look cool, or perhaps they think that kind of behavior makes them appear crazy, dangerous."

"It does that," Aryan said from his corner chair.

Leeland couldn't decide if the young Kapoor was commenting on their coolness or their craziness. Perhaps both, but he didn't pursue it. He could tell from Aryan's body language that he was still angry, and perhaps embarrassed, from their last meeting. Leeland was feeling much the same.

"Does it give them an edge in some way?" Triple-B asked. "Does it make them harder to grab?"

"The lack of fur certainly makes it harder, yes," Bullseye answered. "But the ink provides no oil or grease to the touch in any way. So, it's one of two things, in my view: there is some personal or religious reason why they do it, or they think it makes them look ominous and crazy. Either way, one thing we know for sure: after playing them, the other team looks almost as blue as the Weasels with all that rubbed off ink."

Bullseye pointed to the vid screen. It was showing the Weasels late in their game against another corporate team known as the Arch Rivals during the seeding rounds. The Weasels were way ahead and had a lock on the finish, but Bullseye was right. The bright yellow and green uniforms of the Arch Rivals had a decidedly blue tint about them, and their players' faces, hands—whatever piece of skin was showing—were streaked with blue ink.

"Is it legal?" Leeland asked.

"There's nothing in the rules that prohibits it," Bullseye said, "and they've played through all three of their seeding games with no forceful objection, other than opposing coaches complaining about having to wash their teams' uniforms afterward, and some players moaning about having to shower with pumice soap. They only beat the Arch Rivals. They fell to their other two opponents; close games, but losses nevertheless. Beyond the oddity of the blue ink, they play their games like any other Veer-Myn team."

Leeland nodded. "Fast and chaotic."

The Vipers' 2-1 finish in the seeding rounds had given them the fourteenth position. Certainly not what Leeland had expected, based on his own calculations. The Blue Weasels were a nineteenth seed, so he'd take it. And perhaps it was best to stretch the Vipers' endurance from the beginning. The Veer-Myn would get up and down the pitch quickly.

"The key will be to hit them, and hit them hard," Bullseye said. "And we must castle the back goal. We cannot allow them easy three and four point shots. We have to slow the game down."

Leeland nodded, though he hated castling. It parked too many valuable assets in front of the back goal, assets that could be used more opportunistically down the pitch. But if the Weasels got three or more points ahead at any time during the game, it would all be over.

"Brutus," Leeland said, looking at Triple-B, "I give you leave to knock the stew out of any and all blue rats that get in your way. Just... don't get thrown out of the game for it."

Everyone chuckled as Triple-B struck his open palm with a giant fist.

"Our jacks and strikers will have to play a prevent defense," Leeland continued, "spread our forces out to shadow every blue striker they have. Shyler and Frankie will have to hone their ball-stealing skills before the game. And as I say, I want Brutus and Shadrack knocking heads. We only have to win by a point, so slow them down and don't worry about the blue ink. If at the end we're as blue as they are, perhaps they'll make the mistake of handing the ball over to one of ours, confused as to who is who. My brother Victor was renowned for taking advantage of such situations, so we'll try to use their oddity to our advantage. Veer-Myn don't throw the ball very well, but we do need to worry a little about their guards. I suspect they will start with only one on the pitch, try to get a fast pace going right away. The first four rushes will be key. If we can knock a few into the Sin Bin by then, and if our castle holds, we should be able to wear them down."

"Who are you going to use as the point man on the castle?" Bullseye asked.

Who indeed? Certainly not Shadrack or Triple-B. They needed the freedom to roam and to slam. Strikers were far too important to lock into one place on the pitch. And Conner Newberg was still on the bench, awaiting the appeal on his suspension. He would have been the most obvious choice.

Leeland sighed, then looked at Aryan. He smiled. "We'll use your man, Mr. Kapoor."

***

Hello sports fans, and welcome to the first round of the Third Sphere Invitational DreadBall Tournament. My name is Faraj Chaudhry from Vitala-TAV, the finest sports and new programming network in all the Third Sphere. If you love Dreadball… we got it!

Thirty-two teams will face off in sixteen games to be played today and tomorrow. The competition will be fierce, bloody, and oh so exciting. I haven't seen such a diverse lineup of teams in an age, and if my budget was large enough, I'd have had a color commentator here with me in this tiny booth to discuss the nuances of every move, every slam, every score. But alas, it's just me. Perhaps by the end they'll spring for more talent. Perhaps, they'll even bring in big guns like Elmer and Dobbs. Right… like that'll ever happen.

But I digress. Thirty-two teams fighting for the chance to win and thus, be invited to play fulltime in the First Sphere Invitation Dreadball League (the FSIDL). That, ladies and gentlemen, is the big leagues, and a chance of a lifetime for many of these players. Rookies and veterans alike have been cobbled together for your viewing and listening pleasure, but do they have the sauce to rise to the occasion? Well, let's find out.

The first game today will be the Vitala Vipers versus the Blue Weasels, and I've got to tell you, I've never seen a team as strange as these Veer-Myn, shaved head to toe, and covered head to toe, in blue ink. They look like walking cotton candy dolls. But can the Vipers match them speed for speed? Unlikely. They'll have to break bones and cause chaos to win. The Vipers have veterans and a coach that some are calling a ghost from the past. Leeland Roth has a scandal sheet a mile long, if all the rumors are true. Can he put his past behind him and rise to the occasion?

The teams are lining up, and it looks like Coach Roth will go against his better judgment and start off in castle, which is a defensive formation that puts three players around the back goal in order to keep a speedy team, like the Blue Weasels, from making three and four point shots. But castles rarely last forever, and it appears as if Coach Roth has decided to use slam-fodder to head off the endeavor. Wow, trusting slam-fodder could be a big mistake. One wonders how long this match will last.

Let's tune in and see…

***

Leeland almost felt sorry for Petr Mogumbo, the young man that Aryan had forced upon the Vipers as payment for a debt. The boy stood on the point of the castle in front of the four-point goal, shivering in his uniform as if he were barefoot and the floor that he stood upon was ice. Almost sorry, for what did Aryan think might happen if the lad were placed into a violent sport with no skills, no training? What did his father think? Casualties and complications mount and everyone, even Mogumbo, had to participate. Now there he stood, trying to keep crazed, blue-inked Veer-Myn from taking the lead. He was doing reasonably well, all things considered, but then, most of the action had been on the other side of the pitch.

The Blue Weasels had begun the game skittish, chaotic, as Veer-Myn often do, making some critical mistakes early that put them behind by a point. Then they settled down and began using their speed and agility to negotiate through the Vipers' prevent defense. The castle had held, thankfully, but holes were beginning to form in Leeland's clever plans. The Vipers' tenuous lead evaporated about mid-way through the game, as Skeevak Surick, the Weasels' star striker, struck a two-point goal to give the Weasels the lead by one.

Time was running out, but Shyler Coch had the ball and the Weasels weren't castling.

"Take it to the four!" Leeland shouted from the sidelines, pointing to the Weasels' deep goal. The crowd was thin for this low seed, first round game. Their roar was more of a muted drone that barely registered on the decibel reader. He could be heard easily, and Shyler nodded as he dodged a Veer-Myn's attempt at another steal.

Steals had been down in this game, thankfully. It had taken a while for Leeland's insistence on strong ball protection to seep into Shyler's thick, prima donna head. The striker preferred a looser play style, which would allow him to shuffle pass the ball to awaiting Viper gloves more readily. Having the ball held tightly against one's body didn't lend itself to subtle, fluid play, but the order had stuck in Shyler's mind. So, the Weasels were playing with a level of frustration that Leeland found hopeful. They couldn't easily snatch the ball away, and so they were committing more fouls than was normal for a Veer-Myn team, trying desperately to find a point of advantage through a rigorous defense perpetrated by Shadrack and Triple-B. As many Weasels were being thrown out of the game on fouls as were being sent with sore heads to the Sin Bin. But those injured were coming back, and one had just returned that gave Leeland pause.

"Watch your nine!" Leeland howled to Shyler as the striker was making a circuitous route through the Weasels' backfield to try to give Triple-B a position advantage on a charging Veer-Myn guard. "It's coming in!"

A second and fresh Veer-Myn guard swaggered onto the pitch from the entry door, swung its long, thick tail around Shyler's leg, and yanked.

The striker went down hard. The ball appeared to come loose, but it did not strike the floor or the wall. Instead, it ricocheted off the blue shoulder pad of a Weasel striker, and right onto the glove of Little Frankie, who now had a clean shot on a goal.

The rookie striker paused a moment after holding the ball tightly against his body. This allowed Shadrack to slam a Weasel striker away with the concussive power of a grenade. Blue ink, sweat, and Veer-Myn blood spattered Little Frankie's helmet. The boy shook his head clean and made his move.

***

Wow, what a power shot! I don't know this Shadrack Menapi very well, but that slam gave me a warm and fuzzy feeling. Can we dare to hope for more of that kind of carnage?

Looks like the Vipers now have a clear shot to score. The balls in a rookie's launcher. Little Frankie did well in the seeding rounds, but this is the time for him to show his true worth. Let's see if he can…

***

Little Frankie was in a fine position to take a two-point shot. This would put the Vipers up by one. "Take the shot!" Leeland screamed. Bullseye screamed. Everyone on the Vipers' sidelines screamed. The crowd screamed.

"*Take the shot!*"

But Little Frankie made a small juke which put another Veer-Myn striker on the floor, and then he raced to the high strike zone.

Leeland craned his neck to get a better view of his player. His line of sight was blocked by too many bodies angling for the ball. All he could see was a wall of blue as the Weasel ink, as warned, covered everything. Leeland had hoped that the Weasels would have been confused about who to give the ball to as a result of so much discoloration, but it was Leeland himself with the inability to tell his players from the enemy's. Who was who? Even the cybernetic referee was scrambling to find a good view of what was going on. So many fouls being committed in that morass, and yet it and the Eye in the Sky couldn't get a good read of events.

Then Little Frankie broke through, covered head to toe in blue ink, blood, and gore. He still had the ball. He took a step forward, then another, and another, pulling his body free of the pile. He took a final step, placed his left foot on the furthest spot in the back strike zone, and then shot the ball toward the four-point goal before he was crushed by bodies. The ball sailed effortlessly through the goal. Red lighted klaxons blared. Waving strobe lights flickered madly.

Score!

The crowd's roared approval broke the decibel reader. Leeland's heart leapt as he gave Bullseye a hug in recognition of Little Frankie's excellence.

The Vipers were now ahead by three, and the game was in their...

Wait! We're still playing.

The ball launched back into play at the centerline, and it was scooped up by Weasel striker Skeevak Surick, who was sitting back in his team's left forward strike zone just waiting for it.

Leeland waved violently and shouted at Shadrack, "Fall back! Fall back! Defend the castle!"

Triple-B was tied up in a death struggle with the Veer-Myn guard that had tripped Shyler, so he was out of the picture. The only strong defense the Vipers had left was Shadrack, and he was out of position.

Shadrack backpedaled as fast as he could, but Skeevak Surick was so fast, so quick, that it was hard to place a finger on him. The rest of the Viper team raced after him, even Shyler, who was recovering from the trip. He had had the wind knocked out of him and was struggling to come to speed, and Skeevak Surick was giving a master class on how to dodge.

From the sidelines, Conner Newberg barked at his jacks, pointing frantically to guide them into position. "Choke the lanes, choke the lanes," he ordered, and Leeland let him bark, even though Conner was not officially an assistant coach. For all intents and purposes, he was, since he could not play, and anyway, he was not wrong. They could not beat the Veer-Myn striker at his own game. They simply had to slow him down, force him to make turns and moves he had not planned.

Little Frankie now fell into pursuit, though it was clear that his last pile-on had injured his leg. He was limping and finding it difficult to catch up.

Skeevak Surick performed a full three-sixty and lost Shyler in a slick spray of blue ink. The rat's juke put Shyler down again, and Leeland could hear his striker cast foul obscenities as the Veer-Myn star raced toward the Vipers' deep strike zone.

Jack Petr Mogumbo awoke from his inaction, suddenly realizing that he was the object of a Veer-Myn guard barreling toward his position. A Viper jack, under Conner's direction, tried to slow the beast's progress, but the jack was tossed aside like a used handkerchief. Nothing now stood between Petr and an angry, mouth-slathering, Veer-Myn guard.

Petr fell into a defensive position, like he had seen other jacks do many times in practice, but it looked like a child's pose, trying to fend off a playground bully. He hadn't bent his knees enough to lower his center of gravity sufficiently. He stood almost straight, like a scarecrow wavering in the wind. Both Leeland and Conner tried screaming at him to get lower, lower, you fool, and take the slam!

Before they could utter the last word, the Veer-Myn guard slammed into Petr, lifted him off the floor, then shoved him back down onto the pitch and rode him like a sled into the far wall. Sparks flew from Petr's glove as it scraped a gash into the floor. Bits and pieces of his uniform were left in their wake. Blood, gore, and blue ink followed.

The castle was broken, and no one now stood between Skeevak Surick and a four-point score.

***

Well, you know what they say: you dance with a devil, you sometimes get burned. Rookie Mogumbo is—what did they call that ancient dish—Gumbo on the floor. A big mistake to put that poor boy in the castle, but you live and learn. Now, those blue rats have a clear lane to the back goal. Let's see how it goes…

***

The only Viper close enough to stopping Surick was Shadrack, who had slipped on a spot of congealed blood, but was now recovering and galloping dog-like on all fours toward the determined Veer-Myn striker.

Leeland took a step onto the pitch to get a better view, and then stepped off as the red dividing light between the pitch and the sidelines erupted and gave its warning. One more warning and Leeland would be tossed out of the game.

"What's happening?" he shouted at Bullseye, who presumably had a better view of the action. "I can't see anything."

"Surick is making his move," she said.

"Kill him, Shadrack," Leeland said, howling the order like a yodeler on a mountaintop. "Kill that furry little runt!"

But the guard was not in a position to do such a thing. Centimeters were miles in a DreadBall match, and Shadrack could only fling himself forward, arms stretched out like a diver off that same mountaintop from which Leeland had shouted. Skeevak Surick could have easily moved forward a few more paces and given himself a sure three-point goal, bringing the score back down to zero and sending the game into overtime. But he was arrogant, as most strikers were. He stepped back thrice, into the four-point space, and raised his arm to throw.

Shadrack's fingers only grazed Skeevak Surick's glove. It was a light touch, but just enough to move the launcher a centimeter more to the right.

Skeevak Surick released the ball in a perfect rotation off its electromagnetic perch. The crowd hushed as everyone, including an anxious, fearful Leeland, watched the ball strike the goal and bounce once, twice, thrice, then fall harmlessly away.

No score, the game was over, and the small number of Viper fans in attendance erupted in joy.

But the guard was not in a position to do such a thing. Centimeters were miles in a Dreadball match, and Shadowy could only fling himself sideward, arm stretched out like a diver off that same mountaintop from which Lenard had strayed. Sleevok Suticks could have easily [illegible] a few more paces and given himself a huge three-point goal, bringing the score back down to zero and sending the game into overtime. But he was arrogant, [illegible]. He stepped back three times into the four-point space, and raised his arm to throw.

Shadowy Vinges only grazed Sleevok Suticks's glove. It was a light touch, but just enough to move the launcher a centimeter or more to the right.

Sleevok Suticks released the ball in a perfect forearm off, its [illegible]. The crowd [illegible] as everyone, including an anxious [illegible], watched the ball strike the goal and bounce once, twice, thrice, then fall harmlessly away.

No score. The game was over, and the small number of Vinerians in attendance erupted in joy.

Chapter Ten

"Petr Mogumbo suffered three broken ribs, a punctured lung, a dislocated shoulder, and an impacted spine," the team's physician said as they reviewed the poor boy's case in Leeland's office. "He's also in a coma. He's expected to recover from that, at some point. But he's done. He'll not be taking the pitch again in this tournament."

Leeland breathed a sigh of relief. *Thank the gods for small favors,* he thought as the entire Viper team gathered in their conference room to discuss their next opponent and review video.

As the players took their seats, Leeland reviewed some of the action from the tournament's first round.

The number one seed, The Sledgehammers, had advanced as predicted and would face off against another Forge Father team known as the Grimson Graybeards. The analysts were not giving the Graybeards much of a chance against their far superior brethren.

A surprise of the first round was the twenty-fifth seed Crystallan Solarium Diamonds beating the eighth seed Yndij Millstone Mountaineers. The bluish, silicone-based Diamonds had the analysts all in a huff, as no one had predicted such a result, and fingers were pointed left and right.

The unlikely Neo-Bot Nova Station Redshirts had defeated their twenty-first seed opponent, the Veer-Myn Cellar-Dwellers. It wasn't a surprise that a twelfth seed had beaten a twenty-first, but the Redshirts were coached by a two-bit amateur coder by the name of Richardo Vasa, a heavily-bearded, google-eyed toothpick of a man who had done time in the very sanitarium as Triple-B. No one had expected the likes of him to have any success, but he had proved them all wrong.

The tenth seed Rebel team, The Polmak Resisters, had easily defeated their weaker Hobgoblin opponent, The Darkheart Dandies, though the Dandies' Hulk guard had put six Reb players into the Sin Bin during play.

The second seed female Corporate team, the Golan Banshees, had defeated a Sphyr team known as The Surge.

The twenty-second seed Zee team, The Whitestar Chimps, had (like the Solarium Diamonds) defeated a much superior Meta-Bot team known as the Steel Dragons. In Leeland's mind, that was an even more impressive upset. A Zee team is rarely ever expected to win, but when they do, it feeds a narrative that grows and grows until even the little squirts themselves believe the hype. At that point, a Zee team could become deadly and unpredictable.

Another surprise of the first round was the twenty-eighth seed corporate Arch Rivals beating the fifth seed Yellow Scarabs. According to reports, the insectoid Z'zor had gone into the game acting as if they had already won, as if it was an insult that they even needed to play against such a low seed. The Arch Rivals went in with nothing to lose. It turned into a rout.

And finally, as everyone in the room knew, the Vitala Vipers had defeated the Blue Weasels. Up next for them were the third seed Kilmerain Coalminers.

Leeland's heart sank. He hated Brokkrs.

"Settle down, everyone. Quiet!" He worked his still-sore jaw back and forth. The memories of the brawl at the bar still rang loudly in his mind. "Let's get to work."

He waited until everyone had found seats, then he said, "All things considered, we got off easy with the Weasels." He looked at

Little Frankie's silver walking cast, which blinked red and faint green lights along its length to indicate healing progression. The greener the better. It wasn't there yet. "How's your leg?"

Frankie nodded. "Fine, coach, fine. Ankle's still a little puffy, but I'll be ready for the next match. No worries."

"Good," Leeland said, and hoped it were true. The team physician had not been so certain. "I'm going to need your speed and improved scoring skills for the next game. If you're not a hundred percent, I need to know—"

"I'll be ready," Frankie insisted, moving as if he were going to rip off the walking cast. He nudged Shyler instead. "Besides, someone needs to be in the game who's young enough to keep this withered old crone from embarrassing himself."

A burst of laughter forced Shyler to push him back. "Oh, shut up, rookie! You got lucky. Don't get too cocky, young man, or some Brokkr will come up and kill you with one punch."

The room began to stir again. Bullseye brought it under control and Leeland finally continued with the meeting. "So, we beat the Veer-Myn, but that's behind us now. Now, we have to focus on our next opponent, who won't be so easy to beat."

Leeland flipped on the vid screen. "The Kilmerain Coalminers, the 'Killer' Coalminers as they like to call themselves, use a formation that I call the 'flexible wedge'." He punched a few buttons on the touch-screen, and the players changed to simple colored X's and O's. The Brokkr's were the X's.

"They line up in standard wedge formation to start the game, as you can see, with guards here, here, here, and here." Leeland used a laser pointer to denote where the Coalminer's big guys were positioned. Those X's flashed green. "Their standard lineup are four guards, two jacks."

"They don't start with any strikers?" Shyler asked.

Leeland shook his head. "No. They don't care about scoring, as silly as that may seem. What they care about is knocking heads, and they do it very effectively." He adjusted his jaw again. It cracked as he moved it side to side. "They start in wedge formation, but as the first few rushes develop, they shift to a soft V." He let the video run as he talked. "The guards fall back, with this guard falling into a kind of semi-castle position right in front of the back goal. The jacks push out to the walls to protect the flanks. The inside guards wait for opponents to be funneled into the V. Watch."

The O's of the opposing team moved to engage the X's. As the Brokkr wedge fell back, the O's were funneled into the belly of the V. When that was accomplished, the X's simply closed in and slaughtered the O's. One by one, the red O's blinked off. When there were only two O's left, the Brokkr's rotated one of their strikers onto the pitch, scooped up the ball, and scored. Game over.

Leeland turned off the screen. "Now, that was a perfect example of how they utilize the flexible wedge. Their use of it is not always that clean and effective, of course, but I wanted you to see it in its purest form so you understand that that *could* be our fate. They will try to use it against us. They're grizzled miners. They're tough, steady. They won't go down as easily as Veer-Myn. They can be injured, indeed, but they will fight to the last. They will try to close off any easy advance we take toward a goal. The key to our success, then, is to make sure that we do not fall into the belly of the V."

"How do we accomplish that?" Shadrack asked.

"Through speed... and superior skill. Brokkrs are slow, and if we can match their brawn with quickness, we can make a few easy scores. If we can get ahead three or four points, they'll panic. They'll begin to make mistakes, overcompensate, shift out their guards for strikers, but by then, it'll be too late, and we'll have them."

Shyler huffed. "Sir, with respect, don't you think that they know all this? I don't know their coach personally, but they tell me that Hector Silverhorn is a master tactician. He must be sitting with his team right now doing pretty much the same thing we're doing."

Leeland paused in his response, flashed a look at Bullseye who, more so than Leeland, was about to burst. He could see the muscles in her jaw working overtime as she tried to restrain herself from ripping the arrogant striker a new one. She clearly had had enough of Shyler's constant complaining and second-guessing of the coaching staff.

"Of course he's planning," Leeland said to keep Bullseye from jumping in, "just like us. With respect, don't assume that I—that Bullseye and I—aren't aware of it. But the only team that beat them in the seeding round was a female corporate team called the I-Corps Tigers. They did the exact thing I'm talking about and won. And as far as I can tell, the Coalminers have done nothing to shore up that weakness. They are vulnerable to speed and to fast scoring, so that is what we are going to do."

"And you'll be happy to know this, Shyler," Bullseye said, keeping her anger in check and coming up to take the laser pointer away from Leeland, "that we're going to start with three strikers, two jacks, and one guard."

"Which guard?" Triple-B asked.

Bullseye smiled. "You."

There was another ruffle among the players. Since Shadrack had been the star of the previous game, it came as a bit of a surprise that he was not starting. Triple-B's performance against the Weasels had been admirable, but not stellar. It had been Shadrack's deflection of the ball, or rather, his bump of Surick's glove, that had made the Veer-Myn striker's score attempt fall short. That was what the analysts and pundits were saying on all the news feeds, though Leeland was disappointed that Little Frankie's name wasn't mentioned as well. It was, after all, Frankie's excellent score at the end that had put the Vipers ahead for good. Oh well, such was the ebb and flow of the ongoing game narrative. Careers were made and destroyed by perception more often than truth.

"Me?" Triple-B seemed just as surprised with the announcement.

"Yes, you. No disrespect, Shadrack, but Brutus is more suited to play against these Coalminers. He... knows them, after a fashion." Bullseye shot a glance toward Leeland, who returned her stare with a crack of his jaw. "He also brings a psychological piece to the puzzle that you do not. We'll cycle you in during play as needed."

"Really? Oh, that's good news, Coach." Shadrack's voice was laden with sarcasm as he scowled with arms crossed. "That's wonderful. I'll just twiddle my thumbs and wait for that signal."

Triple-B chuckled and slapped his counterpart on the back. "Don't feel too dejected, Shaddy, ol' boy. I'll carry the water for both of us while you keep my seat on the bench warm."

Shadrack shrugged off Brutus's thick hand. "And while you were warming bedpans in prison, I was winning games."

Triple-B shot out of his chair. Shadrack did the same.

The two walls of flesh faced each other, Triple-B a full foot taller than Shadrack. But Menapi held his ground and stuck his face out so that his nose was close to Triple-B's lifeless iron collar. Sweat glistened off each man's gruff face.

"Sit down, the both of you!" Leeland barked. "We don't have time for this. We're a team, dammit, not an individual's highlight film. You stroke your egos somewhere else. Bullseye and I are going to field the team we think is best against these goons, and that's final. Trust me, Shadrack, when I tell you that we have a plan and—once you see it unfold - you'll understand why Brutus is the best choice to start this game. Sit down... please."

The two men took seats, away from each other this time, their backs turned.

Bullseye waited a few seconds, then continued. "Now, as much as I like it, we're not going to employ a castle in this game. There's no need against a Brokkr team that doesn't field strikers right away. We're going light on defense in this one."

Leeland stepped up and concluded the discussion. "I want the ball constantly shuffled from one player to the next. Keep it shifting back and forth. Don't give them time to focus their power against the ball carrier. That's how they win: they funnel opposing players into the V, catch the ball carrier, and then eviscerate him. Keep it moving, keep it mobile. Shyler, you have my permission to carry the ball loosely in this game. Just make sure that if you're under pressure, you dump it off to Frankie or whomever else is nearby. If you don't score in this one, so be it. If it's only jacks that score for us, so be it. The key is to win, and we can if we move fast, think hard, keep our wits about us, and keep options fluid."

"Speaking of jacks, where's Conner?" Little Frankie asked.

"He's on a recruiting mission." Leeland shook his head. "Petr Mogumbo is no longer a member. We need a replacement. Several, in fact."

"When's Conner going to suit up again?"

Leeland shook his head. The appeal to his suspension had been submitted. They were waiting for Digby's final decision.

"Soon, I hope."

The fact that Mogumbo was no longer on the team seemed to brighten the spirits of everyone in the room. Leeland understood fully. He had felt that way himself when the physician had given him the diagnosis. On record, it was always sad to see a fellow player fall, but one as poorly equipped as that boy was worth losing. It was disrespectful to rejoice in a teammate's pain, but Leeland let it go. The

Vipers needed all the good news they could get.

"If there is nothing further?"

"When are we getting paid?" Frankie asked.

When, indeed. Aryan Kapoor was late in handing out paychecks and signing bonuses. The coaching staff had only been paid once. The players not even.

"I'm going to speak with Kapoor right now. I'll find out."

No one had anything further to say, so the meeting was adjourned.

Leeland watched Shadrack and Triple-B leave the room, their eyes throwing daggers at each other. When they were gone, Leeland fell into a chair, sighed, rubbed his eyes, and said to Bullseye, "I worry about those two."

"They're proud men."

"They're arrogant, headstrong, and they'll be at each other's throats if we're not careful."

"Don't worry, Leelee," Bullseye said, touching him lightly on the shoulder. "I can control Triple-B. I assure you, he won't ring Menapi's neck."

"It isn't Menapi's neck that worries me."

"Don't worry about Brutus's either. Trust me. Everything will go as planned."

Leeland nodded at his assistant coach, but he knew one simple truth about DreadBall.

Nothing ever went as planned.

***

Aryan Kapoor's office was on the tenth floor of the Kapoor family tower. Leeland rode the glass elevator up and marveled at the Vitala skyline, a dazzling mixture of dark, brooding industrial concrete towers and colorful vid screens of shifting advertisements, Third

Sphere news casts, wildly fanciful entertainment, and corporate announcements. It was near dusk, and the sky was a blood red from the setting sun. A blood-red sky often denoted danger, death, Leeland knew, but he could not feel anything but grandeur. It was a beautiful city, a beautiful planet. Not quite as posh or as splendid as a First or Second Sphere planet, true, but impressive nevertheless. Parts of it were industrial, and those parts represented more of a blot on the eye than a treasure. All cities had their blighted areas, this one included, but the blue-glass towers in the distance caught the rays of the setting sun and spread light across the urban sprawl that made Leeland's troubles and anxieties drift away. For a little while, anyway.

Then the elevator door opened, and his anxieties returned.

A Gaelian jack from the Polmak Resisters passed him in the hallway outside the elevator. Leeland knew it was Gaelian from its height, double torso, and hoofed feet. The fact that it was wearing a hooded black cloak to hide itself from identification was a joke. The creature towered over Leeland and had to bend down to all fours just to enter the elevator. And he knew that this Gaelian was a member of the Rebel team because of its wild, rope-like green tattoos that covered its hands and stocky legs. It nodded to Leeland as the elevator doors closed. Leeland nodded back reflexively and then felt bad about doing so. He wanted no part of any Reb player outside the pitch.

Aryan's office took up half the tenth floor. Leeland made his way through a maze of cubicles, now dark and empty due to the end of the workday, to find it. Aryan was still there, however. His door was cracked a few centimeters, and pale white light bled through into the hallway. Leeland followed the light to Aryan's door and knocked lightly twice.

"Come in, come in."

Leeland did so and closed the door behind him.

Aryan was sitting with his feet up on the largest dark mahogany table Leeland had ever seen. There were papers and vid tablets strewn across it as if Aryan had been hard at work, but it looked more like he had just awoken from a nap. The young Viper owner seemed content. He had his arms up and his fingers locked together behind his head. He smiled. "Hello, Leeland. What can I do for you today?"

"Why is a Gaelian jack visiting you after hours, Aryan?" Leeland asked.

"Why do you assume it was visiting me?"

Leeland pointed to the door. "Because there's no one else here but you."

"And how do you know that he is a jack?"

Leeland was already growing tired of this. "I saw the tattoos, Aryan. The Polmak Resisters wear their Rebel tattoos as a sign of solidarity to the oppressed races that they represent. I'm not ignorant of the social situation in the GCPS, and it's entirely inappropriate for you to be visiting privately with members of opposing teams."

Aryan swung his legs off his desk and sat up. His smile disappeared. He gave Leeland a stern look. He worked his jaw muscles. "Just as inappropriate as you giving out autographs for free to Brokkr guards?"

He was a guard? Made sense, given the power of the dwarf's punch. "That's entirely different, Aryan. That was out in the open, on a street, and I did not go out that night with the intention of meeting anyone. It's one thing for a coach to glad-hand opposing players; that happens often prior to a match. It's another thing entirely to meet with them, all cloak-and-dagger like, in a dark office."

Aryan huffed and pushed papers and tablets out of his way. He leaned forward, put his elbows on his desk, and ran his fingers through his dark, thick hair. "Okay, you caught me. I met with a Gaelian. He's an old friend of mine. We go way back. He wanted to drop by and see my office, catch up on old times. That's all."

"And you owe him money, I suppose?"

Aryan chuckled. "Who don't I owe money to?"

Leeland shook his head and sighed. Why Digby had allowed a Reb team to play in the tournament was anyone's guess. Sure, there were Reb teams in various leagues throughout the spheres, but there weren't many. They were almost always trouble in some form or another. Perhaps Digby thought that by allowing Reb teams to play, that would help appease their race's grievances, give them a platform through which they could vent those frustrations in a less destructive manner than trading bullets on the battlefield with GCPS forces.

"Fine," Leeland said, wanting to move on. "Let's change the subject. How's business?"

Aryan nodded. "Not bad. My pain-in-the-ass father is trying to dictate company policy from life support."

"How's he doing?"

Aryan shook his head. "Not good. I don't see him long for this world, but he's putting in overtime on contrariness. He's driving me and Saanvi crazy." Aryan grew serious again. "How's Petr doing?"

Leeland shrugged. "About as good as your father, I suppose. He'll live, but he's done for the game."

"Great. Old man Mogumbo isn't going to accept an invalid son as payment for a debt, I'm afraid."

Leeland shrugged. "That's the price you pay for playing unprepared in dangerous sandboxes. You have a lot of - forgive me - crappy friends, Aryan."

Aryan nodded. "Well, when you've played in as many dangerous boxes as I have, the sand gets all over you." He raised his arms as if he were presenting his office to Leeland as a gift. "That's why I'm here and have all this now: so I can become honest, respectable, and make the kind of wholesome money for my family that is required of a good son."

"Speaking of money, my players, *your* players, haven't seen a paycheck yet. Contracts were signed, bonuses promised, four games played, life and limbs laid on the line. Nothing. When will they be wired their money?"

Aryan raised a finger and made as if to poke something. "I hold my finger above the transfer button."

"Why haven't you pushed it?"

"My sister has to approve every credit that leaves our company. She wants to meet you first. Wants to make sure you're a good investment."

"Contracts signed, bonuses promised, four games, life and limb... Must I recite it all again? How much more evidence does she need?"

"Just play her game, all right? Meet with her, give her a warm, fuzzy feeling. Smile at the appropriate moments, take a picture or two for the press, and I promise you, she'll approve the funds. She's like my father: she enjoys the pomp and circumstance of wealth, power. She has to feel like she's a part of it all."

Leeland huffed. "If she's interested in playing games, perhaps we should suit her up and put her on the pitch. She can replace Petr."

Aryan laughed. It was a nervous laugh, one that Leeland had heard before from pampered, privileged children who despised their siblings. But in this case, it was clear that Saanvi held all the cards. Aryan might be the manager of the team, and perhaps even the owner on paper, but Saanvi owned the paper, the ink. She owned Aryan.

"Very well," Leeland said, turning to the door. He was done talking, done with everything today. "Invite her to attend tomorrow's practice. I'll give her all the warm and fuzzies she requires."

He reached the door, opened it, and then said, "And just for the record, if salaries aren't wired to my guys soon, I promise you, Aryan, you'll have your own little rebellion to treat with."

Chapter Eleven

Saanvi Kapoor arrived near the end of practice. Her jet-black hair was pulled back in a short, perfect ponytail. She wore a beige power suit and sensible shoes. She was flanked by two security officers whose bulk was rivaled only by Shadrack's. Leeland could not see their pistols but was sure they were packing lasers. She walked in with confidence, like a woman who knew that everyone and everything in the room was hers. She had a billion megacredit smile.

Leeland ignored her at first and continued barking plays to his jacks and strikers as they moved up and down the pitch in scrimmage, preparing for their match against the Coalminers. Bullseye was working with her guards at the other end of the pitch, working overtime to ensure that Shadrack and Triple-B behaved themselves. Tensions were high. It was not a good time for a corporate visit.

But Saanvi was here, and Leeland had foolishly invited her. He could not back out now.

She approached with her hand extended. He took it.

"Hello, Ms. Kapoor," Leeland said, with as broad a smile as he could muster. "Thank you for coming."

She had a firmer grip than expected. She kept smiling. "So good to meet you finally, Mr. Roth."

"Please, call me Leeland," he said.

"And you may call me Saanvi," she answered. "Ms. Kapoor makes me sound old."

"Yes, I understand that." He motioned to his players. "They like to call me Coach, or Boss. I personally consider that too formal, but I guess we have to maintain some professional distance, don't we?"

Saanvi nodded. "And you seem to handle them well."

"Handle? No. Honestly, every man on the pitch could probably wring my neck if they wanted to, the strikers included. But they're professionals. And they know the stakes are high. You have a good team here, Ms.—I mean, Saanvi. A good team that deserves its pay."

Perhaps diving right into the deep end was not wise. Perhaps the bread needed a little more buttering before taking a bite. But he didn't have time for niceties.

"Yes," Saanvi said, looking at her shoes as if she were embarrassed. "I must apologize for the delay in that. Our accountants had to make sure that no money was being laundered."

Leeland shook his head. "I—I don't understand."

Saanvi looked left, then right, as if she were afraid someone would hear. Then she leaned in and whispered, "May I have a private word, Leeland?"

"Of course."

He asked Conner to take over, then he walked Saanvi into the furthest corner away from the practice pitch. She held up her hand to keep her guards from following.

When they were alone, she said, "It should come as no surprise to you that my brother is... well, let's be diplomatic... not the most focused person on Vitala. I love my brother, you understand, but he hasn't lived up to his potential, as Father might say. He has debts to so-called 'friends' that aren't always patient. Some require payment and require it fast."

"Yes, I have some understanding of what you are saying."

Saanvi nodded. "So, my people had to track the digital coding trail to make sure the credits weren't being shaved away into another account. It happens more often in business that you might know, Leeland, and not just here on our pleasant little planet of Vitala. Money laundering is a significant problem for any corporation, especially one like Kapoor Industries."

"And you suspected that Aryan might do such a thing? I agree... he isn't the most focused person, as you say, but he doesn't strike me as criminal."

Saanvi shrugged. "When you've run with the kind of crowd that Aryan has done most of his young life, the lines between proper conduct and criminal enterprise can become blurred, confused. What do they say: the criminal is the good guy in his own story? Robbing from the rich, giving to the poor? I'm sure Aryan thinks he's utterly innocent of everything, just a young man who's never been given the chance to prove himself. A young man who's so misunderstood, so oppressed by the system, by his father. Utter nonsense."

Leeland could detect the derision in Saanvi's voice. Her expression changed from mildly pleasant to dark agitation. Saanvi might say on the record that she loved her brother, but Leeland could see the truth on her angry face.

"With respect," he said, "if you suspected that Aryan might be capable of theft, then why did you give him a DreadBall team to manage?"

"That was my father's idea, I assure you. I lobbied against it. It was too much, I told Father, too much responsibility to heap upon the boy. But Damon Kapoor has a kind heart, a noble spirit. He wanted to give his son and heir another chance."

A last chance, Leeland thought as Saanvi stood there and brooded in her own words. *Perhaps our team should have been called Aryan's Third and Final Chance.*

Again, Saanvi's expression changed on a knife edge. She shook her head, smiled, and said, "But it seems as if Father was right. The

Vitala Vipers are doing well. I have to believe that that's because of you. My brother picked the right man to run the show."

Leeland blushed in embarrassment. He looked away. He didn't like it when people praised him to his face. Again, his brother Victor had been better at accepting praise and giving it back tenfold. Leeland had never mastered the art of false humility.

"Well, I do what I can," he said. "But it's not just me. Bullseye and Triple-B, and Conner—"

"I don't know much about the game, Leeland, but they say a DreadBall team is a reflection of its coach. And from what I can see, the Vitala Vipers are in good hands." She put her hand out again, and Leeland took it. This time, it was soft, warm, inviting. "Don't worry about salaries... they'll be wired tonight; and in eight weeks, I'll be proud to see you win this tournament."

Leeland laughed nervously and put up his hands as if he were holding her back. "Whoa, now. One game at a time. We have the Coalminers next, and then four more games after that... assuming we get that far. There's a lot of competition left, Saanvi. Don't jinx us."

She smiled and nodded. "Well, whatever happens between now and then, whatever happens, I want you to know that you always have a place in Kapoor Industries."

Leeland was about to give his thanks, when he heard the nastiest, deepest scream he'd ever heard.

He turned to the practice pitch. There, Triple-B was on top of Shadrack, and Bullseye was on his back, trying to keep the collared guard from bringing his mighty fist down into Shadrack's face, screaming "Release! Release! Release!" It didn't seem to be doing any good.

Leeland ran. He was a striker by trade, so slamming was never a requirement for him. They did have to fend off attacks now and then, so over the years, he had developed some skill putting a shoulder in where it was needed. He pushed his way through players who were gathering to witness the fight. He lowered his shoulder, lowered his head, and struck Triple-B square in the arm.

The big man fell backward with a shout of his own. Bullseye went flying. Shadrack tried to get up and pursue, but Conner and several others were quick enough to contain him, though they did receive an elbow or two for their troubles. Leeland tried holding the big man down, but Triple-B flicked him off as if he were lint.

"Release!" Leeland shouted as he fell hard from the toss. Triple-B pursued. Leeland tried to fend him off, but the man was too big, too strong. He hoisted Leeland into the air by the scruff, holding him aloft as if he were a balloon ready to pop.

"Brutus Backhoe Bertuchi," Leeland said, trying to catch his breath. "I am your coach. I order you to release. Now, or you will be kicked from the team!"

That did the trick. Triple-B's raging, red face suddenly stilled. He closed his mouth, blinked several times, and then dropped Leeland to the pitch. Leeland struck it with a groan, but otherwise, he was in good shape.

"You keep that Zwerm away from me, Boss," Triple-B said, as he walked toward the locker room, "or next time, I'll kill him."

Leeland collected himself as Bullseye called an end to practice. One by one, players drifted away, even Shadrack, who was still quite miffed at the confrontation. Bullseye had her arm around his waist and was speaking to him gently. Leeland watched them walk away, then returned to Saanvi.

She had come back to the practice pitch. Her goons were standing at her side. The tall one was bent low, whispering in her ear. Her expression of excitement turned sorrowful.

"What's wrong?" Leeland asked.

A tear rolled down her cheek. She wiped it away and said, "I've just got word. My father... he's dead."

***

Leeland hated funerals, but as a courtesy to Saanvi and Aryan, and to the Kapoor family, he had accepted their invitation to attend. Bullseye had been invited as well but begged off, wanting to take the time to try and fix the rift between Triple-B and Shadrack before the next game and to soothe frayed nerves overall among the players. The Vipers could not go into a match with the Killer Coalminers with so much discord. Internal strife on a team was a recipe for disaster. Leeland knew that a lot of the team's anger and frustration was due to not having been paid. But true to her word, Saanvi had wired all back pay and any signing bonuses promised. Leeland was afraid that the sudden death of Damon Kapoor would prompt another delay on that front, but no. Money had been sent, and that was a great relief, for Leeland knew that a man could put up with a lot of crap, so long as he was getting paid to do it.

As family tradition demanded, Damon Kapoor's body lay at the family complex for twenty-four hours so that any and all who mattered could come and pay their respects. Then his body was cremated. By tradition, his ashes were to be spread over some place of importance, and that's where the delay had occurred. Aryan wanted his father's ashes to be preserved in an urn and placed in honor as a cornerstone for a new high-rise that was being built on the complex itself. Saanvi wanted them scattered in a river. Other family members—aunts, uncles, cousins, half-sisters and brothers—had other ideas. Ultimately, it was Saanvi's wishes that prevailed. "She always gets her way," Aryan whispered into Leeland's ear as the funeral procession wound through ample flower gardens toward the Godavari River, part of which ran through the Kapoor complex. "Saanvi always gets her way."

Leeland and the rest of the non-family members stood along the bank of the Godavari as the family piled onto their private yacht and motored to the center of the river. There, they conducted a small ceremony behind a privacy wall of white gossamer, and then Damon Kapoor's ashes were sifted into the waves.

Watching it all, Leeland remembered his brother's own funeral, just four short days after that fateful game five years ago. It had been a splendid day, much like today, and scores had attended. Fans and teammates and well-wishers of all stripes. Even players from other teams had come, even members from races that had no clear understanding of human funerals. It was rare to see Teratons and cyborgs and Crystallans and Asterians all standing together around a dirt hole, watching a box being lowered slowly into place. His brother's coffin; Victor's box.

Leeland had attended, but he had stood apart from all the others, several headstones away, a hood drawn over his face so that those in attendance could not see his tears, his shame. Every spiritual utterance from the pastor in attendance had raked like nails across his back. Every prayer, every fond word spoken about Victor from the pallbearers and his coaches and admirers who simply wanted to breathe a few last words into the memory of this great DreadBall player, felt like shards of glass in his gut. He was responsible for them being there. He, Leeland Roth, had caused the death of the man in the box, and for what good purpose? No good purpose. The reason had been quite simple but terrible: because my brother had made me mad, had violated some perceived trust between us. *I killed my brother… for no good reason.*

After the funeral, Leeland hadn't even stayed to thank the attendees. He simply turned, climbed into his tiny hov-skiff, and drove away.

"Are you all right?"

Startled, he turned to the voice. It was Saanvi. He hadn't even realized that the yacht had returned to shore.

"I'm fine, thank you. More importantly, how are you?"

She shrugged. "I'll be fine. His illness was long and arduous. It was expected."

"Still, one is never quite prepared for the loss of family." Leeland bit back a tear.

"No, I suppose not."

"Ahh," Aryan said, coming up from the bank. He smiled ear to ear. His breath stank of expensive spirits. "You two seem to be getting along."

Saanvi rolled her eyes. "Please, Aryan, don't make a scene. Not at your father's funeral."

"What scene am I making?" Aryan asked. "I'm simply stating a fact. It's important that you get along, since I'm sure your plan was to take over the team as soon as Father died."

Leeland tried to step away. "Well, I guess I better get—"

"That's nonsense," Saanvi snapped back. "Don't be boorish in front of our guests. You're drunk."

"Of course I'm drunk! Our father is dead, and you now control the company. Congratulations, my sweet sister. Things couldn't have worked out better if you had planned it that way."

Saanvi moved forward and grabbed her brother's collar. She pulled her face up to his, red anger in her eyes. "What are you implying, you little zit? Are you saying I'm the cause of Papa's death? Is that it? Huh? How dare you!"

Aryan tried to break Saanvi's hold of his shirt. He grabbed her arms and tugged at them. Security was on them instantly.

Leeland jumped in, on Aryan's side, though not to force Saanvi's hands off his shirt, but to try to pull Aryan back and control him, to ensure that Saanvi's goons didn't rough him up for touching her aggressively. All the other friends and colleagues that had attended the funeral looked as uncomfortable as Leeland felt, and they scrambled away from the riverside to disappear in their various modes of transportation. Aryan's and Saanvi's scuffle became a larger shouting match between other family members, and for a short time, it seemed as if the entire Kapoor funeral party would devolve into a fight. But Leeland managed to grab Aryan and pull him away. The young, intoxicated fool shouted expletives at his sister as he was dragged from the riverside. Saanvi threw a few curses of her own back, but she was crying, sobbing in between. In contrast, Aryan shed no tears for the situation or for his father whose ashes were now floating away with the river current.

"Are you that stupid?" Leeland asked, as he all but carried Aryan up the riverbank and to the parked vehicles. He dropped Aryan onto the asphalt. The man grunted as his hip struck the hard ground. "She writes the checks, Aryan. And she just did so after a long, long delay. Are you trying to force her hand? Are you trying to damage the team?"

Aryan scooted away with a harsh kick of his dress shoes. The scuffle had disheveled his white shirt, white pants, and tie. He really looked like he was drunk now, as if he had awoken in an alley. "She knows what I meant. You saw all that false concern and sadness on her face. She didn't even wear white today, just some bland blue salwar kameez. Lies, all lies. She couldn't wait to see him dead, so she could take over the company."

"I thought that was already understood," Leeland said. "I thought she was supposed to take it over."

Aryan shook his head. "No, not officially. I'm the son and heir. It's mine, but she's got her claws sunk into everything, everyone on the board. She doesn't give a zit about the Vipers, Leeland. What she cares about is keeping me occupied so I'm not an embarrassment, so she can steal the company away from me when I'm not looking. Trust me, I know what I'm talking about."

Leeland stood silent, not certain what to say. There really wasn't anything to say. He wasn't part of the family, understood little of the Kapoor family dynamic, and this wasn't really his concern, or business, so long as the team was cared for. In truth, he wanted to say what he really felt. *You aren't qualified to head the company, you immature, alcoholic little…* He kept his mouth shut. That kind of talk would serve no purpose. Aryan was the manager and owner of the Vitala Vipers, whether Leeland liked it or not, and Leeland would do what he had to do to preserve the integrity of the team, for as long as he was charged to do so.

He stood there for a good while, looking at Aryan who sat against the humming side of one of the luxury hover vehicles. He was a mess. His new white suit was ruined. Finally, Aryan spoke.

"Do you miss your brother, Leeland?"

He nodded. "Yes. Every day."

Aryan huffed, nodded. "When I think of my father, I miss my mother. She died three years ago. She believed in me, when everyone else did not, and I tried to be as good a son to her as I could. Father didn't deserve my respect, or—" he swallowed, "—my love. He was a harsh, bitter man. Mother softened him, as best as she could, but when she died, he turned away from me and devoted himself to the company and to Saanvi. It's always been Saanvi. She was the jewel of his eye."

Leeland looked around for an exit, any excuse to escape this uncomfortable situation. He was no one's judge or confessor, nor did he want to be. He sympathized with the young man. He understood where Aryan was coming from, but he had no answers. And he didn't have time to find any.

"I'm sorry, Aryan," he said. "I'm sorry for your loss. I'm sorry that you had such a difficult relationship with your father. I really have nothing else to say about it except... win. Any anger or disappointment or hesitation that anyone in your family or the Vitala community has about you is easily washed away by victory. Winning, Aryan, is the best medicine in the world." He leaned in. "Win the tournament, and you will win their respect."

Aryan looked up at him, then smiled. He offered his hand. Leeland helped him up. "Well, that's up to you, my friend. Are we going to win the tournament?"

It was absurd to say yes, and dangerous. It wasn't up to Leeland, not entirely. It was really up to a million little things that had to fall into place before he could hoist the trophy at the end of the line. But Leeland was stuck. He had foolishly blurted it out to try and soothe this broken little man, and now he could do nothing but nod. "We can. We will."

Aryan turned to walk away. "Can I give you a lift?" Leeland asked, pointing to the Zaigor-model mid-sized hov-sedan he had purchased with his signing bonus. A beautiful skimmer of red and gold.

"No, thank you. I'll find my own way... I always have. Don't worry about me, Coach. I'll be fine." He paused, turned, and winked. "Worry about Saanvi."

Chapter Twelve

Hello sports fans, and welcome to the second round of the Third Sphere Invitational DreadBall Tournament. My name is Faraj Chaudhry from Vitala-TAV, the finest sports and new programming network in all the Third Sphere. If you love Dreadball… we got it!

And have we got a game for you today, boys and girls. Yes, though the tournament is in its infancy, the competition is starting to come into sharp focus. The Kilmerain 'Killer' Coalminers will face off against Coach Roth and his intrepid Vitala Vipers. This is going to be a game of inches, not yards, and who takes that last inch will be the winner.

I expect both teams to come out swinging, and if the rumors are true, Coach Roth has already traded blows with some of the Coalminers in a barroom brawl not long ago. Brokkrs are tough, as tough—if not tougher—than their Forge Father brethren, so I expect them to employ their 'wedge' technique as they have done in the past and crack as many skulls as possible. For the Vipers, I expect them to try to up their speed, go with strikers and keep the ball and action fluid. But, since I'm not a color commentator, I wasn't given the full readout of each team's starting lineup, so I cannot share with you my wit and wisdom any further today. But, just between you and me, I expect the Vipers to rely heavily on their striker veteran Shyler Coch. He's a right arrogant little sot. Let's hope he can stow the attitude long enough to do some good out there…

***

A desperate throw, a muffled catch, and Shyler Coch was in business. The ball ricocheted right into his magnetic scoop and he was off, with three howling Coalminers at his heels.

The Brokkr striker in pursuit was demolished by a side slam from Triple-B. The hit was so deadly that even the collared guard had to shake it off. That left two Coalminer guards in pursuit. Shyler smiled. He was loving life.

Throughout the match, the Coalminers had tried castling their back goal, but the Vipers had broken it twice. No luck, however, actually making a higher strike on that goal and so the Vipers had been content with swapping one-point scores throughout the match. They were down by one right now, and Shyler had a clear path to a strike zone.

The Brokkr that had tried to punch Leeland's face off at the bar was suddenly in Shyler's way, having come off the bench. He was spitting blood and bile from an earlier slam from Shadrack, who had also come off the bench earlier, but the little zit had paid him back in kind with a counter-slam that had put the veteran Viper guard in the Sin Bin ever since. The Vipers had only one guard on the pitch, and their paltry medical staff was busily treating jack wounds.

As he had been directed in practice, Shyler looked quickly for someone to dump off the ball, but Little Frankie was just coming back in from a minor injury and was out of position. Whatever was lying in front of him, Shyler had no intention of throwing the ball backward, and Leeland didn't want him to anyway. Leeland waved his striker forward, come hell or certain death. Shyler had to take the shot.

The Brokkr guard held his arms out as if he were a great net, catching fish. Shyler tried to dodge the Brokkr's left arm, got nicked on the waist from a gauntleted finger, and felt the tear of his jersey and skin. He winced and twisted. The ball wobbled on the launcher, but he held firm, maintained his balance by putting a hand onto the floor, and kept moving.

His next threat was two Brokkr jacks who had assembled into an ineffective two-man mini-castle and were protecting the goal Shyler was targeting. The new human rookie jack, Jerold Minata, who had been drafted to replace Petr Mogumbo, was moving into position to try and disrupt the meek castle. Shyler let him take the lead and waited, dodging another attempt by the Brokkr guard to put him down. Shyler did a one-eighty and left the guard on his face.

Leeland clapped and shouted his satisfaction. "Shyler's doing well today," he said to Bullseye standing next to him. "He's actually following instructions."

"There's a first for everything," Bullseye said in agreement. She winked, smiled, and they both turned their attention back to the pitch.

It was clear to Leeland that the Coalminers were tiring. His strategy of speed, speed, and more speed had taken its toll on their short, stocky legs. Shyler was making them look stupid, and Leeland was pleased.

"Take the shot!" he shouted as Shyler reached his destination.

Jerold had disrupted the castle enough for Shyler to see the goal, but it was so tempting to simply step back one space and try for a two-pointer and possibly win the game. Shyler took a step in that direction, then heard Leeland's call. Leeland could see the striker struggling with the decision, fighting against his natural tendencies to ignore authority. But this time, Shyler obeyed his coach. He stepped forward.

A clear throwing lane emerged from the brawl before him, and Shyler took the shot.

Score!

***

There it is, there it is! Didn't I call it? Veteran Shyler Coch put the chicken in the pot! I love it when I'm right. Listen to that crowd!

But there's still a lot of game to be played, and the Coalminers are now stomping mad. They'll get the ball back, my friends. You can count on it. We've got a lot of rushes coming.

I wonder what Coach Roth has up his sleeve to bring this to a satisfying conclusion for the Vipers…

***

The game now swung back to zero, and Leeland could barely hear himself think over the roar and stomping of the crowd. The stadium shook with kinetic energy. Most in attendance were in support of the Coalminers. They had packed the stadium and were shouting their discontent at a lowly fourteenth seed daring to compete with their precious third seed team, a team that Leeland was sure most of them assumed would advance easily. And perhaps they still would. The game was far from over, and now the ball was in Brokkr gloves.

The ball was shot back into play at the center line and it bounced into the launcher of a Coalminer striker, a wicked-fast little player known as 'The Dove.' But there was nothing soft or pleasant about him. His face was festooned with red scars upon scars that could be seen even through a forest of thick white facial hair, and he never mishandled the ball. The scouting report on him had shown Leeland that, in the seven years the Brokkr had been playing DreadBall professionally in one league or another, he had never had the ball stolen or torn from his glove. One had to take The Dove out of commission to get the ball back.

Triple-B was on him instantly, flailing his arms such as to create an almost dervish-like storm of fists. Leeland had seen the move before and was confident that it could halt, or at least stall, any striker. But The Dove had apparently seen the move as well and knew exactly when to pause and when to jump, skip, and slide right through it.

Leeland's breath caught in his throat as he saw The Dove moving to score on the back goal. "Bullseye, we have to spring the trap. Now!"

"Are you sure?" Bullseye asked, holding the small activation device that was connected remotely to Bertuchi's collar.

He didn't want to do it, but what choice did they have? This was the whole reason they had started Triple-B and not Shadrack. Time was running out, and he certainly did not want to go into overtime with Brokkrs.

"Light it up."

Bullseye nodded and waited until Triple-B got closer to The Dove in pursuit. When he was near, she sighed, closed her eyes, perhaps prayed, and pressed the button.

A line of red lights erupted inside Triple-B's collar, and although Leeland could not hear it, he could see the collective gasp that spread around the pitch among both Vipers and Coalminers alike. The lights came on and blinked in swirling patterns around Triple-B's collar, and everyone, including The Dove, scattered.

Everyone, except Little Frankie, who was the only other player on the Vipers who knew what was going on. While everyone paused to see Triple-B writhe around on the floor, clawing desperately at his collar, terror in his eyes, the human striker sneaked up behind The Dove and plucked the egg from the nest.

Little Frankie was across the center line before anyone could pursue. Only those preserving the castle had stayed in the backfield, and Frankie didn't care about that goal.

He casually stepped into the two-point space of the right goal and checked his six to ensure that no one would come up on him at the last moment and disrupt his shot. Then he released, a tight, fast spinning ball that flew down the scoop and into the goal with ease.

The Vipers went up by two.

The ball was again released at the center line, but the wind was out of the Coalminers' sails. Everyone was trying to get their bearings on what had just happened. A Brokkr jack scooped up the ball and tried to make a play, but his pocket was easily picked by Shyler who then spent the rest of the game playing keep-away from stunned Coalminer guards.

The game ended, the Vitala Vipers were declared the winners, and the riot began.

Coalminer fans, enraged by what had happened, stormed the pitch and tried to tear Triple-B apart. They had help from the Coalminer team, who was still on the pitch and was trying to find any Viper to slam. Even their strikers were pounding faces, shouting, and kicking groins.

"We have to get in there," Leeland said. "We've got to get him out."

Bullseye nodded, tucked away the collar activation device, and joined Leeland as they fought their way through the morass toward Triple-B.

Shadrack was holding off three Brokkr fans who had makeshift knives of steel and glass and were trying to gut Triple-B. He smashed the nose of one of the fans, took out the legs of another, and was trying to pull the third off his own back. Leeland got there just as the fan was trying to deliver a shard of glass into Shadrack's ear, pulled him down, and stomped his face.

A fist from somewhere struck Leeland in the side of the head, but it was a glancing blow, and Shadrack was on the perpetrator immediately.

"Don't worry about that," he told the guard. "Grab Triple-B. We've got to get him out before that collar really does blow!"

They found the brute at the bottom of a pile. Shadrack threw bodies aside. Leeland grabbed up his guard, but he was too big and too thick to secure a good grip. Bullseye and Shadrack helped.

Security klaxons bellowed as the wall on the edge of the center line separated and armed men stormed in. Leeland helped guide them out as he waved to his players to order them off the pitch. The Vipers fell back. Security swarmed them and held off the rest of the crowd while they pulled Triple-B to safety.

They were led down the long hallway to the Viper locker room. They dragged Triple-B between them, and when everyone was in the room, security closed and locked the doors behind them.

Leeland took a moment to catch his breath, then said, "That was close."

A stone silence held comments in suspension as everyone watched Triple-B collect himself. He took a couple steps toward Bullseye. His face was red and slimed with spit and blood, his own and probably Brokkrs'. The collar around his neck was again cold and dead. Anger bled out of his eyes like heat. Leeland caught his breath, not certain what would happen. He made a move to try to put himself between the guard and his defensive coach. Then Triple-B halted, and a broad smile spread across his face.

"Close indeed," Triple-B said, winking a watery eye and then throwing his arms around Bullseye.

The room erupted in cheers and champagne, which had been held in reserve just in case, was now uncorked. Leeland endured a shower of it and even accepted a full glass. He sipped modestly.

"Wait, wait, wait," Shadrack said, raising his hands and trying to get everyone's attention. "It was all a ruse?"

Bullseye nodded. "Yep. Only me, Leeland, Brutus, and Frankie knew of it."

"And you didn't bother to tell the rest of us?" Conner asked. "I nearly had a heart attack when I saw those red lights. And I wasn't even on the pitch."

"And that was the whole point," Leeland said. "We needed it to look real, as if the collar was going to blow. We needed the fear to be real. It was the best way to trick those cagey Brokkrs."

"Wait," Triple-B said. "The lights were red. They were supposed to be green."

Bullseye nodded, and then looked as sheepish and as contrite as Leeland had ever seen. "Yes, well, you see, I pushed the wrong button."

"The wrong button?"

"Green indicates an activation, but not an actual countdown," she said. "Red... means a countdown."

"You mean my head could have blown?"

"No... well, yes. But we had another thirty seconds before anything bad would have happened. I turned it off in time."

The room fell silent again, and then everyone—except Triple-B—burst into laughter.

Leeland laughed so hard his sides hurt. He collected himself, raised his champagne glass, and said, "A toast! For the Vitala Vipers, a sniveling little fourteenth seed beating a third. They ruled us out in this game, but we endured. A little trickery, yes, but that's how the game's played. Also to Brutus 'Backhoe' Bertuchi, for playing the role of terror so well..."

"My mother always wanted me to go into the theater..."

"... and to Shyler Coch, who played his best game. So... where are you, Shyler? Get out here!"

Everyone looked toward the showers, thinking their star striker had already gone in to clean up, but he did not emerge. Leeland was going to call for him again when a knock came at the locker room door.

Leeland answered it, and outside in the hall, facing him, was the Brokkr he had fought with in the bar. In the guard's left hand, held by the scruff, was Shyler Coch.

The Brokkr dropped Shyler at Leeland's feet and said, "Here's your price for winning. Congratulations. I wish you well in the coming games."

The Brokkr nodded, turned, and disappeared down the long hall.

Chapter Thirteen

Leeland knew that Snyler Cody was dead even before the Vipers' medical team confirmed it. He had seen enough death in his long career to know what it looked like. They confirmed the cause: blunt trauma, massive internal bleeding, a severed spine, and a broken neck. It wasn't to protect Tripp [illegible] from the same fate. Leeland had forgotten to protect all of his players. The Brokers had been right; this was the price that they had to pay for their stunning victory over a much superior team. It was the price Leeland had to pay for a lot of things.

Thirteen Blades fans and two Goldminer players were being held on various charges, one of which was murder. Since the death had clearly occurred after the game, players could be charged. One of them, however, was not the guard who had delivered Snyler's lifeless body to the Vipers' locker room. Leeland didn't know if the brute was responsible or not for Snyler's death. The fact that he had delivered the corpse was no evidence of that. He may have been the one to pull the striker from the crowd and had felt honor-bound to deliver him personally to Leeland. There was an unwritten rule between DreadBall players that, no matter how intense and deadly the competition became on the pitch, after the game, no player was ever targeted for assault or death. Two players on the Goldminers had violated that unwritten rule, and Digby was determined to see justice delivered to whoever had killed Snyler Cody. They had committed a de-

Chapter Thirteen

Leeland knew that Shyler Coch was dead even before the Vipers' medical team confirmed it. He had seen enough death in his long career to know what it looked like. They confirmed the cause: blunt trauma, massive internal bleeding, a severed spine, and a broken neck. In his rush to protect Triple-B from the same fate, Leeland had forgotten to protect all of his players. The Brokkr had been right: this was the price that they had to pay for their stunning victory over a much superior team. It was the price Leeland had to pay for a lot of things.

Thirteen Brokkr fans and two Coalminer players were being held on various charges, one of which was murder. Since the death had clearly occurred after the game, players could be charged. One of them, however, was not the guard who had delivered Shyler's lifeless body to the Vipers' locker room. Leeland didn't know if the brute was responsible or not for Shyler's death. The fact that he had delivered the corpse was no evidence of the crime. He may have been the one to pull the striker from the crowd and had felt honor-bound to deliver him personally to Leeland. There was an unwritten rule between DreadBall players that, no matter how intense and deadly the competition became on the pitch, after the game, no player was ever targeted for assault or death. Two players on the Coalminers had violated that unwritten rule, and Digby was determined to see justice delivered to whoever had killed Shyler Coch. They had assured Leeland personally of their commitment to such.

Their promise didn't keep his players from falling into a deep rage or cold depression.

Triple-B wanted to kill someone, anyone, for Shyler's death. It took half the team and Bullseye's consummate patience and soothing voice to keep him from fulfilling that promise. Little Frankie disappeared for two days, and Leeland began to wonder if he'd ever return. But on the third day, he showed up with a messy black beard, smelling like Aryan had the day of the funeral. But he was ready to play on, vowing to keep Shyler's memory intact with a win. Everyone else dealt with the loss in their own way. Leeland even canceled practice twice just to allow everyone a chance to deal with the loss and heal psychologically.

No one particularly liked Shyler. He was arrogant and self-absorbed and possessed a host of other failings, but there was no denying his skills and star power. His loss was significant. Leeland did not know if they would be able to recover from it in time for their next match. Who was out there that they could recruit to take his place? They had other strikers on their roster, yes, but they were only competent at best. Competence alone would not give them a victory in the next round.

The sixteen-team round that had just ended continued to surprise sports analysts and defied modern thinking in terms of which teams could and could not advance.

As predicted, the Saltborne Sledgehammers sailed through the round by beating the Grimson Graybeards, another Forge Father team who just seemed ill-equipped to match their brethren's high-powered balance.

The Solarium Diamonds edged out a very competent opponent in the Pious Priests, a Judwan team that forced overtime play but ultimately could not hold.

The Marauder Polstar Privateers upset the Asterian Knight Hawks in what was the shortest game to date. Normally, it would be the Asterians, due to their speedy striker lineup, that would break into an early lead, but the Privateer guards were unstoppable. In one particularly gruesome moment, an Asterian striker raised his glove to accept the ball, only to find that his launcher had failed and thus, the ball ripped his arm and glove off at two hundred and thirty miles clocked. By the middle of the game, the Asterians could only field two players, and thus forfeited with a two point deficit.

The Neo-bot Nova Station Redshirts, the current darlings of the media, continued to dazzle with their win over the corporate Arch Rivals, a team that Leeland had expected to reach the top eight. But the Redshirts were defying expectations and winning crowds. At present, they were playing the most efficient game of anyone.

The female corporate Golan Banshees defeated the corporate Brickshank Socialites in an overtime win that captured the attention of the analysts and sent them into a panic about who would, and would not, reach the final four. The Banshees were just plain impressive, and no one on the team was even well-known. They had no previous stars, no one of name recognition whatsoever—but they understood the definition of 'team.' Everyone worked together to the last rush.

Continuing to defy the experts, the Zee Whitestar Chimps defeated the Marauder Blacktooth Terrors. As powerful and deadly as the Polstar Privateers were in their game against the Knight Hawks, the Terrors were reduced to sniveling wimps against the Chimps. Like most teams, they went in expecting an easy win and came out with a bloody nose. The Zee even managed to kill one of their goblins and severely injured two others. In Leeland's mind, it should be the Zee who were held in highest regard by the analysts, more so than the Redshirts. But it was difficult for anyone to take the Zee seriously. It would take more than a few wins to change perceptions that had been formed over decades of weak Zee play.

The Reb Polmak Resisters defeated the more competent female corporate I-Corps Tigers. Defeated them handily, in fact, though rumors abounded that suggested that they had stolen the Tigers' game plan prior to the match. No official Digby investigation had been called for, but hearing this, Leeland thought back on his encounter with the Gaelian at Aryan's office. Could Aryan have fed the Tiger's gamebook to the Rebs? Did he even know anyone on the Tigers? It seemed ridiculous on the surface, but then, given the Kapoor family's wealth and influence, and if he were paying debts, it was possible.

And finally, of course, the Vitala Vipers defeated the Kilmerain 'Killer' Coalminers in a very controversial game that left the Vipers' star striker dead.

Round two games were finished, and the final eight teams were matched.

The Saltborne Sledgehammers would face the Solarium Diamonds.

The Polstar Privateers would face the Nova Station Redshirts.

The Golan Banshees would face the Polmak Resisters.

The Vitala Vipers would face the Whitestar Chimps.

Despite knowing better, Leeland did breathe a small sigh of relief. The Zee could be tough, indeed, and they could badly damage or kill an opposing player from time to time, but the chance of losing a player against them at any given time due to injury was small. The Vipers needed a game where injury and death were secondary, even tertiary, concerns. They needed a game like that now more than ever.

Some of the higher seeded teams that had been eliminated early had drafted a joint complaint that Digby's seeding determination had been flawed and that the tournament should start over. Digby, of course, would not hear of it, now that the tournament was moving into its final rounds; and besides, the press that they were getting about all the 'underdogs' beating superior teams was translating into big revenues. The Third Sphere tournament was getting more positive press than the Second Sphere, where its tournament was seemingly dull by comparison. So, things would move forward at pace, regardless of complaint.

Leeland now had to turn his attention, and his distracted team's attention, toward the Whitestar Chimps.

***

Aryan ordered Leeland to plan a press conference. It had been a while since they had held one, and the wolves were howling. "A fourteenth seed that has gotten so far in the tournament must speak to the media, must avail itself for questions," Aryan said curtly. "You must!"

Now here Leeland stood, at a semi-opaque podium with vid input that flashed the Viper logo between pictures and stats for each player, while taking the slings and arrows of the press.

"How do you account for the Vipers' success so far, Coach Roth?"

Leeland cleared his throat. "Quality players, a sound coaching staff. Good support in the front office. All of these things have come together."

"*With the death, or rather, murder, of Shyler Coch, how do you move forward with your offense? Do you have options to replace such a stellar player?*"

Leeland nodded. "Yes, we're going through the process of seeking a replacement. It's difficult now, of course, so far into the tournament, but there are free agents worthy of a shot, corporate teams that have just recently lost whose players are looking for a job. As far as moving forward otherwise, I've been in this game for a long time.

Circumstances change very quickly; the fortunes of war, as they say, turn on a dime. It's the nature of the game. We'll adapt, we'll overcome, and we'll move forward."

"*There is great controversy surrounding your last game against the Killer Coalminers. Some are saying that Triple-B's activated collar during the game was a violation of the rules. Do you wish to comment?*"

Leeland snickered and then shook his head. "Players on Convict teams have collars that either shock or explode. They are allowed by Digby. The collar does not violate any rules."

"*Some are saying that the activation of his collar was a ruse and that there was never any chance of it exploding.*"

"Whoever 'some' are, I can assure you and them, that the collar could very well have exploded."

"*Is it too much of a risk to allow your team to be potentially blown apart by a faulty collar, especially in a tournament where a loss means you're out?*"

"No. Every time we take the pitch, there's a risk that we will lose, someone will be severely injured, or die. That is the nature of the game, and anyone who has actually suited up and played understands that. Triple-B is one of my finest players. He understands the risk of his collar, more so than anyone, and he chooses to play. And we choose to play with him, despite the risk. His service to the team and to the sport should be admired, not questioned."

"*How do you intend on handling the Whitestar Chimps?*"

"Very delicately." That got a laugh from everyone in the room. "No, but seriously, as I explained to my staff recently, never underestimate the Zee. The Dragons and the Terrors did, and they are now going home. We will try not to make the same mistake. I've played many games against the Kolossals. I know how Zee play. We'll be ready."

He hoped so, or in retrospect, if they were to lose against the little apes, this press conference would look like boastful arrogance.

"*Coach Roth, the Polmak Resisters are going up against the Golan Banshees in the final eight round. If you win against the Chimps and the Resisters beat the Banshees, you'll be facing them again. Will you be changing tactics to play them any differently this second time around?*"

Leeland shrugged and pursed his lips. "No. We'll study their game footage and prepare like we do against any other team. I'm familiar with Reb tactics, and I don't anticipate that they'll alter their strategy overmuch. They'll be a little more seasoned, like we all are, but I don't anticipate having to make any serious adjustments."

"*And you have no opinion about allowing Reb teams to play in DreadBall Leagues?*"

"My personal opinion on the matter has no bearing on how I conduct myself against them on the pitch. As far as I'm concerned, politics is left at the door when a team takes to the pitch. Perhaps that's a naïve stance, but we've no time to resolve galactic conflicts during a match. I'll let those within the GCPS whose pay grade is higher than mine worry about politics."

"*There are rumors that the Resisters have been receiving their opponent's game plans prior to their matches. Do you wish to comment?*"

Leeland shook his head. "I've heard the rumors, but I've no comment on it."

"*If such rumors were to be found true, would you be in favor of disqualifying the Resisters?*"

"If the rumors were found to be true, I'm sure Digby would take the necessary steps to handle the situation. That's all I have to say. One more question."

He picked a woman in the back who had had her hand up the entire time.

"*Coach Roth, today is the sixth anniversary of the death of your brother, Victor Roth. Do you wish to comment on that?*"

Six years? Yes, of course it was. Now he remembered. He was so preoccupied with the Vipers and their problems and challenges that he had forgotten. *What kind of brother am I? The kind that forgets killing his brother.*

"I miss him, and if he were here today, I'd tell him how profoundly sorry I am." He put up his hand. "Don't insult my intelligence by asking me what I'm sorry for. You know the answer to that question. All I will say right now is that I am dedicating the rest of the tournament, however long it lasts for us, for the Vipers, to my brother. And I hope, wherever he is, he's playing DreadBall, dodging slams, stealing balls, and making scores. He was the best."

Leeland left the podium and disappeared behind a black curtain to the howls of the press corps asking further questions. He tuned them all out. The last question was the only one he remembered, the only one that mattered.

The day had been long, and Leeland was tired. He had canceled the day's practice because of the press conference. Tomorrow, they would begin planning for the Whitestar Chimps. But now, all he wanted to do was go back to his private apartment that the Kapoors had loaned him, drop into a hot, soaking bath, and forget everything.

He walked to his hover car in the underground parking lot. The Gaelian claw that he saw sticking out of an open window on a black luxury vehicle gave him pause. The man who stood in front of the window, speaking to the Reb player inside, made him angry.

As the black hover car sped away, Leeland jogged across the poorly lit parking lot, grabbed Aryan by the scruff, and pushed him against the wall. "Are you that stupid?" he asked, easily holding off Aryan's attempts at breaking free. "At the press conference you insisted on, no less? Did Damon Kapoor raise a stupid boy?"

"Let me go, you Zwerm. Let me go!"

Leeland let him go but stood in his path and didn't let Aryan walk away. "The Gaelian again? Is he the same one I saw at your office? Do you understand how foolish this is, Aryan? The press is all over the rumors that the Resisters are getting team game plans. Are you providing them?"

Aryan fixed his suit, shook his head. "No. I'd never do that."

"It looks like you are." Leeland glanced around, hoping no one was hearing this. He lowered his voice. "Look, I don't give a Zee's rear what debt you owe this Gaelian, or whether you are just simple friends. It's totally inappropriate, and now dangerous, for you to be speaking with him. So you aren't going to talk to him again, you understand me? You aren't going to utter one word, and you definitely won't be giving them our game book. You do that, and I'll knock your sorry ass into *Naraka*, whether you believe in a Hell or not. I'll rag you out to the press and to whomever else will listen. Do you get me?"

Aryan pointed a shaky finger at Leeland's face. "You speak to me again like that, and you're fired. You get me?"

Leeland backed away and spread his arms out, palms up, and shrugged. "You don't own the team, remember? Saanvi does. You said it yourself."

Leeland turned and walked toward his hover car. He was angry and sweating, his face blood red, his pulse rapid. He wanted to punch the ornate pillar that he passed, but worried that being so enraged, he'd bring the whole garage down upon them. He felt like he had the power of Triple-B.

"You don't coach the Vipers anymore!" Aryan screamed at him. "You hear me? You're done."

Leeland ignored the petulant child's rantings. He opened the driver's side door on his red and gold hover, got in, and sat there for a long moment, listening to Aryan's muffled threats. Then he punched buttons to start the engine, backed up, and drove away.

Good, he thought, turning into the driving lane and toward his apartment. Let him fire me. *They're better off without me.*

Chapter Fourteen

Leeland was not fired the next day. Instead, his presence was requested at Saanvi's office at the Kapoor Industries' corporate headquarters.

"Aryan cursed you for over an hour," she said, pouring Leeland a hot tea. Leeland sipped. It was good but needed a little sweetener. "And then another thirty minutes or so, accusing me of sabotaging his efforts. He would not explain to me why he was so upset with you, but in the end, I convinced him not to be so foolish. You're still the coach of the Vitala Vipers."

Wonderful! In truth, now that he had had time to calm down, Leeland was glad. His service to the Vitala Vipers was more now than just satisfying a corporation's desire for more wealth and notoriety. With everything that had happened to date, not to mention his dedication to his brother, it was personal to him now. "That's good to hear."

"Yes," Saanvi said, "and it wouldn't have worked anyway. If such a thing were to occur, I'm sure the rest of your coaching staff and half the team would walk as well. The Vitala Vipers would be no more." Saanvi sat down next to Leeland on the soft couch in the center of the room. She sipped her tea and smiled. "You're the heart and soul of the Vipers, Mr. Roth. You should be proud."

Leeland nodded and cracked a small smile. "Thank you."

"But, I would stay away from my brother for a while, just to let everything calm down. And he will calm down. The good thing about my impetuous, short-attention-span brother is that he always clams down and moves on to the next shiny object."

"I will tread lightly."

They sat in silence, each sipping their tea. Leeland watched Saanvi as she sipped. She was a beautiful woman and most capable. Even drinking tea, she seemed to hold the entire room in suspension, as if every particle of dust in the air waited for her to give it the nod to fall. But there was a seriousness, a concern in her expression right now that worried him, as if she were mulling something dangerous over and over in her mind. She sipped and then rotated the cup and sipped again. Over and over as if she were about to explode.

"Is there something wrong?" Leeland asked.

Saanvi blinked rapidly and pulled herself out of her trance. "No...well, yes. I'm sorry, Leeland, I don't mean to burden you with this, but I'm worried about my brother. It goes beyond his selfish behavior, his immaturity." She looked him straight in the eye. "How well do you know Aryan? I mean, how much have you spoken to him? Have you seen him do anything, or speak with anyone, that might be considered... untoward? I mean, beyond foolish notions of firing you as our head coach."

Yes, Leeland wanted to say but kept his mouth shut. It was on the tip of his tongue to blurt, *Yes, yes, he's been speaking to Rebels, to a Gaelian.* But the words caught in his throat. Speaking to a Gaelian in and of itself was no issue, but the clandestine way in which her brother was doing it, that was cause for alarm. Leeland wanted to confess, wanted to explain why Aryan had threatened to fire him since Aryan had not divulged the reason why to his sister. But something in his mind made him pause. Something Aryan himself had said.

Worry about Saanvi…

"No, nothing. Obviously, we've had our severe differences in team management, in personnel issues, but nothing else."

Saanvi nodded, sipped again. "Okay, well, if you see anything, anything at all, please let me know. My brother has been known to sympathize with causes that are... let us say, incompatible with our family's business. That was another reason why Father let him manage the Vipers: to try to get him to care about his future, about the family's health and well-being. Let's just hope he takes it to heart."

Leeland nodded. "I'll try to keep an eye on him."

He finished his tea, then moved to stand.

"Would you like to join me for dinner tonight?" Saanvi asked him. "Nothing fancy or formal. Just us, here. We can discuss the team, discuss its future, even beyond the tournament." She then stepped forward a pace and smiled. She was very close now, and Leeland could smell her perfume, see her long, dark eyelashes. She was even more beautiful up close. "I promise, nothing uncomfortable. We'll discuss business, have a laugh or two. Wine and good food."

It was tempting, oh so tempting. Leeland felt himself swoon in her closeness, and if the situation were different, he wouldn't hesitate to accept. But, "Thank you, Saanvi, for the invitation, but I am putting in a long night of prep for the Chimps. Some other time, perhaps?"

Saanvi nodded, blinked her impressive eyes, smiled, and Leeland could not detect in her any disappointment or sorrow. "Very well. If spending a night with tiny chimps is more interesting than spending it with me, good wine, and good music, you go right ahead."

Leeland laughed, seeing no anger or frustration in her jest. "Well, it isn't, I will grant you, but necessary. One must never take the Zee for granted."

Saanvi led him to the door, shook his hand, and gave him a small peck on the cheek. He swooned again. "Thanks for coming by, Leeland. Let's speak again soon. And remember, if you see anything, anything at all, please let me know. It's for my brother's benefit more than mine. We want to help him stay on the straight path."

Leeland nodded again and walked away, player X's and O's in his mind and the scent of her perfume still in his thoughts.

***

"The Whitestar Chimps... how do we beat them?"

It was a valid question, and one that Conner Newberg, still benched unfortunately, tried to answer. "We show up."

Everyone in the meeting chuckled, even Triple-B who, surprisingly, had taken Shyler Coch's death the hardest. Perhaps he felt guilty for being the main reason why Shyler had been put into that deadly situation; it was Triple-B, after all, that had recommended that Shyler be put on the team. But it wasn't the guard's fault at all. If it were anyone's, it was Leeland's. And Bullseye's, perhaps, but he wasn't going to let anyone else take the blame. *It's my fault*, he thought, as he allowed the team a few fleeting seconds of levity.

"That is normally the case," Leeland said, "but these little cloned apes have defied the odds, beating both a Metabot and a Marauder team on their way to us. We are a higher seed than they are, so Digby has parked their GCPS Cruiser, the *Dread*, in low orbit over Vitala, thus giving our fans more tickets and us home field advantage. That'll help, but I've watched video of their play and their practice, and I can tell you, they are pros. They are serious, dedicated, and ready to go. All jacks, of course, but that makes them even more serious: they have something to prove, and they've done so. We need to be ready."

He turned on the vid screen. The Whitestar Chimps' last game appeared and was nearing the halfway mark, and all that anyone could see was a field of white-and-yellow armor and the Chimps' white starburst logo emblazoned on a yellow field like a jewel. There were Zee everywhere on the pitch.

Leeland paused the game. "They work in tandem, and they swarm. Swarm, swarm, swarm. They do not care about slamming their opponent. They do not care if they are the weakest team in the tournament when it comes to hits, injuries, deaths. They want to score. They approach the game like the Asterians do. All they care about is getting the ball and finding lanes to the goals. And cheat; gods above, do they cheat! One of their games in the seeding rounds had nearly half their numbers out for cheating, and they still had enough to field a full team. They are going to agitate us until we're spent... if we let them. But we're not going to let them.

"Triple-B will command the castle," Leeland said, pointing at him in the second row, "and you will pulverize any Zee that gets in your line of sight. Understood?"

The big man nodded.

"Shadrack will roam the pitch and knock heads. These little fellows are the antithesis of the Brokkr. We don't have to worry about taking many slams from them, but they will swarm our ball carrier and bite and claw and rip our gloves to shreds to get it. Trust me, I know. I want you, Mr. Shadrack, to keep the swarms at bay. Follow our ball carriers, and disrupt any Zee attempts at piling on. Little Frankie and our other strikers will do the rest."

The rookie striker held up his hand but did not wait to be called upon. "Have you found a replacement for Shyler?"

It was a mild sore point for the other strikers on the team who warmed the bench most often. They wanted their chance, and Leeland was planning to give it to them. Newly-acquired Spencer Mills, even more rookie than Frankie, would be moved off the bench and into the starting lineup right away. Others would be rotated into play when required, but the Vipers still needed that one star striker that the late Shyler Coch represented so well.

"We're looking at several candidates right now," Leeland said. "Both the Arch Rivals and the Brickshank Socialites were defeated in the last round. Their strikers are looking for work."

"Is that legal?" Conner asked, in a mildly petulant voice. "Since they have already played in the tournament and have been eliminated. Doesn't seem right, does it, that they can move on in the tournament with another team, and I'm stuck on the bench."

Leeland nodded. "Yes, I agree: it doesn't seem right. But with respect to Digby—and I say that reluctantly—your situation is slightly different than other players from defeated teams. Their teams are out, and there is no chance that they might face their previous teams in the tournament again."

"But they may face them again in league play," Conner said, continuing to press the point. "If one of their strikers signs on with us, and then we lose in these last few rounds, the Third Sphere is planning to create a league with as many rejected teams as possible. If the Vipers then sign on for that league and the striker we get stays on as a teammate, wouldn't they be in violation of their contract?"

Leeland did his best to keep calm. He sympathized with the man, but now was not the time. "Maybe, but we don't have time for a legal discussion right now, Conner. The situation is what it is. I don't make the rules. If I did, trust me, you'd be suiting up. Right now, my concern is getting a top-shelf striker to fill a seat."

"When will my 'situation' be resolved?"

"Soon," Leeland said. "Digby has promised Saanvi that they will make a ruling right after the Chimps, which could be too late, but that's the best she could do."

"Oh, it's 'Saanvi' now, is it?" Shadrack said, giving his coach a little wink. "On a first name basis with the boss, eh?"

Leeland shrugged. "I call you by your first name."

"Yes, but I'm not a hot babe who..."

"All right, all right," Leeland said, tamping down chuckles. "That's enough of that. We don't have time for anything else right now but the Chimps. If Bullseye were here, she'd smack you across the face for such talk. Now, let's refocus."

"Okay," Conner said, "then who is the leading candidate to take Shyler's place?"

Leeland swallowed. "Jimbo Threpe."

A collective moan spread across the room. "Not him!" Shadrack looked like he had eaten a bad grape. "Where's Shyler Coch when you need him?"

"In the ground," Triple-B said in his most sorrowful, lowest bass voice.

After that, the room erupted into scores of meaningless conversations, both pro and con, of the man known as Mackinaw Jim.

Leeland sighed, shook his head, and ended the meeting immediately.

Chapter Fifteen

Jimbo Threpe, aka Mackinaw Jim, aka Mack 'in-awe' Jim was quite possibly the most arrogant and narcissistic striker in the tournament, and perhaps anywhere. He made Shyler Coch's self-absorption look quaint by comparison. And despite his moniker, his skills on the pitch weren't particularly awe-inspiring, save for his throw. He had - some would say - a poetic throwing motion. If he got into a strike zone and had an unfettered view of the goal, he would score. End of discussion. The Vitala Vipers didn't need head-knockers or field generals, but they did need a scoring machine.

He arrived at the next practice wearing his infamous techni-colored Mack, his fancy top hat with pseudo swirling colors of nebula fire, and a diamond-studded walking cane which he claimed had a blade for protection. He wore sunglasses that looked like two tiny black holes on his face. He had a mustache and apparently no other body hair, so the stories told. He had once famously asserted that body hair slows down a striker, though how that was possible being covered head to toe in armor was anyone's guess. He had a personal manager, an analyst, and brander. He was independently wealthy. He didn't need to play the game, but 'I love it so,' he would say again and again at press conferences. And he did seem to love the game. The pomp and pageantry of it, anyway.

He practiced his throwing and spent a little time catching passes from the coaching staff. He spent a lot of time in conference with his manager. He signed a few autographs for fans that had come to watch the practice. He took a few calls. He got into a scrape with Shadrack who grew frustrated by his lack of concentration and lack of seriousness in practice. There was pushing, some shoving, but all in all, it was a productive day. No one got injured. A practice without injuries was always a good sign.

On the day of the game, Mackinaw Jim showed up twenty minutes late, though luckily the game hadn't started due to a technical malfunction with the Vipers' back goal. Leeland spent a few minutes ripping into Mackinaw for his tardiness. The preoccupied striker simply winked and said, "Don't worry, Boss. I've got everything under control." He nodded toward the technicians working on fixing the problems with the back goal. Leeland didn't know if it was a nod to that specific activity, or to the pitch itself, as if to say he was ready to play. A man of Mackinaw's wealth and contacts, it was possible that he had the connections to make things break down, to delay the game for whatever reason. Leeland considered asking for a clarification but decided against it. When it came to nefarious activities on and off the pitch, it was sometimes best for the coach not to get involved.

The game began, and as predicted, the Zee swarmed like hornets.

The Vipers snagged the ball first, with Little Frankie getting it on a toss-back from Spencer Mills, who seemed a little shell-shocked at suddenly being in the big game. Spencer went under a wave of Zee jacks. Little Frankie moved to score.

Shadrack shadowed Little Frankie, and as practiced, he smacked away Chimps who were trying to climb Little Frankie like a mountain. Already the Zee were cheating, as one in tandem would try a legitimate steal of the ball while his partner would try to restrain the target before Frankie could move clear. The Chimps were experts in this illegal activity, however, and while one restrained, another kept the referee's attention elsewhere. It was all Shadrack could do to break their hold on Little Frankie. He was dealing with climbers of his own, not to mention their foul breath and teeth snapping at the soft, exposed uniform seam at his throat.

The red foul lights blinked and clamored. The referee had finally seen the Chimps' illegal restraint and had ordered the Zee off the pitch. Frankie was back in action.

He twisted and turned his way through the dividing ocean of Zee, slid into the closest strike zone, and threw the ball at the goal.

Interception, as one Chimp flew into Frankie's line of vision at the last moment and scooped the ball out of the air. The crowds roared. The little interceptor rolled, righted himself, and took off down the pitch.

For his troubles, Little Frankie suffered a sucker punch undetected by the ref and was sent into the Sin Bin.

Damn! Leeland did not like that, though Frankie seemed only mildly shaken by the illegal attack. He'd be back, but Leeland knew that the first score attempt in any DreadBall match was oftentimes the most important, as it set the tone for the rest of the game. Now, the Vipers had to transition into a defensive stance, and he didn't have the personnel on the pitch for that.

Triple-B, along with two jacks, were holding the castle in place. Leeland was not worried about that, as it was obvious that the Chimps had watched video of previous Viper play and had witnessed his collar light up. They were keeping a wide berth of the guard and focusing on making two- and one-point scores. Zee weren't known for their throwing skill, so Leeland knew that they'd try to sneak in closer to the goal. That gave the Vipers some flexibility in how they were going to defend.

Bullseye was all over it.

"Pedal back!" she screamed to Shadrack and the Viper jacks who were trying to slow the Zee roll. "Don't turn away. Pedal backward and keep your eyes on the ball hugger!"

In a match against the Zee, one had to keep an eye on the ball because the Zee moved in tandem and kept the ball moving back and forth between the partnership, thus confusing their opponent as to exactly who had the ball at any given moment. And despite their small stature, they kept the ball on their tiny launcher and out of sight until the last minute.

This was when Shadrack's long experience paid off. He had played against Zee as well and knew how they operated. He pedaled backward, as directed, but made sure that he did not obscure the view of the referee. He pedaled to the left but did not move so close to the oncoming white-and-yellow traffic that he couldn't readjust if the Chimps so chose to shift their entire group, like a flock of birds, in the other direction.

And that's exactly what they did. As they neared the right side strike zone, the ball carrier and his partner shifted to their left, so quickly that they left Little Frankie fumbling at his heels. The only thing between them and a score now was Shadrack and one frightened Viper jack.

Shadrack pushed his teammate out of the way. Leeland didn't like his players man-handling others, but in this instance, it was warranted. The rookie jack, which, like Spencer, had just been brought into the lineup as a new starter, looked as if he were shaking in his boots, and the Zee had an uncanny ability to sense fear and exploit it. With him out of the way, the only thing the non-ball carrier could do was face Shadrack and his Viper-fanged fist.

The tiny Zee must not have known what hit him, as his helmet cracked under Shadrack's blow and flew off his head. Nasty spit, blood, and Zee bile arched through the air like a line of mixed paint from an artist's brush. It was followed by the Zee himself, who flew in chase and then crashed unconscious on the pitch, smearing his own blood and making a right mess of the floor, like an ancient drip painting. Tiny servitor robots scrambled across the floor to clean up the mess, while a medibot dragged the unconscious (and perhaps dead) Zee away.

The ball carrier hesitated, just for a few seconds, in awe or perhaps fear, of what had happened to his partner, and this was enough time for Mackinaw Jim to sneak up and pluck the ball right off the Chimp's glove.

The star striker was down the pitch immediately, but unlike a humble person, he strutted and waved, zigged and zagged, and played to his adoring fans. For a moment, it looked like the Zee would recover and swarm him before he reached a strike zone. At the last minute, after bowing as if he were catching bouquets of flowers at the end of a theater production, he flicked the ball toward the goal like a piece of lint. It arched through the air like the shattered Chimp had just done and pierced the goal with a precision that, Leeland had to admit, was poetry.

The Vipers were suddenly up two points and the stadium was rocking.

"He keeps it exciting," Bullseye said.

Leeland nodded. "Yeah, but guys like that can become weights around your neck. One of these days, his flash and fancy will pale, and he'll do something stupid and lose us the game. I wish we had gone for someone else, Carla. Someone more stable."

She huffed. "In this game? Good luck finding one of them."

From that moment forward, the whole tenor of the game changed. It seemed as if, at last, the Whitestar Chimps had lost their drive. They still played hard, still fouled excessively, but their speed, their nerve, was gone. They managed to score a few times, bringing the total back down to moments where it seemed that they might take the lead. But then, they'd fall behind again, and once the Vipers were up four points, Bullseye ended the castle and allowed Triple-B a chance to get in on the action. By the time he and Shadrack were finished, they had racked up six casualties between them. The pitch was slick with gore, and the game had to be stopped twice so the little servitor robots could clean up the mess. In the end, the Vitala Vipers crushed the Whitestar Chimps by five points, and Mackinaw Jim had scored them all.

***

Amidst the celebration in the locker room, Leeland pulled Mackinaw aside.

"Did you pay them off?" he asked, whispering. "Did you pay off the Chimps?"

Mackinaw pulled back, "What are you talking about?"

"They just shut down after your first score, just went through the motions. This was not their style. If the Zee were going to fall back on their worse tendencies, they'd have done it already. There was nothing in their portfolio that suggested to me that they were going to do this. They had fallen back in games before, and they didn't just give up. If anything, they became even more determined. A two point deficit is easy to overcome, yet they never tried to do it. They were giving a good show for their fans, but I've been around the block many times, Jim, and I can say with certainty: they were not playing to win. So, I'll ask you again, did you pay them off?"

Mackinaw stared at his coach, and there was real confusion, and perhaps anger and insult, in his glare. He leaned in. "Look, I gave the technicians a little incentive to delay the start of the game. I was running late, and I didn't want that to be the reason we lost. I'm an arrogant waste of space, Coach, and perhaps a little too flashy for my own good, but I'm not stupid. Digby would be all over me if I were to fix a game. This isn't Xtreme... I know that. All I did was delay the start. That's all."

Leeland nodded, not being able to divine any falsehood in the striker's words or demeanor. "Very well. But you keep it clean from here on out, you understand me? We're not going to lose this whole thing because one of my players makes a bone-headed mistake. If you're late, fine. I'll bench you if you do it again, see if I don't. You play it clean, and maybe we'll get out of this with something to be proud of. Play it clean."

Leeland walked away and let his players celebrate.

He left the locker room and walked the hallways throughout the ship. The *Dread* was massive, and there were places on it that he was not allowed to enter. He kept to the sanctioned paths and walked and walked, letting his mind work through what had just happened. He was happy that the Vipers had won. Why wouldn't be he? He was their coach, and it was his responsibility to share in his players' happiness. They had played well. They had come together after the tragic loss of Shyler Coch and had done their duty.

Still... someone had tampered with the Chimps. It was, indeed, possible that they had just lost their drive, their nerve, their luck. It was possible. In DreadBall, a team could win extraordinarily and then, in the next game, look like rank amateurs. It was possible. But it just didn't feel right to him. Not right at all.

Someone had bought off the Whitestar Chimps. Who was it? Aryan? Saanvi? Someone else? It was hard to know. But it had happened.

And Leeland didn't like it.

outrageous waste of space, Coach, and perhaps a little too flashy for my own good, but I'm not stupid. Gabe would be all over me if I were to fix a game. This isn't 'Gremlins,' I know that. All I did was delay the start. That's all."

Leeland nodded, not being able to divine any falsehood in the catcher's words or demeanor. "Very well. But you keep it clean from here on out, you understand me? We're not going to lose this whole thing because one of my players makes a hare-brained mistake. If you're lying, fine. I'll bench you if you do it again. If you didn't, Vic, play it clean, and maybe we'll get out of this with something to be proud of. Play it clean."

Leeland walked out, and let his players celebrate.

He left the locker room and walked the hallways thinking about the thing. The Dread was massive, and there were places on it that he was not allowed to enter. He kept to the sanctioned paths and walked and walked, letting his mind work through what had just happened. He was happy that the Vipers had won. Why wouldn't he be? He was their coach, and it was his responsibility to share in his players' triumphs. They had played well. They had come together after the tragic loss of Skyler Corh and had done their duty.

Still, someone had tampered with the Chimps. It was, indeed, possible that they had just lost their drive, their nerve, their luck. It was possible. In Dreadball, a team could look extraordinarily good and then, in the next game, look like rank amateurs. It was possible. But it just didn't feel right to him. Not right at all.

Someone had bought off the Whipstar Chimps. Who would? Anvil? Security? [illegible] But it had happened.

And Leeland didn't like it.

Chapter Sixteen

There were four sky boxes on the *Dread*, normally for wealthy fans with season tickets. However, for this tournament, they were reserved for the coaching staffs of the final eight teams, so that they may attend the games that they most cared about and be able to do some analysis and scouting during the competition.

Three of the final four games had already finished, with the Saltborne Sledgehammers defeating in overtime the Solarium Diamonds in what was being called 'The Score Heard Round the Sphere,' as the Sledgehammers won on a ball ricochet off the shoulder pad of a Crystallan jack diving for a deflection. But it was widely believed that if the jack had actually missed the block, the poorly thrown ball would have fallen short, and the Diamonds would have advanced as a final four.

Continuing to defy their critics, the Nova Station Redshirts defeated the Polstar Privateers in the deadliest match of the tournament to date. At the end, only one goblin jack faced off against four Redshirts in their last rush. The goblin refused to leave the pitch despite his coach's plea for 'mercy.' The little fellow even managed to steal the ball for a split second. Then he was crushed under the weight of two neo-bot guards and dragged off the pitch in smears.

The Vitala Vipers, of course, defeated the Whitestar Chimps, and so only one game remained. It was being played right now, as Leeland, Bullseye, and Triple-B entered the sky box in business casual.

The Polmak Resisters were facing off against the Golan Banshees. It was proving to be an exciting match. The winner would face the Vipers.

Saanvi greeted all three as they entered, and then to Leeland's surprise, bid farewell. "I apologize, but I have important family business to attend to," she said, "but please, help yourself to all the food and drink. Stay as long as you like. You three deserve it."

The entire team deserves it, Leeland thought to say, but he let her go with a simple nod.

The rest of the team had decided to watch the game in the Vipers' team meeting room on the ship. They did not want to dress fancy for such an event. They just wanted to kick back, unwind, and not be in the midst of their coaches who would, Leeland hoped, use this time in the box as a working lunch. Unlike the other teams that they had faced, they could not spend as much time on pre-game analysis. The two semi-final matches would be played in five days, and that barely gave anyone time to plan.

"We've already played against the Resisters, so we know a little about their game," Leeland said as he piled cheese slices and crackers onto his plate. He took a sip of a deep purple wine, winced at how tart and dry it was, cleared his throat, and continued. "Rebs are Rebs. They push, ram, pummel, jump... everything you'd imagine. Don't know much about the Banshees, though. They're the ones I want to look at closely. What can you tell me about them, Carla?"

Carla had forgone the wine but had piled her plate even higher, adding a Vitala chickpea dip, carrots and celery stalks grown in an ion-retardant greenhouse, and small crab puffs. Triple-B had done much the same, though he chose to forego a wine glass and instead gulped from the bottle.

"They're good at interference," she said, stepping out of Triple-B's way so as not to get knocked over as he lunged for the crackers. "They won't give us many lanes for scoring. They're fluid and very agile, very athletic. Their premiere guard is tough, too. Brenda McGinty, Big Bertha they call her. She's a good friend of mine. She's every bit as dangerous as Shadrack and much faster. She'll be a handful, assuming we play them."

Leeland nodded as he found a comfortable chair near the balcony. He now had a great view of the game. "You comfortable with coaching against a friend?" He took a sip of wine as he asked.

Bullseye looked at him with insult. "I'm a professional, Leelee. We've all had friends on the other side of that dividing line, including you. You know me better than that. When it comes time to play them, if we play them, I won't hesitate to lower the boom."

He knew that. He didn't know why he was even asking the question, but all the commotion of the past few weeks, with Saanvi's and Aryan's feud, Aryan's utter lack of discretion when speaking to Rebs, Shyler's death, game manipulation from Mackinaw Jim, Leeland needed assurance that, at least, Bullseye was clean. The stakes were going up. The Vipers had made the final four. To come this far and not make the championship game... well, it was too painful to imagine. Two final games stood in their way, and one of the two teams below would face them next.

Both teams were playing reasonably well, though it did seem as if the Banshees were putting in a slightly better effort. The Big Bertha that Bullseye had mentioned was throttling a Ralarat striker that was trying to drag itself across the pitch in an attempt to avoid being stomped by its own teammates. The Gaelian jacks were doing better with the Banshee's own jack line. A nasty back and forth had developed at the center near one of the ball entry cannons, and somewhere in the middle of the morass was the ball. Leeland couldn't see it from where he sat, but he'd been in enough of those scrapes to know that the ball was probably sitting harmlessly at their feet, while everyone was pairing off with another assuming that someone, anyone, in the pile had the ball. Finally, the Rebs' Rin guard kicked the ball out of the pile. A very tall and spry Banshee striker saw it, went after it, and scooped it up on the run. She dodged an impressive slam attempt by a Gaelian jack - one that looked just like the one Leeland had seen at Aryan's office - and then slid into the strike zone. She raised herself on tiptoes to get an even better view and angle on the goal than her height allowed, and threw. Score! And just like that, the Banshees were in the lead.

Leeland nodded. "Impressive. They're fast and accurate and tenacious. They have a good eye for the ball." He leaned over and whispered to Bullseye, "Honestly, I'd rather play them. Tough, but easier to predict. Their game is more straightforward. You never know what you're going to get with Rebs."

"It does not matter who we play," Triple-B blurted through a mouthful of crackers and cheese. "We'll break them either way."

Leeland scoffed. "More humility, my good man, would suit you." He winked.

"Humility is for the weak!"

Leeland had nothing to say to that, so he let it go with a nod and smile. He was glad to see his star guard so enthusiastic about their next opponent and knew that that enthusiasm would translate into excellent play, but—

"Where's Aryan?" Bullseye asked, turning to look at the door. There was a Kapoor Industries security goon standing there, waiting, but no Aryan.

"He's running late," Leeland shrugged, "so he said. But he's been very absent of late. We should just view and analyze our competition without him."

So they did, spending the next several minutes observing and then commenting on the game as it unfolded. Bullseye took notes and scribbled potential plays and maneuvers that the Vipers could employ against either team. Then the Banshees went up by three, before a Resisters' striker got a lucky goal on a bounce. Leeland was about to comment, but something was going on near the Resisters' Sin Bin.

"What's the ruckus over there?" he asked, pointing.

Bullseye shook her head. "I don't know, I—"

A vibration spread through the sky box as if something had struck the *Dread*. Then another small shake, and then a third, more powerful, one.

The lights flickered, and Leeland gripped the armrests of his chair. "What the—"

The game stopped, and the ruckus near the Sin Bin became a full-on brawl. A Sorak jack pulled a las pistol and fired at a Banshee across the pitch. A spear of red firelight struck the unsuspecting woman and she fell dead.

Leeland could hear the crowd scream. He tried to get up, and then the *Dread* was struck hard.

The lights went out. There was silence, another explosion, and then the *Dread* listed left.

***

Red emergency lighting filled the sky box. Security klaxons blared.

"A Reb attack!" Bullseye shouted over the alarms. "Where's my assault rifle?"

"You don't have it here," Leeland said, feeling his way to the exit. The Kapoor security guard was trying to open the door. It had locked automatically due to the ship's listing.

"We haven't lost gravity yet," Triple-B said, joining the guard to try to open the door.

"Yes," Leeland said, "but we will if the *Dread* keeps getting hit."

"What do we do?" Bullseye asked. "I need a gun!"

"It may be best to stay put," Leeland said. "Let the *Dread's* own security put this down."

"But the Vipers," Bullseye said, as she joined them all at the door. "Our team. They're here. They may be in trouble. And those sons of Zees have guns!"

Bullseye pointed through the red light to the pitch which was alive with screaming, dying, laser and small arms fire. How did the Resisters get guns through security? And how many cohorts did they have in this attack? Surely, the bulk of their fan base was helping; many of them, anyway. It was too difficult to think about how many innocents were dying down there where an honest game was, just a moment ago, being played to cheering fans. *The Resisters must have been planning this from the beginning,* Leeland thought, *to bring shame and discredit to the game, to Digby, to the GCPS. Bastards!*

Triple-B pushed the guard out of the way. He pulled back himself, then lowered his shoulders, took a deep breath, and then struck the door. Again and again.

It crumpled and crashed outward on his fourth try.

The corridor was filled with red flashing light. The klaxons were even louder now as Triple-B collected himself and stood guard as Leeland, Bullseye, and the security goon filed out of the room.

The *Dread* seemed to right itself, and then Leeland felt air pressure return to normal. The *Dread* shook again, but this time, he knew it wasn't from taking Reb fire.

"We're firing back," he said. "Good!"

"Do you have a gun?" Bullseye asked the security guard.

He nodded. "Yes, miss."

"Let me have it."

He shook his head. "I cannot. Security regulation 135—"

"Screw your regulations. I'm an ex-corporate marine. Give me the gun!"

"You better do as she says," Leeland said. "She's a much better shot than you."

The guard wavered for a moment, sighed, then pulled the pistol away from its magnetized holster and handed it over. Bullseye checked it. It was a standard laser pistol with an optional adapter for a smart bullet clip. "Okay," she said, "follow me."

They followed her down the corridor to double doors that led to a small flight of stairs. People were running everywhere, fans mostly. Security was mobilizing, but it seemed like a slow response. Leeland could still hear muffled gunfire through the walls. The *Dread* kept taking fire, but it was definitely now in the battle. How many ships did the Rebs have? Not too many for sure. The Rebs never acted in large numbers; raids mostly on GCPS outposts. To plan and activate such a stab at the heart of the GCPS, literally attacking in broad daylight, against a GCPS Cruiser no less, was unthinkable. Which was why it was succeeding. Nobody, not even this ship with its large crew, was prepared.

"Wait!" Bullseye ordered, putting up her hand.

They halted at the top of the stairs, listening. A gang of Rebs were ascending. Bullseye crouched, checked her pistol again to ensure it had the proper power. She waited, waited, until the first head appeared. Then she aimed at the center of that head and fired. A clean, white-hot stream of light cut through the stairwell. The Reb at the receiving end of that deadly stream dropped.

Shouts and gunfire answered as they fell back to cover themselves from a dumb bullet spray up the stairwell. The fire subsided. Bullseye crawled over to the stairs again, aimed the pistol down, held her breath, and fired thrice.

Three additional kills.

The door behind them slammed open. A Reb Grogan with an assault rifle appeared. The bulky humanoid shouted and raised his weapon.

Triple-B ducked behind the Kapoor security guard. The poor man took several shots from the rifle and dropped dead before the Grogan's clip was empty. When he heard the click of an empty magazine, Triple-B leapt forward, took the Grogan by the throat, squeezed, screamed, and ripped its larynx out. For good measure, he drove his boot heel into the beast's head as it fell. Then he reached down and ripped the rifle from its massive hand and gathered up the scattered clips.

Triple-B hefted the rifle and pushed his way past Leeland. "Let's move!"

Bullseye held him up. "You go down those stairs, and you die. Let's get a few more before we try it."

Triple-B popped a fresh clip into place. "Nope."

Bullseye tried again to reason with the brute, but Brutus's blood was up, Leeland could see. He was angry, and no amount of reason was going to stop him. No use of 'release' was going to work.

"Okay," she said, letting him go, "but don't hog all the shots. I want my kills."

Triple-B was now in the lead, followed by Bullseye and then Leeland, who wished he had a gun. It wasn't fair, and frankly, it was embarrassing, not to be carrying. But that matter was resolved quickly, as Triple-B sent small bursts of laser fire into retreating Rebs as they descended. In a matter of minutes, there were several guns to choose from, laying on and about dead Reb bodies.

Leeland paused before choosing a laser pistol like Bullseye's, though it did not appear to have the optional smart bullet adapter. He wanted a gun. He needed one. He needed it to defend his friends, his team members. He needed one to defend his own life. But to kill again? Could he do it? Victor's face appeared to him through the confusion, his battered, broken little face. *Can I pull this trigger?*

Ahead of him, a Reb showed its own face and Leeland took a nervous shot. He missed. The Reb fired back. Leeland ducked and then realized that this was no time to doubt. He'd have plenty of time to do that later, when shots weren't flying over his head. The Reb showed its face again; Leeland aimed and took another shot. This time, he cooked meat.

Bullseye paused, aimed, and sent another Reb to its death. Return Reb dumb bullet fire peppered the stairs and sent them to cover. Triple-B held his rifle up out of cover, sideways, and answered with a spray of his own. Then he screamed.

"You hit?" Bullseye asked.

Triple-B grunted, spit. "Just a graze."

"I told you not to get too cocky. Didn't I tell you not to get too cocky?"

"No, I believe you said, 'don't hog all the shots'."

"Don't play semantic games with me, you big oaf. You knew what I meant. I—"

"Shut up, the both of you!" Leeland barked. "We either go forward or back. Choose."

He heard an empty clip drop and a fresh one click into place. Triple-B stood and cycled the chamber. "Forward."

They were almost there, almost at stadium level. Another firefight erupted as they rounded the last corner. Triple-B took another shot, this time to his shoulder, and another graze to his leg. Leeland winced. *He's done. He won't be able to play in the next game.*

How could he be thinking of the game in a time like this? *What's the matter with me?* Leeland didn't have a good answer at the moment. People were dying all around, and all he could think about was his star guard's ability—inability—to play. Leeland's anger at himself fueled his response to the Reb fire. He leaned over the rail and fired a light stream into the mass of Rebs barring their descent.

Even with a wounded arm, Triple-B emptied his clip into the enemy. Bullseye finished off the rest, and they kept moving.

"Are you okay?" Leeland asked as he helped guide Triple-B off the stairs.

The big man nodded. "I'll live."

They stepped over a pile of Reb bodies. Leeland downed a Sorak that tried crawling away. With each shot, his heart sank. He'd killed again, and he didn't know how he felt about it. Now didn't seem like the time to contemplate its meaning. This time, he had done so to defend himself and his friends, and that felt like a better excuse.

Security seemed stronger on this level than it had coming down the stairs. Made sense to Leeland. The stadium was on this level, and so if they were to regain control, they'd have to do it here. Squads of armed guards were running up and down the corridor. Fans that had escaped the carnage were being ushered to escape pods. Members of other teams were doing so as well.

Leeland got the attention of one of the passing guards. "What's the situation?"

The young man was nervous, scared. He breathed heavily. His eyes darted back and forth as if he trusted no one. "Reb attack."

Leeland fought the urge to swear. "I know that. Has it been brought under control?"

"Only their ships have been destroyed. But the *Dread* is hemorrhaging life-support, and the Rebs still control the stadium."

He darted away. "Come on," Bullseye said. "Let's get to the team."

Their way to the locker room was clear. They had to pause and show credentials twice as anxious guards wondered why they were carrying weapons. They could have legally confiscated them, but chose not to do so, and instead waved them away. Leeland thanked them and kept moving.

They reached the Vipers' locker room. The door had bullet holes and black scorch marks from the Reb attack, but it had held. There were Reb and *Dread* security bodies everywhere. Leeland drew his access card and swiped it across the lock. It took three tries, but finally, the lock acknowledged and opened.

Triple-B ducked Shadrack's punch and grabbed his arm before he had a chance to strike again. "Stand down, Shad. It's us."

The guard was lying in wait, fearful that whatever came through the door was the enemy. His eyes lit up as he saw his coach. "We thought you guys were dead."

"Not yet," Bullseye said as they entered and greeted their players with delight and joy. Everyone came up to give hugs and pats on shoulders, including Mackinaw Jim, who seemed genuinely relieved.

"Is everyone all right?" Leeland asked. "Everyone accounted for?"

Shadrack nodded. "We wanted to get out there and kick some ass, but it was a madhouse for a while. You see the bodies outside?"

"Yes. The Rebs were trying to get in?"

Shadrack nodded. "They wanted a massacre, Coach, but they were fought off."

"I'm glad they were. I'm just glad everyone is safe."

"Not everyone."

Leeland turned and saw Bullseye. She was staring up at the vid screen, which was still on and still broadcasting from the stadium.

Leeland looked in horror upon what was happening on the starting line of the pitch. He dropped his pistol.

The Polmak Resisters were executing Banshee players.

Chapter Seventeen

"Brutus!"

Bullseye was out the door and chasing Triple-B before anyone could stop her. The entire team followed.

All entries to the stadium were being held by armed Rebs inside the ten small incline walkways to stadium seating. They were perfect choke points, and *Dread* security had yet to penetrate any of them.

"Slowly, Carla," Leeland said, trying to keep up with his defensive coach who was moving from entry to entry seeking access. "Slowly. Don't let those guards mistake you for a Reb."

"They're going to kill them all," Bullseye shouted as she moved. "We have to get in!"

Finally, Bullseye had had enough. She tried muscling her way past security at one of the entryways, but she was stopped by a guard holding a rifle. "You can't go in there!"

She took a swing at the guard's head. He moved to duck, but Triple-B grabbed her and held her back.

"Let me go!" she shouted and nearly broke from his grip before Shadrack came up and helped hold her back. "I'm not going to let anyone stop me. I'm going to get in there and kill them all!"

Leeland stepped into the middle of the scuffle and said, "Sir, tell us. What's going on?"

The man, clearly angry with Bullseye's attempt at striking him and looking like he wanted to raise his rifle and fire, finally calmed, and said, "They've blocked off every entrance. They're heavily armed. Attempts at breaking through have been unsuccessful."

"Why are you still broadcasting?" Leeland asked. "You're giving them what they want."

"They've commandeered the network. It can't be shut off."

This was an inside job. Had to be. No Reb force would have the pull to do such a thing. "Overload an entry point. Hit them with twice their men. Three times."

"We've tried," the guard said, "but they killed five outright on the attempt and have threatened more if we try it again. There are a lot of innocents in there, sir. A lot. We go knocking down doors, and they'll start killing wholesale. Our orders are to contain the situation and wait for reinforcements."

"And when are they going to arrive?" Triple-B asked, still holding Bullseye back.

"Any minute now."

Leeland huffed. Any minute could mean five minutes or five hours. The 'reinforcements' that he spoke of were off-ship, for sure, perhaps coming from Vitala, perhaps from another ship that would have to slide into the system beforehand. That wasn't enough time. Banshees were still being killed.

Leeland looked up at the vid screen. Another Banshee had been muscled to the starting line, pushed to her knees, a pistol trained on her temple. The Gaelian jack that held the gun was spouting demands so quickly that Leeland could barely understand them. As he spoke, he became more animated, angrier, until at last he fired. The bullet popped right through the Banshee's skull, and she dropped.

"No!" Bullseye was crying uncontrollably now. "Please... help them. Make them stop."

The guard, clearly moved by Bullseye's grief, shook his head slowly. "I'm sorry, miss, but I have my orders. There's nothing we can do."

"I can do something."

Triple-B, still holding Bullseye back, finally let go. She fell to the floor. Then Triple-B rifled through the pocket of her coat and grabbed the activation device.

Bullseye tried stopping him. "What are you doing? Give it to me. I order you to hand it to me. Stand down, stand down!"

Triple-B shook his head. "No, Carla. Your orders worked because I allowed them to work. Not this time. We've run out of options, and I can no longer see you suffer like this. They will all die, unless we stop them, and if these useless guards won't, I will."

Triple-B held up the activation device for his collar and clicked it with his thumb.

Shadrack moved to stop him. Triple-B slapped him aside, dropped the device, and then smashed it with his boot. The iron collar around his neck pulsed red.

"Goodbye, Carla," Triple-B said, giving her a wink. "You're the best."

He turned and ran, and the next couple minutes flashed past Leeland so fast, he almost missed them.

Triple-B got up a good momentum, despite his injuries. His weight and muscle propelled him forward, much like it did during a game. He held his right arm close against his chest as if there was a ball on his glove, as if he were trying to score. In those last few minutes, Leeland imagined Triple-B a striker, dodging guards like himself to secure a score and the win. He plowed through a line of guards to an access tunnel as if they were nothing, as if they were trash thrown to the wind and he was simply brushing them aside. They did not fire at him as he crashed through, dazed perhaps, or confused about what was happening. The Rebs inside the tunnel did much the same, shocked at seeing a lone man, screaming, cursing obscenities at them as he came on. And when they finally collected themselves and began to fire, it was too late. Triple-B smacked them all aside like Judwan strikers. *Let them pour a dozen or more bullets into his back*, Leeland thought, watching it all on vid. Nothing would stop his star guard now from scoring. His first score attempt. His last.

The Rebs on the pitch, holding rifles, were just as paralyzed with fear as everyone else, and those brief moments of pause gave Triple-B the advantage. He was halfway to the starting line before they opened fire.

The remaining Banshees under Reb control broke free and scrambled for safety. As the ladies ran, Leeland watched the vid screen and round after round struck Triple-B in the chest, the arms, the legs. But nothing stopped him. He took three more steps, strong, wide steps as if he were winding up like an old toy. And then he struck.

Triple-B launched into the air as the red light on his collar began to blink rapidly. Leeland could hear the echo of the collar as he watched it all. The move was both beautiful and terrible, bold and foolish, and he wanted to close his eyes to it. But he could not. It would be an insult, he realized, not to witness such a sacrifice from his player. Triple-B flew through the air and struck the pitch near the center line. His impetus slid him several meters further. The Rebs on the pitch fell back firing. The collar blinked even faster, sounded even louder.

Then it blew.

***

The explosion knocked out every Reb on the pitch, and finally, a smart security officer, seeing the advantage, ordered a full assault against the stadium.

Minutes later, the Rebs and their fan compatriots surrendered. After a few rigorous firefights, *Dread* security got the upper hand and ended it by killing every member left alive on the Resisters. True to their word, as soon as the assault commenced, the Rebs began killing hostages, but only a dozen or so were hit, and most of them only wounded. Before the matter was brought to a close, four Banshees, including their coach, were dead. Thankfully, 'Big Bertha' McGinty was not one of them.

Triple-B's remains were claimed and collected by Digby. Bullseye, inconsolable, could not participate in the collection, nor would she see the remains back to Brutus's home planet for proper burial. She left the *Dread* by shuttle craft. Where she went, Leeland did not know, but he let her go.

No charges were brought against Bullseye for trying to strike an officer. Nor were charges brought posthumously against Triple-B for violating *Dread* security orders. If anything, he was being hailed as a hero.

A few days later, Bullseye returned and paid Leeland a visit in his office. She looked like she hadn't slept at all. They hugged in silence. Leeland offered a chair, and she took it.

"What's the verdict?" she asked.

"The verdict?"

Bullseye nodded. "What are they going to do about the tournament?"

"They've put a halt on it for ten days. They're giving everyone a chance to recover, to regroup, repairs to be made to the *Dread*, both inside and out. Honestly, I'm surprised that they haven't ended it, just washed their hands of it all."

Bullseye shook her head. "That would be giving in to the Rebs and their terrorism. That cannot be allowed."

"The ratings are fantastic too. The semi-final and final games may be the most watched games anyone can remember, so long as the Banshees can reconstitute in ten days. They lost some good people and their coach. They were ahead when it all went down, so they've been given the win."

"I'm aware of the Banshees' situation, Leelee," Bullseye said. She leaned forward a bit and arched her back so that she looked taller in the seat. "That's why I'm here."

He paused and waited for the next shoe to drop. He knew what that shoe would be. "You're leaving us?"

Bullseye strained to keep from crying. Leeland could see tears well in her eyes. "I don't want to, but I can't coach the Vipers anymore. I keep seeing Brutus flying through the air at that last moment. Everywhere I go. In time, I'm sure the image, and some of the pain at least, will go away, but not fast enough. I can't coach Shadrack, or Little Frankie, or Jimbo Threpe without seeing Triple-B. I just can't." She paused, then, "I've agreed to be the interim coach for the Golan Banshees."

Leeland sat back and shook his head. He couldn't believe what he was hearing. "So, you can't coach for us, but you can coach against us?"

"You don't understand."

"No, I don't. Please explain."

"Brutus and I—well, we were once lovers."

Leeland nodded. "Yes, I gathered that from our sanitarium visit."

"It wasn't just a fling, Leelee. It was serious. Believe it or not, we had planned to marry once I retired from the game. But, you know how it is, how difficult relationships are."

"I do indeed."

"But he had anger issues, as you know, and I—well, I'd lived my own life for so long that I just couldn't live with someone else, couldn't abide by compromising my personal freedoms to accommodate a live-in partner. I tried, but it didn't work out. I called it off. Brutus was so upset that he ended his retirement and went back into the game.

"It was then that he acquired the collar. When he finally left the Lifers, he gave me the control box for it. He put his life into my hands, Leelee. That's how much he trusted me. So for him to violate that trust, to take his own life because he saw how much pain I was in seeing Banshees being killed and not being able to take independent action to stop it, took a courage that I cannot betray. Brutus wanted to save their lives for me. The least I can do is complete his mission.

"The Banshees need me, Leelee. They don't have time to find a fully qualified replacement coach. I'm the only one."

Leeland sighed, trying not to let his growing anger overwhelm him. "Carla, I'm sorry about Brutus. I really am. But Sheera Rainwaters from the I-Corps Tigers is available. She's not doing anything these days since they lost."

"They don't want her. They want me."

"Big Bertha wants you, you mean."

Bullseye blinked away the tear. She gritted her teeth as if she were ready to take a bite out of Leeland's neck. "What are you saying, Leelee?"

He sat up in his chair, a flush of blood in his cheeks. "I'm saying you're playing favorites. I asked you in the sky box if this was going to be a problem, us playing the Banshees, when you have good friends on that team. You said it wouldn't be a problem," he held his hands up and out to the side, "but clearly it is."

"Don't hand me that crap, Leelee. That was then; this is now. Everything has changed. I just explained to you my reasons. I don't care if you believe me or not. What do you want to see happen? The

Vipers jumped right into the championship? That sounds like a coward talking."

"What I want is my defensive coach to stop wasting time, buck up, and get back to work. Brutus is dead. He was a good man, a heroic man. I'm truly sorry for your loss, Carla, but you have to deal with it!"

"That's rich, coming from you."

"What's that supposed to mean?"

"Oh, I think you know what it means. You killed your bother. Get over it!"

Leeland could tell that Bullseye was about to blow her stack. She glared at him with eyes that, if they were knives, would have been plunged into his chest by now. She said nothing, and they stared at each other, both short of breath, both ready to tear the other apart. *She went there*, Leeland said to himself. *I can't believe she went there*. But he should have known that she would. Bullseye had been a sniper and was one of the toughest ladies he'd ever known. The toughest. She wasn't about to allow him to accuse her of emotions that he himself could not keep in check.

"I'm surprised they would allow it," Leeland finally said quietly as a way to contain his anger, to temper the situation. "Seems like a terrible conflict of interest."

Bullseye breathed. She nodded. "It is, but under the circumstances, Digby would rather take criticism for that instead of, as I say, allowing you to have a bye and jump right into the championship. They'd rather have the game than the controversy."

"They'll have both, either way. Have you spoken with Aryan? With Saanvi?"

"No. I was hoping you'd do that for me."

Leeland chuckled. "So you want me to cut my own throat."

"Come on, Leelee, you know this isn't easy for me. I just can't serve the Vipers anymore. If Brutus had died normally, on the pitch, playing the game, then that would have been one thing. But not this way, not sacrificing himself the way he did. I am responsible for that, Leelee. If I hadn't been such a blithering idiot, if I hadn't shown so much emotion for the Banshees, then perhaps he wouldn't have felt the need to do it. I did this, and I just can't look the team in the face anymore, always wondering if they'd rather see me dead than Brutus. I have to leave."

What she was saying was ridiculous, Leeland knew. No one on the team would accuse her of Triple-B's death; the notion was farcical. Brutus 'Backhoe' Bertuchi had a death wish; he was a troubled man, with a troubled past, a troubled soul. He wanted to die, and he found a way to do it, to go out in a blaze of glory, as they say. One last wild ride. One last hurrah.

But there was no changing her mind at this point. Bullseye was gone; her mind was set, and no further discussion would change that.

"I don't have much of a team left," he said, "and I don't know how much I can improve our situation in two weeks."

"Half the Banshees are gone," Bullseye said, "so it'll probably be an even match."

They both managed to laugh at that. Then they were silent again, looking at each other, both wanting to say more, but knowing that further words would be useless. They were in opposite camps now, and so the nature of their conversation, their relationship, had to change.

"See you in two weeks, Bullseye," Leeland said, standing and offering his hand. "We'll show you no mercy."

"Nor will I," Bullseye said, taking his hand and gripping it tightly. "Prepare for a beating."

She left, and Leeland dropped back into his chair. He nursed a headache for thirty minutes, and through the pain, tried to figure a way out of this mess. Brutus was gone. Bullseye was gone. And it seemed as if no one, other than the Rebs, were going to be accused of the attack. But that was nonsense. It was an inside job. It had to be. Too many Reb sympathizers and too many weapons had been smuggled onto the *Dread.* An attack of that magnitude could not have been handled by Rebs alone. Someone else was to blame.

If you see anything, anything at all, please let me know…

Saanvi's words rang in his mind like a bell.

[illegible]

The [illegible] reaction to the movement in the Third Square was called the Third Solareal Garden Front. The [illegible] immediately disavowed any knowledge of connection with the attack, which officials and learned had been committed by a small Rab terrorist group known as the [illegible] Freedom Fighters. Many of the Promar Resistance had been members, officials learned, and the vicious assault was apparently 'payback' for a massacre of a Pakarus community just a few [illegible] ago. The Rebs had blamed the [illegible] for the assault. The DCPS, of course, had denied it, claiming that they had been ambushed by outlaws in the Kolona town and were simply defending themselves. Exactly how the Rebs had commandeered the Dart was still under investigation, but one thing was clear to Leeland: they had to have had help from the inside, and a lot of money, to pull it off.

Leeland finally broke down and told Sabah about her brother conducting the meeting with the [illegible]. Shortly thereafter, [illegible] Kapur was arrested on suspicion of conspiring with the terrorist group. They found him [illegible] in his office, a whiskey bottle in one hand, a charged Holter pistol in the other. The arrest was easy, however. He had fallen [illegible].

Three days later, Leeland visited Ayon at the Vitoki Maximum Security Prison to see for himself the man he had ratted out to Sabah, to see the guilt and shame on his face that would confirm the suspicion. But seeing the bruises and cuts on the boy's cheeks and

Chapter Eighteen

The main Reb resistance movement in the Third Sphere was called the Third Sphere Liberation Front. They immediately disavowed any knowledge or connection with the attack, which officials had learned had been committed by a small Reb terrorist group known as the Zaigor Freedom Fighters. Many of the Polmak Resisters had been members, officials learned, and the vicious assault was apparently "payback" for a massacre of a Ralarat community just a few star systems away. The Rebs had blamed the GCPS for the assault. The GCPS, of course, had denied it, claiming that they had been ambushed by agitators in the Ralarat town and were simply defending themselves. Exactly how the Rebs had commandeered the *Dread* was still under investigation, but one thing was clear to Leeland: they had to have had help from the inside, and a lot of money, to pull it off.

Leeland finally broke down and told Saanvi about her brother's clandestine meeting with the Gaelian jack. Shortly thereafter, Aryan Kapoor was arrested on suspicion of conspiring with the terrorist group. They found him locked in his office, a whiskey bottle in one hand, a charged laser pistol in the other. The arrest was easy, however. He had fallen asleep.

Three days later, Leeland visited Aryan at the Vitala Maximum Security Prison to see for himself the man he had ratted out to Saanvi, to see the guilt and shame on his face that would confirm the suspicion. But seeing the bruises and cuts on the boy's cheeks and forehead, seeing the defeat in the way he carried his shoulders low when guards brought him into the visiting chamber with a clamor of shackles around his wrists and ankles, Leeland regretted his decision immediately.

Aryan was thrust into a chair by a rough guard. He almost fell to the floor. Leeland found himself helping the guard keep him upright. Aryan looked drugged. His face was flushed. He stared, seemingly, into a void. His dark eyes were watery.

They said nothing for several minutes. Then Aryan spoke first. "How's the team?"

Leeland shrugged. "As well as can be expected, under the circumstances. We're lucky that the GCPS, that Digby, didn't open up an investigation on me or the entire team. Your arrest seems to have satisfied everyone."

Aryan chuckled. It seemed to hurt his ribs; he winced and squirmed in his chair. "Then there is a pot of gold at the end of the rainbow. I finally did something noble."

"But did you do it?" Leeland asked, not allowing himself to be lured into a self-pity party. He had had enough of those for himself over the past several years. "Did you help those Rebs?"

"On advice from my counsel, I cannot answer that question on the grounds that it might—"

"Don't play that game with me, Aryan." Leeland almost fell out of his own chair as he moved forward to get right into the boy's face. He whispered, "Did you do it?"

Aryan shook his head. "Saanvi says I did. That's enough to convict on Vitala."

"She's that powerful?"

"My family's that powerful. You've walked into a hornet's nest, Leeland. You better bug off before you get stung."

Too late for that. "You invited me in when you hired me to coach."

Aryan nodded, winked. "You didn't have to say yes."

And right now, Leeland wished he hadn't. He now realized that he had accused an innocent man of conspiring with Rebs. And why? Because he was mad about losing Triple-B, about losing Carla. Good things to be mad about, indeed, but not to this extent. Aryan's recent behavior had made it so easy to snitch.

"Why did you meet so openly with a Gaelian, you idiot? Didn't you know that it would draw suspicion?"

"As they say, I'm not the brightest bulb." Aryan raised his shackled hands to move a strand of hair out of his eyes. "I had no knowledge of what they were planning, I swear it. We weren't speaking about any of that. We spoke of old times. I paid him back a little money I owed him. That's all. If anyone was going to complain, it was how you did it: angry that perhaps I was sharing team secrets. I could have lived with that suspicion. I'm loyal to my friends, Leeland. I don't have many, and that Gaelian was one of them. He saved my life once, dragged me out of a puddle of muddy water when I was dead drunk and face down. I'd have drowned in my own vomit if he hadn't saved me. Yes, yes, it was foolish to have so many secret meetings with him, but I never thought they'd do something like this. I never thought he'd betray me like that. I guess he wasn't a friend after all."

Aryan slumped his shoulders again, and the hurt in his eyes, like the puffy lacerations on his face from the abuse he had gotten in prison, was evident.

"How do I prove it was Saanvi?" Leeland asked.

"You don't. The matter is closed. It's been arranged. The sentence has been handed down before the trial even begins. Just step aside and let it play out. Your job here is to take the Vipers to victory, if you can. Saanvi will let you do that. You have real value in her eyes now that she owns you and has full control of the team. Just step aside, do your job, and forget about good ol' Aryan Kapoor. The rest of Vitala already has."

The guards came in again and hoisted Aryan from his chair. They dragged him out of the room. Leeland tried to protest, but the door was closed behind him before he had a chance to pursue.

He left. His headache had returned. He didn't know what to do. Should he do anything? He certainly didn't have the pull or the clout to call for an investigation into Saanvi Kapoor. And even if he did, he'd need evidence that it was she who had conspired with the Rebs. But Aryan was right: Saanvi was far too smart to be so openly foolish with her scheming. She had most certainly covered her trail well, and the power of Kapoor Industries could crush any investigation into its broader involvement, if such involvement existed. The old adage, 'When you're in the wolves' lair, you play by the wolf's rules, or get eaten,' was apropos to the situation. Leeland could not forget that.

But, the galaxy was vast and there were people with contacts that extended beyond any reach of a Third Sphere corporation. Leeland knew exactly whom to call.

The phone rang three times. Mackinaw Jim answered. "Jimbo," Leeland said, getting into his sedan and activating the engine, "meet me in the locker room, and let's discuss strategy."

***

The first semi-final match featured the Saltborne Sledgehammers against the Nova Station Redshirts. No one doubted the Sledgehammers' presence there, they being considered the top team in the bracket. Many were still surprised to see the Redshirts, despite their having earned the right. Those cagey Neo-bots were considered by the commentary class to be the darlings of the tournament, but few were willing to say it out loud, lest their misplaced enthusiasm was seen as jumping on the bandwagon. Their concerns were well-placed, for when the ball was released, the opening slam was a kill.

Sledgehammer star guard Thorgus Oakbiter, who had amassed the most kills in the tournament to date, waited for the ball to fly by. Then he took three steps forward and drove his gauntleted fist into the nearest Redshirt jack and smashed its core processor. All of its systems crashed before it fell to the pitch with blue electricity arching across its metal body.

The game was on.

It appeared as if the Sledgehammers had no intention of scoring. They had left their strikers on the sidelines for the opening rush and did not bring one in until halfway through the game. By then, however, the Redshirts had lived up to their name. They had suffered one kill and three heavily damaged players licking wounds in the Sin Bin. When a Sledgehammer striker did appear on the pitch, he easily scooped up the ball and scored two points. That score remained in place until near the end, when the Redshirts finally showed up to play.

A Neo-bot striker named K-934 easily picked the pocket of Sledgehammer striker Borus Dakport. It then zigged and zagged its way toward the Sledgehammers' back goal. The castle there had been temporarily broken, and the Neo-bots' linked technology allowed them to move in concert, thus harassing Forge Father efforts to block avenues of approach. At the last moment, when Thorgus Oakbiter stepped into the path of K-934 to try to put his shoulder into the discussion, the Neo-bot striker leapt over him, and in mid-flight, took aim at the goal and scored, thus giving the Redshirts a one point lead.

The Sledgehammer coach tried to call the shot illegal because the passer was in the air and not technically touching the strike zone. But that accusation was ridiculous since there was nothing in the official rules that required a player to have contact with the strike zone during a score attempt, so long as the body was in the strike zone area. The play and score were declared valid. It was clear to everyone that the Sledgehammers were just trying to cause a little friction, a little mischief, in an attempt to sew doubt—at least in the eyes of their fans—about the outcome if the game came down to that one score. The last ball was launched back onto the pitch.

The Sledgehammers got to work. Borus Dakport took the ball on ricochet and, with the aid of Thorgus Oakbiter and two angry jacks, managed to work across the pitch and set up for an easy one-pointer to even the score. But the arrogant Dakport took a step backward into the two-point strike zone and tried a shot. It failed, but a fortuitous bounce put it into the glove of an unsuspecting Forge Father jack, who wisely dunked it into the goal as time expired.

The game went into overtime.

Luckily for the Sledgehammers, the Redshirts were so banged up that they could field only five players. Despite being exhausted, the Sledgehammers made short work of the remaining Neo-bots and scored an easy shot to put the match away.

The Nova Station Redshirts' meteoric run through the tournament had come to an end, and the number one Saltborne Sledgehammers were going to the championship game, as 'everyone' had expected.

They now awaited the winner of the Golan Banshees versus the Vitala Vipers, another high seed versus low seed match. Would the results be the same, the analysts wondered, as they wasted valuable vid time arguing over every facet of the upcoming game. But the recent Reb attack had put both teams in a difficult situation. No one was willing to put their faith in one team over the other. The betting money was even, with perhaps a slight lean toward the Banshees, since they were the higher seed. Finally, one analyst threw his holopad into the air and said, "Screw it! Let's just watch the game and see what happens!”

Leeland couldn’t argue with that logic.

One bit of good news came a day before the semi-finals: Dubois had finally concluded that Conner Meadows could play. His previous contract with the Brewer team was not in conflict with his current career endeavor.

There was much rejoicing in the Viper locker room.

"Don't go out there and try to be a hero, Conner," Leeland told [illegible] as the Vipers suited up. "I know you're proud of [illegible] and anxious to [illegible] some punks, and you have something to prove, but you know that the flow and pace of the game is different in the real than in practice. I don't want my star jock sent to the Sin Bin before the game even starts. You're too valuable to lose, especially now."

Conner looked [illegible] protest, but instead said with a smile and wink, "Don't worry, Boss. We got this."

There was controversy surrounding the game. As Leeland had predicted, the hues and cries were plentiful. Some wanted the Bumshots to play another quarter-final game against the [illegible] Tigers who had lost to the Reivers in the previous round. Others actually wanted the Vipers to get a bye and slip right into the championship. Leeland appreciated the sentiment, but that kind of move would have plagued them to the end, with many post-tournament [illegible] them and accusing [illegible] of buying their way into the final. There was enough controversy swirling around the [illegible] already with the [illegible] and [illegible] alleged participation

Chapter Nineteen

One bit of good news came a day before the semi-final game: Digby had finally concluded that Conner Newberg could play. His previous contract with the Trontek 29ers was not in conflict with his current career endeavor.

There was much rejoicing in the Viper locker room.

"Don't go out there and try to be a hero, Conner," Leeland said as the Vipers suited up. "I know you're mad as hell and anxious to slam some punks, and you have something to prove, but you know that the flow and pace of the game is different in the real than in practice. I don't want my star jack sent to the Sin Bin before the game even starts. You're too valuable to lose, especially now."

Conner looked to protest, but instead, said with a smile and wink, "Don't worry, Boss. We got this."

There was controversy surrounding the game. As Leeland had predicted, the hues and cries were plentiful. Some wanted the Banshees to play another quarter-final game against the I-Corps Tigers, who had lost to the Resisters in the previous round. Others actually wanted the Vipers to get a bye and slip right into the championship. Leeland appreciated the sentiment, but that kind of move would have plagued them to the end, with many post-tournament decrying favoritism and accusing Kapoor Industries of buying their way into the final. There was enough controversy swirling around the Kapoors already with the Reb assault and Aryan Kapoor's alleged participation;

they didn't need any more. Some even wanted the Golan Banshees to be leapt into the final game, arguing that the Vipers were too tainted with the stain of rebellion to be a viable choice for inclusion into the FSIDL. The Trontek 29ers and their general manager Horus Ruth put their support behind that claim, but Digby ignored it all and stuck to their plan.

The *Dread* stadium was packed, and the fans and pre-game music and festivities were so loud that Leeland's headache had returned. He rubbed his temples but then quickly stopped when he saw cameras picking up every expression on his face and projecting it onto big screens set below each sky box. Every move, every expression, everything, would be under the microscope for this game, and dozens of analysts would be watching and judging. *Let them,* Leeland said to himself, as he considered making a foul gesture toward the closest camera. He chose restraint and, instead, took a moment to stare across the empty pre-game pitch toward the Banshee coaching staff.

Bullseye was in the middle of them, pointing and shouting commands, though he could not tell what she was saying. Banshee players wandered up to her, and in a few seconds, she was surrounded by all of her players. They began to rock back and forth and chant, as if they were some primitive tribe worshiping a god around a pit of fire. Bullseye clapped, and they'd clap back. Again and again it went that way until the fervor was so great that the ladies were cursing and striking each other's helmets and shoulder pads. They were fired up and motivated. They were impressive, and they were ready.

Leeland looked at his own players who sat stoically on the bench, as if they had had too much to drink and not enough sleep the night before. His heart sank.

We're doomed.

***

Hello sports fans, and welcome to the fourth and semi-final round of the Third Sphere Invitational DreadBall Tournament. My name is Faraj Chaudhry from Vitala-TAV, the finest sports and new programming network in all the Third Sphere. If you love Dreadball… we got it!

The Golan Banshees will face the Vitala Vipers, and whoever wins will advance to the championship game against the Saltborne Sledgehammers.

I must confess up front: I get a little misty when I look out upon the teams below as they assemble for the game. What tragedy has struck both of these teams! Half the Banshees were brutally murdered in the Reb attack, while the late, great Triple-B sacrificed himself to save the Banshees from a total massacre. And now Carla 'Bullseye' Bock is serving as the Banshees' coach. That's a real gut punch to Coach Roth, I'm sure.

Now, just between you and me, rumor has it that Bullseye and Backhoe were very friendly, and that she just couldn't go on with the Vipers with his memory lingering in her mind. I've been told by the studio that I'm not allowed to provide my 'opinion' about such matters: "just stick to the game," they said. But honestly, who they going to replace me with all the way out here, am I right? Anyway, I believe the rumors and hope that Bullseye finds some peace somewhere going forward. One thing is for sure, whatever the reason, it's going to be a great game.

This is it, ladies and gentleman, boys and girls. Whoever wins here is in the championship. So, let's get to it…

***

All concern Leeland had was laid to rest when the starting klaxon sounded and the ball was launched.

Big Bertha and Shadrack Menapi struck in the center and went at it like an old married couple filing for divorce. The ball buzzed between Shadrack's legs, bounced once, scattered, and struck the glove of Banshee striker Melinda Puck, who accepted the metal sphere gladly into her launcher, and then ran. Little Frankie moved to steal the ball but was stopped by two Banshee jacks slamming into his chest and legs. He disappeared in a pile of roiling shoulders and fists. Luckily, Conner Newberg was close enough to counter-slam the Banshee striker before she escaped from the scuffle. He put a right hook into Melinda's helmet that she could not dodge. The blow lifted her off the pitch. Her arms slacked and the ball soared freely through the air toward the far wall. Puck was knocked cold. She was removed, and another Banshee striker came onto the pitch as her replacement.

Mackinaw Jim was there to scoop up the ball. He was down the pitch before anyone could catch him.

"Watch your front!" Leeland shouted to Jim as he skirted near the edge of the Banshees' entry zone in order to keep away from Shadrack's and Bertha's brawl, which Bertha was cleverly allowing to drift toward Jim's approach near the left strike zone. Nothing Shadrack did could put the big lady down, it seemed, and so she tactically drifted back and back, holding off blow after blow, until she was flanked with two jacks in Jim's path.

Then the striker coming in from the Banshee entry zone made a move to steal the ball. Mackinaw Jim reflexively shifted right to protect it, but that put him too close to a Banshee jack who thrust her shoulder out and caught enough of Jim's glove to dislodge the ball and send it sailing. The lady jack then finished Jim off with a clothesline that rattled his skull.

Jim was horizontal on the pitch, unmoving. Little Frankie was still in the game but slow getting up. And the ball was free.

***

A wicked strike on my good buddy Mackinaw Jim! I hope he'll be able to come back. I'd hate to have to call his mother with bad news. And he owes me money.

Listen to that crowd, ladies and gentlemen. This stadium is rocking, and with good reason. This is some of the best action I've seen in the tournament so far. These teams are out for blood. Whoever wins, I feel sorry for the Sledgehammers.

***

"Blast it, we're losing momentum." Leeland struck jack Jerold Minata's shoulder pad. "Get in there and relieve Jim."

Jerold was through the entrance to the pitch and moving with Conner into a defensive position before the drones pulled Jimbo off the floor and into the Sin Bin. Someone on the Banshees now had the ball, but Leeland could not see who from his position. He glanced up at the big screens, but even the cameramen couldn't get a good angle. A jack, a striker... it was hard to know. He turned away from the screens, stepped aside to allow the medibot through with Jimbo, and squinted to get a better view.

The medibot dropped Jimbo into the Sin Bin and then flew away. Other medibots were on the star striker immediately, jamming smelling salts into his flared nostrils to get him conscious. "Make him well, fellows," Leeland barked. "He's got to go back in soon if he ain't dead."

They couldn't afford to lose strikers, any of them. Leeland still had one more on the bench, but he was loathe to put him in and risk having all three down so early. *Let Conner manage the defense*, he thought as he focused his attention back to the game. *He'll get it done.*

Conner went to work. He used hand signals that he had taught to all of his jacks to order them to spread out and await the coming mangle of Banshee strikers, jacks, and fighting guards.

A Banshee jack had taken the ball from the scramble in the far corner and was trying to pitch it to an awaiting striker named Carmen Goesh, who was making a strong move toward the Vipers' right-side strike zone. Little Frankie had managed to find his feet and had avoided continued harassment by Banshee jacks with some fancy footwork that left them striking each other and falling flat. He moved to shadow Goesh and keep her from receiving an easy pass.

The Banshee jack managed to break free from the roiling brawl. She took three further steps and then shuffle-passed the ball to Goesh. Frankie leapt to try to knock the ball off its trajectory, but he narrowly missed. It flew right onto the Banshee striker's glove. She twisted away from Jerold, who tried gaining position in front of the strike zone, and left him looking left then right to find her. She pushed off his back by placing a boot into this lumbar and gained enough propulsion from the move to sail into the strike zone. She landed and fired the ball into the goal.

Score!

***

My, oh my, but that was good. I love Goesh. I love her! She has to be the best striker in the Third Sphere. With those kinds of moves, I don't see how the Vipers can pull it out. We've got a lot of game ahead of us, boys and girls, but I don't think I'm alone in saying…

Banshee! Banshee! Banshee!

***

Leeland covered his ears from the roar of the crowd and the annoying game commentator's scratchy voice as he barked, "Banshee! Banshee! Banshee!" from his comfortable press box, to the adulations of the Banshee fans. He leaned over and listened to the diagnosis on Jimbo.

"He will be back," the medibot said in its computerized voice, "but not on the next rush."

That next rush started with Conner Newberg finding the ball in his glove and faking a throw to Little Frankie, who had now recovered enough to be effective. The fake throw sent Carmen Goesh flying through the air in a futile attempt at intercepting nothing. Conner tucked the ball against this chest and leapt over her sliding, sore body, finding comfort in a small defensive wedge headed by Jerold and Little Frankie.

"Don't get too close to her, you little Zwerm. Dodge! Dodge now!" Leeland barked across the pitch, but it was too late.

Little Frankie ignored Leeland's order and kept running toward the waiting Banshee jack. An effective move, indeed, if successful, the idea being, get as close as you can to a charging opponent, and then do a quick shift-move left or right, faking out your opponent and leaving them swirling on the floor. But Frankie waited too long to twist, and the Banshee jack didn't bite. She put out her arm, Frankie got tagged and went down hard. The hit didn't knock him out, but he was *out*. A medibot scrambled onto the pitch, grabbed Little Frankie by a shoulder pad, and pulled him to safety.

"He is ready, sir," a sideline medibot said, slapping Jimbo on the shoulder and pushing him to the entry point with its small, mechanical hand. "Lock and load."

Leeland ignored the anachronistic and corny saying and provided one of his own as he slapped the arrogant striker on the helmet. "Make us proud, Jim."

Jimbo nodded and stumbled onto the pitch while the medibot carried Little Frankie to the Sin Bin.

Conner had lost Frankie to throw the ball to, and Jimbo was way behind him. So he held on to the ball and worked his way toward the Banshees' left strike zone.

Meanwhile, both Shadrack and Big Bertha had moved on to deciding who would keep the house in the divorce settlement, and neither seemed willing to hand over their key. But Leeland could tell that Shadrack was wavering; perhaps Big Bertha was too. Their slams seemed less forceful, less precise. Someone was going to drop soon, and Leeland feared that someone would be Shadrack.

"Spencer," Leeland shouted over the pitch. He waved frantically to try to get the striker's attention. When he did, he pointed to Shadrack. Spencer nodded, seemed to understand, and broke off from Conner's move toward the strike zone. That seemed to annoy Conner, who tried getting Spencer back in line, but Leeland was the coach, not Conner. A coach had to look at the big picture, and if Shadrack went down and the Vipers had no power anchor on the pitch, then they were finished. They could afford failing to score at this moment, if Conner could not deliver on his own. They could *not* afford losing Shadrack. As a striker, Spencer could not assist Shadrack in his attack, but, by being nearby, his presence could cause Big Bertha just enough distraction to change the nature of the brawl.

Spencer joined Shadrack, and the tide of battle began to turn.

Conner now worked on his own, and instead of going for the easy one-point shot to tie the game, he changed directions and worked toward the Banshees' back goal. And why not, for it wasn't being protected by a castle, which Leeland found strange, given that they were being coached by defensive-minded Bullseye. Perhaps she didn't have the personnel to pull it off, Leeland thought. Conner was moving to take advantage.

Whatever Conner was, he wasn't a great scorer. Sending Spencer Mills over to help Shadrack could prove foolish, but the die was cast. All Leeland could do was watch and wait.

Conner finally received help. Two Viper jacks were now in front of him, and they worked aggressively to keep their field captain from greedy hands, as one Banshee striker after another tried picking his pocket. But he was a pro, and he kept strong control of the ball and his focus firm. The deep strike zone was now only four steps away, and he was determined to reach it.

Mackinaw Jim had moved fast enough to be just a few paces away from Conner. He shouted, "The ball! Throw me the ball!" But he was still behind Conner, and a toss to him plus additional moves through Banshee jacks was not ideal. It all rested on Conner's shoulders, and he moved to impress.

Perhaps it was anger for being denied so many games. Perhaps it was the energy of the crowd, the sneers from Banshee fans in the stands not far from his position on the pitch. Whatever brought his pot to boil, Conner reached the deep strike zone, though Banshees worked diligently to interfere with his movements. He stood now alone in the center of the deep zone and ducked a screaming Banshee as she tried a leaping tackle at his head. He braced himself, paused two seconds to set, and fired the ball.

Score!

The Vipers now took the lead by two.

Spencer Mills's aid to Shadrack now paid off. At one point during the fight, Bertha put her foot forward to gain positional advantage. However, her ankle buckled and she fell. Shadrack exited the fight and left the clean-up of the brawl to one of the Viper jacks who moved away from Conner and finished the dispute by stomping Bertha with a swift jab of his boot. A foul was called against the jack, but Bertha was sent to the Sin Bin for the next couple rushes.

Thereafter, the game wavered back and forth for several rushes. The need for scoring became a bigger concern as the end of the match drew near. Mackinaw Jim scored quickly thereafter, bringing the Vipers' lead up to three, and it seemed as if they would coast to a victory. But Leeland wasn't running with a castle either, and the Banshees took advantage.

Carmen Goesh scored a quick three-pointer to tie it up, and on that rush, Conner was throttled by Bertha, who had rejoined the action and was gunning for revenge. Shadrack, rejuvenated, sent her back off the pitch with a carefully placed slam to her back. Bullseye protested the slam as a foul. However, replay proved that he had been in proper position to make the hit, and the game progressed.

Little Frankie retook the field after recovering from that wicked clothesline and managed a one-point score to bring the Vipers up by one, and it seemed that it would be impossible for the Banshees to have enough time to score. But the game continued.

The ball was shot back into play, and it bounced off the wall and right into Carmen Goesh's hands, who just happened to be standing a meter from a Viper strike zone. Carmen should have taken three steps left and tried for a two-pointer, but she seemed as surprised to see the ball in her glove as Leeland was, and so she simply turned and scored a point. The game was suddenly tied again before the crowd had stopped cheering Little Frankie's score.

Now the game was close to ending. The ball was launched once more onto the pitch. This time, it flew directly towards Mackinaw Jim's glove.

"Don't play to the crowd, you fool!" Leeland shouted over the fan eruption. It was louder now than he had ever heard it. "Just score!" But it was not in Jimbo Threpe's DNA to 'just score'. He was enjoying himself as he jumped and juked and jiggled his way across a pitch with blood stains and bile and tiny bits and pieces of armor strewn around the floor as little reminders of the brutal competition that had occurred. The lights, the noise, the sagacity of the moment, were too much for the man to pass up. Leeland's heart pounded in his chest as he watched in sheer terror as his star striker made a total buffoon of himself, preening like some jackanapes on a pleasant stroll. The crowd did indeed love it, but Leeland bit through his lip and drew blood. There was nothing he could do. All the bench-warming jacks and strikers and guards on his team had been removed from the pitch through foul or injury. Now, all he had to rely on were his veterans

— Little Frankie, Shadrack, Conner, Jerold, Spencer, and Jimbo. That, indeed, was a fantastic lineup, but if they faltered now, there was no one else he could send in as replacements. This was it, and they had to rise to the occasion and keep the wolves, the Banshees, at bay.

They did so, but at great cost. Conner went down again. Little Frankie and Jerold got into exchanges with angry and desperate Banshee jacks who were now fouling on principle. Shadrack managed to keep his legs and plowed the field as Jimbo followed with fancy footwork.

Finally, he reached a strike zone. He toyed with the crowd by stepping forward and back, forward and back, from the two-point to one-point range. Leeland howled at his striker to take the shot until he was hoarse. Jimbo seemed to acknowledge his coach at the last minute. Almost a minute too late, unfortunately, for Carmen Goesh got through Shadrack's defense and put her hand on Jimbo's glove. The striker lost control of the ball for a brief moment, recovered, and finally, *finally*, took a shot.

Score!

The stadium erupted, and for a brief moment, Mackinaw Jim was a hero, and not just in his own mind this time.

Then he disappeared beneath a pile of Banshee jacks.

Leland winced as he viewed the [illegible] of Jimbo's leg. "That's horrifying."

The physician nodded. [illegible] torqued body [illegible] snapped the [illegible] the bone shard didn't [illegible] the [illegible] totally different conversation. [illegible] pretty bad, [illegible] that his leg wasn't totally ripped away at the knee.

Leland [illegible] leg was twisted a full ninety degrees below the knee. "Can it be fixed?"

"Of course. He'll be walking—limping, at least—in a week or two, with the proper care and therapy."

"Will he be able to play?"

"In time, yes, but not for the championship, I'm afraid."

The championship. It was hard to fathom that a team with [illegible] had made it so far. [illegible] there had been [illegible]. The Vipers [illegible] but it wasn't a display of [illegible]. The [illegible] had it [illegible] along the way. The little [illegible] had stepped up [illegible] skill they had provided.

[illegible] later, Jimbo [illegible] and the [illegible] once more.

Chapter Twenty

Leeland winced as he viewed the x-ray of Jimbo's leg. "That's horrifying."

The physician nodded. "His leg got torqued badly in the slam. Snapped his femur immediately. Luckily, the bone shard didn't hit the femoral artery, or we'd be having a totally different conversation. His tibia and fibula were severed clean. His right knee's in pretty bad shape too. Meniscus and ACL tears. It's a wonder that his leg wasn't totally ripped away at the knee."

Leeland saw how Jimbo's leg was twisted a full ninety degrees below the knee. "Can it be fixed?"

"Of course. He'll be walking—limping, at least—in a week or two, with the proper care and therapy."

"Will he be able to play?"

"In time, yes, but not for the championship, I'm afraid."

The championship. It was hard to fathom that a fourteenth seed had made it so far. Right after Jimbo's score, there had been such joy. The Vipers' fans invaded the pitch, but it wasn't a display of hooliganism or violence. Just happiness and, honestly, surprise. The Golan Banshees had it in the bag, but like each game along the way, the Vitala Vipers had stepped up. Through luck, timing, skill, they had prevailed.

Then minutes later, Jimbo Threpe was found all broken, and the DreadBall gods had reared their ugly faces once again.

"What are you going to do?" the physician asked.

Leeland shook his head. "The game's in one week. No time to recruit. Hardly any time to breathe. We go in with what we got. That's the rule. We've enough players... just not enough skill."

"Sorry for your loss, but congratulations on your win. Good luck to you, sir."

Leeland shook the physician's hand and watched him walk away. He looked at the 3D x-ray once again, and then left the room himself and returned to Jimbo, who was being prepped for surgery.

The striker was half conscious, his eyes glazed over with the flood of painkillers being fed through his IV. He tried to smile. "Sup, Boss?"

"I'm fine, Jimbo, I'm fine." He patted the striker's shoulder. "More importantly, how are you?"

"Feeling great." Jimbo forced a tired laugh. "These painkillers are kicking my butt."

Leeland nodded. "Don't get used to them. You have to get back to the game."

"I won't make it for final, and you know it, Boss. I may never play again." Jimbo swallowed as if he were fighting back true sorrow. "This is the end for Mack 'in-awe' Jim."

"Ridiculous. I've seen guys with worse injuries play even better afterward. You'll be fine."

Jimbo nodded weakly and then fell silent. He closed his eyes, and it looked as if he dozed. Then he awoke quickly. "Did we win?"

"Of course we did. You won it for us."

"That's right. But I should have listened to you, Boss. I should have taken the shot earlier, instead of dancing around, being foolish. I'm sorry."

Leeland was surprised with Jimbo's humility. Powerful painkillers indeed. "Don't worry about that now. The important thing is that we won, and you are the man of the hour. You'll be able to enjoy your laurels soon."

Another moment of silence, and then Jimbo waved Leeland to come closer. "I know a name, Boss. A name..."

Leeland leaned in, and Jimbo whispered the name.

"Are you certain?"

"Yeah. He's legit."

"No tricks or hit jobs, Jimbo. I want clear, truthful evidence."

"It's clear. Find him, and you'll see."

Three nurse servitors entered the room to take Jimbo to surgery. Before they whisked him away, he said, "What you gonna do, Boss? Where you gonna find a new striker?"

"We're not going to find a new one," Leeland said. "We're going to use an old one."

***

"Are you nuts?" Bullseye asked him as they dined alone in one of several beer gardens and taverns hastily opened on the *Dread* to accommodate the expected record-setting attendance for the final match. "The game is faster and deadlier now than in your time, Leelee. You're going to get destroyed."

"You act like I'm a fragile old coot," Leeland said, cutting into a medium rare steak and savoring the sweet smell of barbeque sauce in the small container nearby. "I was playing Extreme when Aryan found me, remember? I can handle myself."

"What does Digby say about it?"

"I've already gotten permission. If they're going to place recruitment restrictions on us before the final, then what choice do they have? We go in with what we got. They've got me. I'm suiting up."

"The Sledgehammers are merciless," Bullseye said, taking a bite from her fresh wheat roll. "I feel like I'm having a last supper with a good friend. Don't make me lose two good friends in one month, Leelee. I can't handle it."

Leeland leaned back in his chair and held his hands out as if he were about to pray. "I can't believe what I'm hearing. Why are you busting balls? I was expecting you to be supportive."

"I am supportive," she said, picking up her salad fork and stabbing the leafy greens as if it were an enemy. "I just don't want the price of my support to be your death. Leelee, winning is not worth your death. If you suit up, I guarantee you that the Sledgehammers will gun for you until you are dead, or, at least, knocked out of the game permanently. There are coaches, and there are players. You can't be both. If you try to be, you'll have a permanent bullseye on your back."

"I want a Bullseye on my side, dammit!"

"You have one," Bullseye said, trying to calm herself before the matter got out of hand, "but I'm not going to sit here and tell you lies, Leelee. That's not what you and I are all about. I'm worried. I'm worried you are putting your life at risk for what... a win? Why does that matter to you so much?"

Again, Leeland couldn't believe what he was hearing. "We're DreadBall players, Carla. Winning seemed to matter to you a week ago, when you were whipping your Banshees into a frenzy before the game. Don't act surprised with me; I saw what you were doing."

"I'm out of the tournament, now," she said. "My perspective has changed."

"Well, here's my perspective." Leeland pushed his plate away and leaned forward, putting his elbows on the table. "I'm not doing this for the win, Carla. Honestly, I could care less if we win or lose. No one expected us to get this far, so we've beaten the odds. We've done what we set out to do. I'm doing this for Conner and Shadrack and Frankie and Jimbo, and Triple-B's and Shyler's memories. I'm doing this for the guys. They deserve a win. And if it means sacrificing myself so they get that win, so be it.

"In my youth, I used to dream about being a Trontek 29er. To get a contract with them as a rookie was the highlight of my life. I thought there was nothing better. And I gave them the best years of my career. What did it get me? The death of my brother. I'm through with dreaming about being a member of a team. My place was never with them, and it took years wallowing in ditches, covered in booze, sorrow, and my own waste, to realize that I'm a Viper. I've always been a Viper. And I will always be one."

Bullseye smiled. Her face beamed as if she had been given a great compliment. She shoved her plate away. She stood and walked over to Leeland. She reached down and grabbed his face with both hands. Then she kissed him on the mouth. But it wasn't a kiss of passion. It was a kiss of support, of love. The kind of kiss a mother or sister would give her child or brother.

"Finally," she said as she pulled away. "You've come to your senses. You're finally back among the living." Her expression then turned from joy to a deep seriousness, and she smacked him across the head. "So now, get up, Leeland Roth, and go win this tournament."

Bullseye walked out, leaving him with the check as always. Everyone in the restaurant was staring at him, expecting him to say something or, at least, react to what they had just seen. But Leeland said nothing. Instead, he sat there, smiling, finishing his dinner, knowing that good ol' Carla 'Bullseye' Bock had, once again, gotten the better of him, gotten him to say, to confess, what he needed to say.

She's good!

So now, he had one more person to win a game for. But before all that, before he could suit up and win that game, he had another person to save.

[illegible]

The stadium on the Dreadnought was dark save for a row of drop lights that ran down the center the full length of the pitch, from one near goal to the other. Leeland was in full Viper gear, running back and forth, ducking in and out of the broken light as if he were dodging ravenous Horse Father guards intent on breaking his bones. He'd worked up a sweat. He breathed heavily as he pretended that an opponent on the left was reaching for the ball. He then shifted hands, controlling the ball even better as his opponent's arms tried flinging it away. He reached the goal, did a one-eighty to twist into position. Then he paused, aimed, and threw the ball into the goal.

Score! [illegible]

"I thought we were meeting in your office."

Saoirse's voice echoed across the pitch as she stepped into the light near the center line.

"Step back!" Leeland shouted. "Now!"

First Saoirse continued, but when she heard the whir of the ball cannon come to life, she stepped back just as the ball was being released. It roared past her, a blur of steel and potential death.

Leeland leapt into the ball's path and caught it before it flew out of the light and across the pitch. The speed and firmness of the ball aggravated his old injuries, but he held firm and said, "Rule number one in DreadBall, Saoirse: don't enter the pitch without your suit, your protection."

Chapter Twenty-One

The stadium on the *Dread* was dark, save for a row of drone lights that ran down the center, the full length of the pitch, from one rear goal to the other. Leeland was in full Viper gear, running back and forth, zigging in and out of the trail of light as if he were dodging ravenous Forge Father guards intent on breaking his bones. He'd worked up a sweat. He breathed heavily as he pretended that an opponent on the left was reaching for the ball. He then shifted right, controlling the ball even better as imaginary arms tried ripping it away. He reached the goal, did a one-eighty to twist into position. Then he paused, aimed, and threw the ball into the goal.

Score!

"I thought we were meeting in your office."

Saanvi's voice echoed across the pitch as she stepped into the light near the center line.

"Step back!" Leeland shouted. "Now!"

First, Saanvi was confused, but when she heard the whirl of the ball cannon come to life, she stepped back just as the ball was being released. It soared past her, a blur of steel and potential death.

Leeland leapt into the ball's path and caught it before it flew out of the light and across the pitch. The speed and impetus of the ball aggravated his old muscles; but he held firm and said, "Rule number one in DreadBall, Saanvi: don't enter the pitch without your suit, your protection."

"I wouldn't have had to if you had stayed in your office as you said in your message."

"My apologies, but I need the practice."

Saanvi adjusted herself, collected her wits, and stepped back into the light. "Wouldn't it be better to practice with real players? You have an entire team, remember?"

"I gave them the night off," Leeland said. "The championship is in three days. They need a break. Besides, this gives me time to hone my skills without humiliating myself in front of people."

"But practicing in the dark? That doesn't sound wise."

Leeland took three long steps forward as if he were about to leap and slam dunk the ball. Instead, he shot it at the back goal, far outside the legal distance. It sailed through the air, arcing from light, into darkness, and back into light as it struck the goal.

No score.

The ball ricocheted left. Leeland let it go. Another ball was launched. He scooped it into his launcher. "My brother and I used to practice in the dark. In our hometown, the local electrical corporation would conduct these rolling brownouts to shift power from one of their facilities to the next. Very annoying and crippling sometimes to the less-than-rich families that had to live with it. Victor and I would have to play in the dark. It proved to be a perfect way to practice Dread-Ball because, from the darkness, you never know what's coming for you. It teaches you never to underestimate what you do not know, what you cannot see.

"Did I ever tell you about my brother Victor? Did I ever tell you how he died?"

Saanvi shook her head. "No, but I'm aware. You accidentally killed him in a semi-final match against the Jade Dragons. Aryan has told me. It's no real secret."

"Did Aryan tell you why I killed my brother?"

Saanvi shook her head. "No, but I assume it was because you were angry. Your team was losing, and you snapped your lid."

Leeland stepped forward and took another long shot on the goal.

Fail.

"Perhaps in that moment," he said, "I was angry. But no. I killed him because I was jealous. Jealous that my brother was better than me in everything... and everyone that mattered to me in the sphere—my coach, my teammates, my fans—were watching. How could I let them see that I was a mere shell of the player my brother was? So, I killed him. It took me a long time to come to that realization, and I will never forget or forgive myself for what I did. I will carry that guilt to the grave."

Another ball was launched. This time, Leeland waited to snatch it until it had almost barreled into Saanvi's side. He snagged it just in time.

"But I think," he said, moving forward to stare into her eyes, "the family dynamic is the same all across the galaxy, no matter how poor or how rich or powerful you are. The relationship between brother and brother, daughter and father, sister and brother... transcends the social stratosphere. And I think that's why you framed your brother Aryan."

Leeland took another shot, this time from where he was standing.

Fail.

Saanvi glared at him with dark, grave eyes. "What are you talking about?"

"You framed him," Leeland said, waiting for another ball to launch. "You were angry, yes, at your father's insistence that Aryan run the company because *he* was the son. And how could that be?

How could something as trivial as gender dictate such an important corporate decision? Damon Kapoor had told the board that Aryan would run the company in his passing, didn't he, so the only thing you could do was either kill him, or frame him for murder and conspiracy? And that was so easy, wasn't it, because Aryan is such a reckless twit, an easy mark. Like shooting Veer-Myn in a sewage pipe, as they say. Thus, once Aryan was out of the way, once there was no chance of him ever heading Kapoor Industries, the board would have no choice but to declare you the CEO. Your jealousy for your brother, whose only qualification for leadership is the equipment between his legs, got the better of you. I understand that, Saanvi, and I sympathize. I've been there."

Another ball was launched. This time, Leeland caught it immediately.

"That's a lie!"

Leeland shrugged. "No, it's true. You conspired with Horus Ruth and his lawyers to keep Conner from playing, didn't you? You also bribed the Whitestar Chimps to make them give up at the end. It wasn't enough to just have Aryan and the Vipers lose; that would have left the team and Aryan intact and thus, able to continue in a Third Sphere league if such an organization were formed. That might have been seen as success. No. We had to win that game in order to be on the *Dread* during the Rebs attack, so that we too could be caught up in the violence and, like the Golan Banshees, slaughtered where we stood. If it had just been me in the sky box that day, you'd have gotten your wish. But you forgot that I was flanked by an ex-professional sniper on one side, and a crazy beast on the other. The plan was almost perfect, but it was too big for you, and the details got out of your control."

"You're wrong," Saanvi said, slowly backing up until she was out of the light. "And my brother was right about you. You're not fit to lead this team, not fit to play. Effective immediately, you're no longer the coach for the Vipers. You hear me, Leeland? You're done. Pack up your stuff, and—"

"Yeah, well, here's the thing," Leeland said, taking a step forward while hefting the ball. He made sure Saanvi saw it on his glove. "I got a name, and I made a call, and there's one further thing you must also learn if you're going to deal with Rebs on a regular basis. A Rebel is only as loyal as the flow of his money, the imperative of his agenda, or the threat to his life. Interrupt one of those three, and he sings like a bird. So no, Ms. Kapoor, I'm not packing my stuff. Your game is up."

Leeland tossed the ball, and this time, he did it like he'd seen Mackinaw Jim do it a hundred times. The right way.

It was more of a straight shot, with only a little arch and curve to the right. It struck the goal.

Score.

The lights in the stadium came on. Around them, in a half moon, stood security personnel, three men in black suits, and a cuffed Gaelian who towered over all of them on powerful hooves.

Saanvi Kapoor turned, paused, looked at all of them, then said in an anxious, quivering voice, "You can't prove anything. No one is going to believe Gaelian trash over me, the daughter of Damon Kapoor, the newly appointed Chief Executive Officer of Kapoor Industries."

Leeland motioned to the Reb. "Tell her what you told me."

The Gaelian's accent was difficult to cipher, but they got the gist of his message. "She promised a ship, all the weapons we could carry, and a safe-base on Vitala from which we could conduct further attacks."

"Lies!"

One of the security personnel pushed a button on his wrist-comp. Saanvi's voice rang out crystal clear as she offered exactly that in her back alley conversation with the Gaelian.

"You thought you weren't being recorded," Leeland said, "but there's another thing you have to know about Rebs: they cover their tails, and in the case of Gaelians... literally."

Saanvi, fear flashing across her face, took two steps back, then tried to run.

Security grabbed her. Saanvi screamed and kicked and punched and threw threats and accusations at everyone around her. Finally, they cuffed her and carried her out of the stadium. Leeland watched as they dragged her through the access tunnel. She made sure he saw her staring at him. He did not like her stare, but Leeland felt sorry for her. Why, he wondered, would she now go to jail when he was walking free? She hadn't killed anyone while Leeland had killed his own brother. Well, Saanvi Kapoor hadn't pulled any trigger, certainly, but a lot of innocent people had died during the Rebel assault. Her hands were bloody, and she would get what she deserved, hopefully.

He sighed deeply, straightened himself to prepare for more practice, and totally forgot that another ball was launched.

Leeland turned just in time to take the ball, at full speed, into his chest. The shot knocked him down and back three meters. He howled as he struck the hard pitch and skidded another two.

He lay there, trying to breathe, feeling the stinging pain of broken ribs with each breath. Leeland opened his eyes, and the stadium spun.

One of the security personnel pushed a button on his desk-top. Saanvi's voice rang out, as clear as she'd [illegible] exactly that in their back alley conversation with the Skeleton.

"You thought you weren't being recorded," Leeland said, "but here's another thing you'll have to know about Reb: they cover their butts, and in the case of Cavaliers, literally."

Saanvi, after doing a [illegible] [illegible], took two steps back, then tried to run.

Security grabbed her. Saanvi screamed and kicked and punched and threw threats and accusations at everyone around her. Finally, they cuffed her and carried her out of the stadium. Leeland watched as they dragged her through the access tunnel. She made sure he saw her staring at him. He did not like her stare, but Leeland felt sorry for her. Why, he wondered, would she now go to jail when he was walking free? She hadn't killed anyone, while Leeland had killed his own brother. Well, Saanvi Kapoor hadn't pulled any trigger, certainly, but a lot of innocent people had died during the Nobel ca-[illegible]. Her hands were bloody and she would get what she deserved, hopefully.

He sighed deeply, straightened himself to prepare for more practice, and totally forgot that another ball was launched.

Leeland turned just in time to see the ball, at full speed, into his chest. The shot knocked him down and back three meters. He howled as he struck the hard pitch and skidded another two.

He lay there trying to breathe, feeling the stunning pain of the [illegible]. Then with every breath, Leeland opened his eyes, and the stadium

Chapter Twenty-Two

Hello, DreadBall fans, and welcome to the championship game of the Third Sphere Invitational DreadBall Tournament. I am Elmer.

And I am Dobbs.

Before we start, I'd like to thank V-TAV for their lovely hospitality in getting us all set up and ready to go. And Mr. Chaudhry, when you get a moment, we're still waiting on those lattes and muffins. Thank you.

Now, let's begin. We've been whisked all the way out here to the hinterland to witness what has become, in DreadBall circles at least, the most anticipated game in recent years. Isn't that right, Dobbs?

It sure is, Elmer. And who would have thought it all those months ago, when thirty-two teams from all over the Third Sphere came together in a one-and-done tournament that has become, in many ways, a poster child for how tough and brutal this sport can be.

You're right about that, Dobbs. Never have I witnessed so many low-seeded teams play at such a high, professional level as I've seen in this tournament. And today's championship game is no exception.

Today, the Saltborne Sledgehammers—a team everyone expected to see in this final—are going against perhaps the most unlikely team, the Vitala Vipers, a team who has been wracked with losses and controversy and scandal from the opening bell. Isn't that how you see it, Dobbs?

With eyes wide open, Elmer. Nobody expected to see the Vitala Vipers here, and in fact, their fourteenth seeding at the very beginning was considered by many to be brought on by bribery at the hands of the Kapoor

Industry board.

There is no proof of that accusation, Dobbs, but you are right: the Vitala Vipers seem to have a demon on their backs. But perhaps they can shake it off for this final—and most important—game in their short existence. They go against a Forge Father team that they met in the seeding rounds, so they know a little about how the Sledgehammers lower the hammer, if you will permit me some verbal levity.

Very little levity, Elmer. The Sledgehammers come into the game leading in injuries, in kills, and in shots-on-goal. If the Sledgehammers get the ball, they take a shot. The only category that the Vipers lead on is actual points scored.

Yes, Dobbs, but that will no longer be a strength for them, as they have lost two star strikers, Shyler Coch and Jimbo Threpe, and guard Brutus 'Triple-B' Bertuchi, may he and Shyler rest in peace. The only stars left in their skies are Conner Newberg, Shadrack Menapi, and their coach, the aged veteran Leeland Roth, who's decided to suit up and play this game in his old striker position.

That man has bigger balls than those shot out of the cannon, Elmer.

Keep it youth appropriate, Dobbs. There are kids listening. But you're right: rumor has it that Leeland Roth suffered a serious injury just a few days ago, so the question on everyone's mind is, can he do the job?

Well, we'll know in about an hour or so. So let's go down to the stadium and see if we can get an update on Roth's condition. Hannah Zeller is standing by. What can you tell us, Hannah?

***

Leeland winced as tape was applied to his sore—his broken—ribs. The pain had subsided somewhat, but it would rise again during the match. He could depend on it.

"You sure you want to suit up, Boss?" Shadrack said as he and Conner watched their coach being prepped for the opening toss.

Through their closed locker room door, they could hear the muffled commotion of the fans as they poured into the stadium. Leeland shook his head. It was going to be a riotous crowd.

"I am," he said. "This may be my last game as a player. What better way to finish up that part of my career than on the pitch with you guys? Besides, you're going to protect me, aren't you?"

Conner and Shadrack traded stares. "Only if you listen to me out there," Conner said with a wink.

"I will follow the time-honored striker code of conduct: I will listen, and then do what I want."

"That's what I'm afraid of," Conner said, helping Leeland snap on his armor. "There can only be one general on the pitch at a time, Boss. Who's it going to be?"

Leeland sighed. "When we're out there together, you can direct the traffic."

Conner looked as if he didn't believe the words, but Leeland stared at him until Conner blinked. "Very well," Conner said. "I'm going to hold you to that."

Leeland stood there in Shyler's old kit since they were similar in build and height. The armor felt a little tight in the midriff, but Leeland figured that was the tape. He turned to Shadrack. "Give me a punch in the ribs, big guy."

"What?"

"You heard me... punch me. And don't play nice." Both Conner and Shadrack stared at him in horror. "Look, we need to know now if I can take a punch, cause it's going to get even worse out there. We need to know now if my armor will hold. So, punch me. Punch me like I'm Triple-B, and I've just insulted your mother."

Leeland thought that that would get a laugh and lighten the mood, but neither Conner nor Shadrack was laughing. "Okay, Boss, if you say so."

The big guard made two steps back to give his massive arm room. He breathed deeply, pulled his arm back, balled up his fist, and drove it into Leeland's chest.

The strike pushed Leeland back three steps. Conner caught him to ensure he did not fall.

Silence.

"Well?" Shadrack asked.

Leeland stood there for a moment, then smiled. "We're ready."

He followed them out into the hallway where the rest of the Vipers were waiting. Down the line, he gave each a slap on the helmet. When he reached the front of the line, he turned and said, "This is it. This is what you've worked so hard to achieve. Whether you go out there and win it tonight is immaterial in the end, for you have proven yourself men, and no one can take that away. But... it seems like such a waste of time to get all dressed up and lose. So, forget what I just told you, and go out there and beat those little punks into the floor. Act like Vipers. Strike fast, strike hard, and pump your poison until there isn't a single one left standing.

"I'm dedicating this game to my brother, Victor. He would have loved a game like this, with everything on the line, fighting against a superior foe, with everyone in the stands shouting for your blood. No one expects us to beat them. Let's go out there and prove them wrong. Let's prove it to ourselves. Let's prove it to the fans. Let's prove it to Victor!"

The team howled, and Leeland howled with them.

They ran down the corridor toward the pitch. Leeland let them take the lead, for he didn't want to be the first one out. This was not about him. It was about Shadrack and Conner, about Little Frankie and Spencer, and all the other Vipers waiting to take the pitch. It was about the team.

And besides, he couldn't run very fast anyway with pain coursing through his body, and the trickle of warm blood down his stomach from the wound Shadrack's punch had reopened.

***

Okay, Dobbs, let's review the lineups.

Here we go, Elmer…

The Saltborne Sledgehammers will start with a basic 2-2-2—two guards, two jacks, and two strikers—and they will try to control the center. Now, most of the players on this team were veritable unknowns when the tournament began, but I assure you, Elmer, that is no longer the case.

For their guards, they have Thorgus 'Uppercut' Oakbiter, who likes to employ his fists with the force of a volcano; Hentor 'Barbarian' Brunka, the one they affectionately call The Pick Axe. For their jacks, they have Stephon Stephonson and Karl Veneer, both of whom are relatively new to the starting lineup but have proven themselves worthy of the position; and finally, the strikers: Gregor 'Musket' Moon, their chief scorer, and Borus Dakport, the fastest striker on the Sledgehammers and considered by many to be the best player in the entire tournament.

Oh, I think you'd get pushback on that last statement from the Vipers, Dobbs.

I'm sure I would, Elmer. Why don't you tell us the Vipers' starting lineup and prove me wrong?

I will, indeed…

Unlike the treasure-trove of noobs that the Sledgehammers have brought to the pitch, the Vitala Vipers are a mixed bag of rookies and aged veterans whose best days are, perhaps, behind them; and yet, they have proven that you don't put a bull to pasture if he can still rut.

The Vipers will start in a small formation of 1-2-3—one guard, two jacks, and three strikers—with the hope of getting the ball first and scoring first. They will rely on speed and veteran experience to bring them the gold.

Shadrack Menapi will be their starting guard, and he has racked up an impressive list of opponent injuries throughout the tournament.

Their jacks will include Conner Newberg and Jerold Minata, one veteran and one rookie, but Conner is considered to be the best field general the game has ever seen. He manages the game like a coach, and he's still got a chip on his shoulder after Digby, due to previous contract restrictions, denied him the right to play most of the tournament.

Finally, we have the strikers: Little Frankie, who came into the tournament as green as an apple, but has quickly become one of the brightest stars of the game; Spencer Mills, who, in my view, best serves the Vipers as more of an agitator and ball stealer and lane denier than a scorer; and finally, the aged, well past his prime, Leeland Roth, whose life and career is socked in with controversy and scandal. He understands the rough-and-tumble environment of DreadBall better than anyone on the pitch, and he will hope to bring that experience to his team as a player.

Okay, so tell us, Elmer, who do you see winning it all?

In truth, Dobbs, I think it's a tossup, but if I had a gun to my head…

And you do, Elmer.

…I'd have to go with The Saltborne Sledgehammers. We've seen time and time again that the team that controls the center, controls the game. And the Sledgehammers will control the center. I think it will be a low-scoring game that will come down to the wire. I don't see it going into overtime, but my money is on the Forge Fathers. What about you, Dobbs?

My head agrees with you, Elmer. But my heart will go with the Vipers. They have overcome adversity every step of the way, and they will get it done. They are, in my opinion, faster than the Sledgehammers, despite popular opinion, and their veterans will bring to the table something that the Sledgehammers do not as of yet possess. I think it may very well go into overtime, but in the end, I think Leeland Roth and his nest of Vipers will prevail.

Okay, so there you have it from the booth. Now all that's left is the game itself.

So, let's get to it…

Chapter Twenty-Three

Just before the ball was released, Conner called for a realignment. He and Shadrack and Jerold, who had been lined up along the center line in a formation that looked like the Vipers would start the rough and tumble, fell back and gave way to Leeland and the other two strikers. The shift confused the Sledgehammers momentarily, as they themselves tried to realign to match. But as the ball was released, Little Frankie took advantage of the Forge Fathers' confusion by leaping over the center line and snagging the ball as the Sledgehammers floundered.

The crowd roared, the game was on, and Little Frankie moved to score.

He was fresh, he was sound of both body and mind, and Leeland couldn't help but smile behind the face guard of his helmet as the rookie first dodged Sledgehammer guards Oakbiter and then Brunka as he worked toward the right side strike zone. The ball was tucked tight against Frankie's body. Leeland was pleased. The young man had learned so much in such a short period of time. Gone were the days of carrying the ball loosely; gone was the indecision that every rookie in the sport fought against. *After the game,* Leeland thought as he strategically backed away to center himself for the inevitable counter-rush, *we'll have to start calling him Mr. Frankie.*

Sledgehammer jack Veneer managed to put himself in Frankie's line of sight. The young striker hesitated just a moment on his score attempt, and that proved to be a mistake, as it gave Sledgehammer striker Dakport just enough time to jump in front of the arching ball and deflect it away from the goal.

Leeland considered moving forward to close the gap in the center, but Conner waved him off and instead ordered Shadrack to come up, for Oakbiter and Brunka were moving to protect their ball carrier.

Gregor 'Musket' Moon snatched the ball on ricochet and headed toward a score. He moved along the edge of the wall, as if he were walking a zip line, and then turned immediately inward to place himself between the safe and powerful trundling masses of his two guards who had already knocked Jerold and Conner to their backs. Luckily, neither was injured, though Jerold looked a little dazed.

With a wince of pain from his ribs, Leeland shifted quickly to his left to try to get into position to either stall the move or steal the ball, if such an opportunity presented itself. But with two beefy Forge Father guards plowing the field, it would be difficult. He decided to shift again and try to come at Moon from behind. However, Spencer was already making a move to that effect, and so Leeland held his ground. A moment later, Thorgus Oakbiter slammed right into him.

Leeland turned just in time to accept the slam on his right shoulder, away from his broken ribs, and so he suffered little pain. Oakbiter then tried to employ his patented upper cut, and it might have worked, had Shadrack not grabbed his arm and forced the raging Forge Father to lose his footing and go down hard, taking both Leeland and Shadrack with him.

Both guards fell right on top of Leeland, and he tried not to shout out in agony. However, a little screech left his mouth as he tried to push himself away from the suffocating brawl that was being committed on top of him. As he tried to break free, Leeland saw the blur of Forge Father legs run past him, and reflexively, he put out his arm and grabbed a dark boot.

Moon howled as Leeland's hand cuffed the striker's steel toe and took him down. As he fell, Moon tried scoring, but his angle was off and the toss weak. The ball didn't even make it to the goal. It bounced three times and then ricocheted hard to the left.

Little Frankie was on the ball again, catching it on his glove and making his way across the pitch toward the Sledgehammer goal he had tried scoring on before. Leeland finally pushed himself free and joined the race.

"Give it to me!" he shouted to Frankie. At first, it seemed as if Frankie was going to refuse the order, but then he pitched it over with a sneer on his face. *You'll have a chance to score later*, Leeland thought as he fixed his attention toward the Sledgehammers' back goal. *I promise.*

Jacks Veneer and Stephonson had fallen back to guard their back goal in a kind of impromptu castle. Leeland was surprised that the Sledgehammers hadn't started that way. Most likely, their arrogance and celebrity had convinced them that it wasn't needed, but Leeland was moving to ensure them they were wrong. A Forge Father team should almost always start the game in castle, Leeland knew, though he himself hated the practice. For some teams, it was simply required.

But even in a hastily-prepared castle, it would be difficult for Leeland to score, and the rest of the players on the pitch were rallying to catch up. The big brawl that Shadrack had started by jumping Oakbiter had resolved, with Moon being lifted off the pitch via medibot, and Shadrack himself slow to get up and still being harassed by Brunka.

Leeland winced again, but this time, not from pain, but from the thought of losing his star guard. But he couldn't worry about that now. Before him lay the back goal, and Forge Father jacks were waiting.

Conner came up, and Leeland faked him a hand-off that totally paralyzed striker Dakport. This gave Conner the opportunity to step ahead of Leeland and put a slam on Veneer, who held the spot right in front of the goal. As they tore into each other, Leeland had to pause and wait for the matter to resolve. This was the part of the game that he hated the most: those moments when a player had to wait, wait, wait, until a clear line of sight opened. Leeland jumped back and forth, into and out of the strike zone in order to find the right position to take a shot over the flailing of jack arms and legs. No lane opened, unfortunately, and Oakbiter was angry and closing.

"Throw it to me!"

Leeland looked to his right, and there was Spencer Mills, standing all alone in front of one of the Sledgehammer's other goals. But standing so close to the goal would yield him only one point if he scored, and Leeland was hesitant. He so wanted to take that four-point shot, for going up that many points early would be so sweet and almost guarantee them the win against a slower opponent. Oakbiter was closing, closing, Conner's brawl with Veneer wasn't resolving, and Spencer was wide open.

Leeland cursed and threw the ball to Spencer.

He wasn't able to see Spencer take the shot, however, because Oakbiter struck him just afterward, driving him into the floor, and riding him all the way to the wall. But Leeland knew his striker had made the goal since the lights in the stadium flashed red and green, the klaxons sounded, and the crowd went wild.

The Vitala Vipers took the lead by one.

***

What a dramatic first score, Dobbs.

Indeed it was, Elmer. Leeland Roth paid for that decision.

He sure did, and look… it seems as if he's taking himself out of the game. He's signaling for the medibot. Have you ever seen a player do that, Dobbs?

Not since Pelgar Mystics' star Vivi Mystino did so in 975AE against the Locust City Chiefs. The medibot had to go back twice for his leg and his arm. You remember that game, Elmer?

Can't say as I do, Dobbs, but I'll take your word for it. How badly do you think Roth is hurt?

Hard to say, but if he's half as bad as Vivi Mystino, it's bad, Elmer, very bad.

***

The pain was excruciating. Leeland tried to bear it as best he could as Thorgus Oakbiter screamed into his face, the guard's spit clouding his eyes. "You're dead, Leelee," Oakbiter said, throwing Bullseye's pet name at him like a knife. "Dead!"

"Not yet," Leeland replied and then signaled for the medibot. He felt dead, but he was still breathing, and wasn't that half the battle in DreadBall?

The bot picked him up, and the game kept going.

He had to stay on the sidelines for a little bit and let the younger folk play it. Now that they were up by a point, it would be okay to take a break. But he couldn't show weakness; not now, not until the final bell sounded and the game ended. And there was a lot of game left.

He collected himself, endured his pain, and worked the game.

Borus Dakport now had the ball, and as the practice film had suggested, he was fast. Amazingly fast, given his stature. He worked his powerful, tiny legs like pistons, dodging and weaving through the

chaos of the pitch as if he were a Judwan striker. But he was short, and so his vision was hindered. Because of that, Dakport was being overly cautious with his move toward a Viper strike zone, allowing his blockers to take out and/or engage pesky defenders. His apprehension allowed Conner to orchestrate a proper defense, and everywhere Dakport turned, he was greeted with a Viper staring down on his head.

Oh, how I wish Bullseye were here, Leeland thought as he too shouted orders to his strikers, corralling them into position to pluck the ball away if the opportunity presented itself. It was too much to ask Conner to not only play, but to act as the *de facto* defensive coordinator. Leeland chuckled. *I'm doing the same thing.* It was hypocritical for him to think Conner couldn't pull it off, and yet—

There Conner went, under a crushing slam by Sledgehammer jack Stephon Stephonson. The Forge Father jack delivered two additional punches to reinforce his move, and then got up and carried on.

Conner did not move.

***

Oooohh… a devastating shot, Dobbs. Conner's gonna be feeling that for weeks. Do we know how long he's going to be out?

Hard to say as this point, Elmer, but we'll check with Hannah Zeller momentarily to get the word. I don't know how many more shots they can… ooohhh… and there goes Little Frankie.

***

Leeland was ready to tag back in, but first he ordered a benchwarmer jack, Raj Butala, to replace Conner. Leeland tried keeping his cool as he slapped the young man on the shoulder and directed him onto the pitch.

"Are you okay, Boss?" Raj asked. "You're bleeding."

Leeland look down, and indeed he was. His ribs. Right though his uniform. He touched the dark spot. It was warm, wet. He shook his head. "Nothing to worry about. Get out there!"

Raj entered the game, and Leeland followed.

Dakport finally found an open lane and took a shot on goal. It rattled out.

There was a scramble on the ball, as it bounced and bounced and bounced in such a manner that no one could get their mitts on it. Spencer Mills was the closest, but he was struck by Sledgehammer guard Brunka and taken out of the equation. Luckily, it was a glancing blow, and Spencer recovered quickly, but he was now out of position, and the ball kept bouncing.

Karl Veneer tried taking it on ricochet off the wall, but Leeland stepped in front of him and got it first. Despite his pain, his blood, he moved quickly to score.

It was like old times. In his mind, at least. Too bad Conner was nursing a headache in the Sin Bin, for it would have been wonderful to see two Trontek 29er alumni working down the pitch once more to the adulation of the crowd, the love of the cheerleaders, the rage of the opposition. But he was alone. Alone, save for Shadrack.

The big man had surprisingly survived an incessant attack against him, and now he led Leeland to the right strike zone. Stephon Stephonson tried blocking their path. Shadrack put his fist forward like a steel press and knocked the Forge Father jack aside as if he were a leaf in the breeze. Leeland kept close and looked for the two-point spot.

The spot pulsed metal blue. Leeland paused just a moment for Shadrack to push Brunka out of the way, and then he slid into position.

It would be a difficult shot from this spot, Leeland knew. Brunka was nearby, as were others. He had the aid of Shadrack and Spencer, who were trying to keep the wolves at bay. But the wolves were violent, and suddenly, Shadrack went down.

"Take the shot!" he heard someone scream. It sounded like a woman's voice. Bullseye? Or perhaps it was his mother. His mother had been dead for many years. Surely, it wasn't his mother. Then the world began to spin, and he felt more warm blood trickle down his stomach.

He took the shot. It bounced out.

But Jerold Minata, who had just arrived from a little spat with Karl Veneer, took the ball on bounce near the goal and slammed it home for one point.

The crowd erupted again. The Vipers went up by two.

Leeland smiled and then passed out.

***

The Vipers are getting banged up out there, Dobbs, but they are up two points. That's a good position to be in.

So right you are, Elmer, though as we know, it won't take long for the Sledgehammers to tie it up. I have to say, though, that Coach Roth is showing some serious grit out there, despite the fact that this is the second time a medibot has had to drag him off. What can you tell us about his condition, Hannah?

Dobbs, I'm standing here in the Vitala Vipers' Sin Bin next to Conner Newberg, who seems to have shaken off the wicked shot he took and is ready to go back into the game. We are awaiting Leeland Roth's body any second now, and once he arrives I'll be sure to get back to you. But let's see if Conner wishes to say anything. "Conner…do you wish to say anything at this time? How's your team holding up?"

Well, that was very rude of him, wasn't it, Elmer, ripping Hannah's mic out of her hand and crushing it under his boot.

Nobody ever said that Conner Newberg didn't have a temper. But let's get back to the game, Dobbs. There is never a pause in the action.

Chapter Twenty-Four

Leeland was laid out on the Sin Bin floor. Hannah Zeller was on him immediately with a fresh mic.

"Coach Roth, are you all right?"

Leeland heard someone say something. It sounded like his mother's voice. "I'm fine, fine, Mama. Don't worry about me."

"He's delusional. And look at all the blood."

A medibot was on him immediately. His expression confirmed what everyone around suspected. "You can't go back in there, Coach. You're gonna bleed out if you do."

"Bull!" Leeland said, grabbing hold of the physician and Hannah to pull himself up on weak legs. "I need some water, that's all. I'm fine. You can tell your Elmer and your Dobbs and whoever else you want to tell... Leeland Roth is fine. Now, get out of my way, and let me do my job."

But he did not go right back in. The water helped, but Leeland knew that, at the very least, he needed a rest. Again, he would be confined to the sidelines, but he would not be moved. This was it. This was the last game, their last hurrah. Now or nothing.

I will not be moved.

Shadrack had survived Oakbiter's slam and was now engaged with both he and Brunka. It was not going well for the big oaf—he was taking punch after punch—but he was holding his ground. The distraction was useful for Conner and benchwarmer Raj, who now tried to position themselves to keep Gregor 'Musket' Moon from scoring. With Leeland out, the Vipers were running with one guard, three jacks, and two strikers. A 1-3-2 formation was good for defense, but Moon was closing on a strike zone.

Moon was not as fast as Borus Dakport, but his body control was sublime. The Sledgehammer striker shifted from left to right perfectly on cue with any whiff of danger. If circumstances were different, Leeland thought it'd be nice to hire Moon as a striker coach, if at the end, the Vipers won and advanced. *But what am I thinking? Focus… focus…* He was so lightheaded, so weak.

"Take him out!" Leeland shouted to Raj who was in the perfect position to conduct a strike. Raj, now in the big game, was clearly nervous, unsure of himself. Leeland had to hold himself back from rushing the pitch. He could enter play, and if the referee did not notice that the Vipers were running with more than six players, it would be legal. But what were the odds of getting away with that in a championship game, with millions watching, screaming, and rooting for his death? No. Leeland held himself in check and instead screamed for Raj to do his duty.

Raj moved to intercept, and for a moment it looked like Moon was stymied. He paused, stumbled back, and looked to drop the ball. But it was all a ruse. He recovered quickly as Raj leaned in for a slam. Moon took a quick step to the left, twisted, and left Raj face-down and flailing.

Moon stepped into the two-point spot, settled his legs, and threw.

Score!

And just like that, the game was back to zero.

***

OMG! Is that Little Frankie dead on the pitch?

I think you're right, Elmer… no, wait. It is Frankie, but he's alive. The DreadBall gods show their mercy. Little Frankie is down, ladies and gentlemen, he's down, but he just moved a finger. And now a foot. Here comes the medibot.

Wow, that was an exciting rush, Dobbs. We have a tie game. Viper slam-fodder Raj Butala took it in the chops as well. It looks like he's injured and is coming out. What an embarrassment for the young man; to be injured by just falling to the pitch.

Like nature itself, Elmer, DreadBall is fickle.

No time for your popcorn philosophy, Dobbs. We've got a game to watch.

Then let's get back to it, Elmer. We have a tie, and time is running out. Whoever makes the next score will win.

***

Oakbiter laughed and waved at Leeland as he stepped over Little Frankie's broken body. Leeland gave him the finger and moved to enter the game.

A hand stopped him.

"Don't do it," Bullseye said. "Don't kill yourself."

Leeland turned, and there she was, tears running down her face. She was trying to be brave, trying to show strength, but the situation had changed since their last meeting in the restaurant. Since then, Leeland had been struck by a ball, punched by Shadrack in a foolish dare by Leeland himself to show courage, and had taken a good beating within the last several minutes. He was bleeding out.

"You know I have to, Carla," Leeland said, pulling away from Bullseye's hold. "I have to. For Victor."

Bullseye shook her head. "Victor wouldn't want to you die, no matter what happened between you two at the end. You can't sacrifice yourself and hope to make things right. He's dead, and there's nothing you can do to change that. The only thing you can do to honor his memory now is to be the best person, the best brother, you can be... alive. Your death will render his death meaningless."

"Winning this game will give his death meaning, Carla," Leeland said. "He was a DreadBall player, a striker, like me. He understood very well that we who play this game have to sacrifice everything for it. If I don't go out there and give everything I have left—give my life if necessary—I insult the *game*. And to Victor, that would be a far greater insult than anything else I could ever do to sully his memory. I have to go out there. I have to. Please... don't try to stop me."

Bullseye moved as if she were going to grab him and wrestle him to the floor. Then she paused, and instead, took his head in her hands gently and gave him a small kiss on his sweaty, cold forehead. She blinked away her fear. "Then go, you stubborn fool. Go, before I change my mind."

Somewhere inside, Leeland found the strength to run across the pitch, toward the mass of bodies fighting for the ball. Somewhere in the pile was every player on the pitch. The Sledgehammers weren't running with a castle anymore. They too had poured everyone they had into this last scramble for the ball. This was it. This was, literally, the game. Whoever came out with the ball, and whoever could score, would win.

It's going to be me.

Leeland didn't know where he got the temerity, the courage, the balls, to make such a private pronouncement, but it wasn't his voice. In his mind, it was Victor who had said those words, and he wasn't going to let his brother down.

He entered the fray. He could not tell who was friend, who was foe. Everyone was shouting. Everyone was kicking and punching and putting their shoulders into it. No one seemed to care where the ball was or who had it. This was war. This was violence on a scale rarely seen even in a DreadBall match. The game had fallen back onto its basic conceit: win by power. And if you can kill more players than your opponent, you'll win. It didn't always work out like that, but for corporate and Forge Father teams, it was a good philosophy to live, and play, by.

Leeland spotted the ball. It was nothing but a blur of blue-and-silver titanium, and it bounced through legs and arms as if it were intelligent enough to be afraid. It bounced through the hands of Veneer, through the gloves of Stephonson, off the spiked pauldrons of Hentor Brunka, and then into the hands of Borus Dakport.

"Give it to me!" Leeland shouted and motioned to get the ball.

And in the madness of the moment, Dakport got confused, panicked, and handed it over.

"NOOOO!" Dakport screamed and tried to strip it off of Leeland's glove, but it was too late.

Leeland was gone.

The crowd roared, and at first, Leeland moved alone, the entire pitch wide open to him. But that didn't last long, as Dakport took off after him. Then Veneer. Then Oakbiter, who seemed to be angrier at Dakport than Leeland. For good reason, Leeland knew, but now was not the time to lose one's cool. Dakport had just done so, and it had cost his team.

Now Shadrack and Conner took to the chase and tried to delay the other Sledgehammer players who were closing fast. But it was Dakport who was closest and the most immediate threat. He caught up easily with Leeland and tried first to get position to steal the ball, but Leeland had learned something by watching Moon from the Sin Bin.

Unlike many strikers who played fast and loose with the ball as they moved to score, 'Musket' Moon always protected it with both arms criss-crossed against his chest. The move created an almost unbreakable lock against the ball, making it near impossible to steal. Leeland tried mimicking the move. Dakport tried to pull Leeland's arm away, just like Victor had done all those years ago. The old memories flooded back as Leeland fought fatigue, nausea, and confusion. For a brief moment, Dakport's face warped into Victor's face, and Leeland almost bought the illusion, almost decided to throw the ball into that face, to keep it from laughing, from accusing, from cheating. But the illusion faded, the smells, and sounds, and lights of the moment flooded back, and Leeland slid into the left strike zone.

Just a one-point shot. That's all they needed. That's all he needed to do. Take the shot, take the shot. But the cold sweat on his face began to burn. The stadium began to swirl. *Which one is the goal?* He wondered. *The one on the right? The left? The center?* He couldn't decide.

Thorgus Oakbiter came into view.

First, Shadrack tried to stop him, but Oakbiter delivered a left hook that put Shadrack down. Jerold and Spencer tried blocking his path, but he took Jerold out with another swing. Spencer—for all his skills—couldn't take the pressure. He simply fell away and out of the opposing guard's path to keep from being struck, leaving the Sledgehammer guard a wide open slam against Leeland.

Take the shot!

Take the shot!

Take the shot!

The entire stadium was screaming it. And Leeland obliged.

"For Victor," he said as he reared back his glove and took the shot.

As the ball flew toward the goal, Oakbiter slammed into Leeland's side and took him down.

The last thing Leeland heard was the roar of the crowd slowly, slowly, give way to static silence.

Chapter Twenty-Five

Leeland awoke with more wires and leads attached to him from a Chromium Chamber. The bedside had tech and monitoring his blood pressure and O_2 saturation. [illegible] next to his bed, and whenever he tried to move, something tugged deep within his bladder [illegible] a mixture of high and low tech medicine whose purpose was, obviously, to keep him alive. If he was alive, and this wasn't some sort of dream where he was floating on a cloud in the afterlife. He was more mummy than man, but he opened his eyes and focused on the lights above his bed. He was thankful. At least the world had stopped spinning.

His bed was automatically raised. Leeland pulled himself up on weak elbows and focused on the man standing beside his bed.

Aryan Kaboor wasn't the only person standing there. Bullseye and Comet were there as well, and they all seemed pleased that he had awakened. Bullseye was taped. Comet had a blood-stained [illegible] wrapped around his head.

"Hello, guys," he said, acknowledging each in turn. He then looked at Aryan. "They let you out of jail, eh?"

Aryan nodded. "Once my sister confessed, they couldn't hold me. Remember, it's not a crime to talk to Reinh. But it is to conspire with them to commit murder and terrorism."

Leeland cleared his throat. "I guess you're happy now. You're out of jail, your sister's in jail, and you can take over Kaboor Indus-

Chapter Twenty-Five

Leeland awoke with more wires and leads attached to him than a Chromium Charger. The bedside med-tech drone monitoring his blood pressure and O2 saturation was beeping its obnoxious noise next to his bed, and whenever he tried to move, something tugged deep within his bladder. It was a mixture of high and low tech medicine whose purpose was, obviously, to keep him alive: if he was alive and this wasn't some fever dream where he was floating on a cloud in the afterlife. He was more mummy than man, but he opened his eyes and focused on the lights above his bed. He was thankful. At least the world had stopped spinning.

His bed was automatically raised. Leeland pulled himself up on weak elbows and focused on the man standing beside his bed.

Aryan Kapoor wasn't the only person standing there. Bullseye and Conner were there as well, and they all seemed pleased that he had awakened. Bullseye was teary; Conner had a blood-stained cloth wrapped around his head.

"Hello, guys," he said, acknowledging each in turn. He then looked at Aryan. "They let you out of jail, eh?"

Aryan nodded. "Once my sister confessed, they couldn't hold me. Remember, it's not a crime to talk to Rebs, but it is to conspire with them to commit murder and terrorism."

Leeland cleared his throat. "I guess you're happy now. You're out of jail, your sister is in jail, and you can take over Kapoor Industries."

"We'll let you two talk," Bullseye interrupted, as she moved from the foot of the bed to his side. "But the next time you do something that stupid, Leelee, I'll kill you myself." She leaned over and took his face in her hands. She kissed him gently on the forehead and ruffled his hair.

Before they departed, Conner Newberg approached the bed with a wide grin. He reached out to pat Leeland on the shoulder, then thought better of it when he saw all the leads and tubes. He took a step back and said, "You did good, Coach. Real good. It was an honor being on the pitch with you."

"Thank you, Conner," Leeland said. "You'll make a fine head coach someday."

Bullseye and Conner left the room. When they were alone, Aryan said, "I'm not happy that my sister will spend the rest of her life behind bars. Despite her mountains of flaws, she is my sister. I relinquished all control of the company to the board. Saanvi was right about one thing: I'm not qualified to replace our father. I'm leaving it to the board to pick someone more suited to the task, and in exchange, they've agreed to allow me to remain owner of the team. My place is with the Vipers."

A light went off in Leeland's head. "Oh, that's right. The game. Did we win?"

Aryan reached behind the foot of Leeland's bed and pulled out a three foot trophy. "Yes we did. Oh, you should have seen your score, Leeland. It rattled around, rattled around, and then bam! It dropped right in. One to nothing. A little riot broke out afterward. Some of their fans rushed the pitch, but overall, the Sledgehammers took it rather well. Although Borus Dakport hasn't been seen since. That was a wicked trick you pulled on him. Where'd you learn it?"

"From my brother," Leeland said, running his fingers over the chrome and polished dark wood of the trophy. It had the Vitala Viper logo emblazoned on the cup. It was beautiful, pristine. "He scored many times by taking advantage of the chaos of the game and mimicking the voices of his opponents. Luckily, I've played enough Forge Father teams in my day to know how they grouse and grumble." Leeland paused and smiled. "I think Victor would have enjoyed seeing me use that trick."

Their conversation paused, then Leeland asked, "How's the team?"

"Fine, fine. As you saw, Conner has a head injury and a concussion. Little Frankie... well, his neck injury is quite serious. He's paralyzed, but the doctors think that with reconstructive surgery, he'll be fine. We'll see."

Leeland lay back down. What terrible news about Little Frankie... *Mister* Frankie. But that was always the way it seemed with DreadBall: joy, followed by sorrow; victory, followed by defeat.

"So," Leeland asked, "when do you enter the FSIDL?"

"Well, that's the thing," Aryan said. "I haven't accepted the invitation yet."

"Why not? Isn't that what you wanted?"

Aryan shrugged. "There's talk of a league forming from the remaining teams, as you know. It may be better to just stay put and compete here, in the Third Sphere."

"Nonsense," Leeland said, pushing himself up again on elbows. His heart monitor beeped faster, his blood pressure rose. "You go through all this trouble, all this pain, and you're going to refuse the invite? Shyler Coch died for this. Triple-B died for this. I almost died for this, and you're going to—"

"Then give me reason to accept," Aryan interrupted.

"What do you mean?"

"I mean, your contract's up. You are technically no longer a Viper. So, give me a reason to accept the invitation." Aryan leaned in close. Leeland could smell a touch of wine on the young man's breath. "Are you still a Viper or not? Are you done with DreadBall or not?"

Slowly, Leeland laid his head back on the pillow. Was he? Was he still a Viper? Should he be? It was something that he had confessed not long ago, but now that the tournament was over, he had a choice to make. Stay, or leave?

He had done what he had come here to do, what he had been paid to do. He had cobbled together an unlikely bunch of newbies and veterans and had won the tournament. His work was over, and he could go now and crawl back into that gutter and wallow again in filth and booze. That would certainly be easier than dealing with the constant up and down of victory and defeat, of pain and joy, that the game of DreadBall brought to everyone that engaged in it.

What should I do?

He raised himself back up, and the minute he looked at Aryan Kapoor, his boss, Leeland Roth knew the answer.

He threw the sheet covering his legs aside and began pulling out his wires. "What are we waiting for? Let's go to work."

THE END

TALES OF MANTICA
DROWNED SECRETS
BEN STODDARD
KINGS OF WAR

TALES OF MANTICA
STEPS TO DELIVERANCE
KINGS OF WAR
MARK BARBER

Tales of Mantica
Edge of the Abyss
KINGS OF WAR
Edited by
Brandon Rospond

THE GREAT MARTIAN WAR
AMERICA IN FLAMES
SCOTT WASHBURN

For more on gaming in the worlds of Mantic Games go to:

https://www.manticgames.com/

and information on Dreadball at:

https://www.manticgames.com/games/dreadball/